KHE

THE AHSENTHE CYCLE, BOOK ONE

ALEXES RAZEVICH

RAZOR STREET PUBLISHER

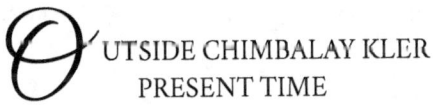
"SHUN the sweetly fragranced flower of desire, for the fruit is poisoned."
—*The Rules of a Good Life*

BEHIND ME THE beasts whistle—three short, low-pitched notes—the pack members on the hunt, calling to each other. There are seven of them, each one-half again as tall as me. They run faster than I can, moving with a cruel grace on feathered, thickly muscled legs, a blur of red and white, like two-legged flames. If they'd seen me earlier, before I made it down the hills and this close to the gate, I'd be in their bellies.

I know the stench of the beasts' foul breath. The calculating looks in their large black eyes. I've seen the damage their barbed teeth and pincher-clawed hands do to flesh. Beasts like these hunted me when I first came to the wilderness and thought it would be my sanctuary. I know better now.

My breath, harsh and ragged, makes white puffs in the air. Thin sheets of ice crackle beneath my feet. I spread my toes as wide as they will go, for balance. My cloak flares behind me as I run across the plain.

The city is tantalizingly near, agonizingly far. Chimbalay rises straight up from the plain, its black glass towers protected by a massive stone wall and a silver metal gate, ten levels high at least. The gate is closed. I have to get inside. For safety from the beasts. To find the orindles, who are my only hope.

The beasts whistle again, their call changed, a sound so

1

low it's almost a rumble. They're spreading out. All twenty-four emotion spots on my neck tingle. I run, my heart knocking against my chest.

A noise like a great rising storm tears across the plain. I'm both afraid to look and afraid not to. I slow a little and glance toward the sound. Down the plain, something hard edged and solid is moving in my direction. I can't tell its speed or what it might be. I focus on the gate, running faster, concentrating on my goal.

Beasts whistle to the right and left. Two run past me, to get in front and press me back to their companions.

The sound of the wind grows louder, the moving thing coming nearer. The whistles of the beasts change, rising in pitch and coming closer together. The calls come so quickly that they are almost a continuous sound—one voice springing from seven points, fighting to be heard over the wail of the raging wind in the still air.

I don't want to slow again to look, but anxiety makes me. I must know what the beasts are doing. Glancing over my shoulder, I see one and then another beast stopped, staring at the thing coming down the plain. The thing hovers a handsbreadth above the land, streaming toward the open space between Chimbalay and me, the way vehicles move. But this is no vehicle. It's close enough now that I can make out the protective outer mud wall and some of the buildings behind it.

A corenta.

My breath sticks in my throat. I've never seen one of the mobile trading villages on the move before. I've never been in an anchored one. Simanca made sure we were protected from that evil. I can't worry about the corenta now. Reaching the gate is all that matters.

The gate is near enough that I can see the words "Chimbalay Kler—Region Seat, Gambly One Region" carved on it in letters nearly as tall as I am. The beast between the corenta and me suddenly stops, throws back its great shaggy-feathered head, and howls in fear.

I keep running.

The corenta keeps coming. The beasts wail and scatter. I would flee from the corenta too, if the safety of Chimbalay were not at hand. I pound against the closed gate, shouting, "Open up!"

The corenta, tiny compared to the massive ring of Chimbalay, settles itself on the plain, not far behind me. Not nearly far enough for comfort. They say not only the doumanas, but also the plants, beasts, and structures in a corenta are alive and conscious. They say the doumanas there have no faith in the creator. The skin on my neck burns as my emotion spots flare gray-green in revulsion. I bang my fist against the gate.

What will I say if someone opens the gate? Perhaps "My name is Khe. I've come from Lunge commune to see the orindles, in hope that they can cure me." Which is the truth, though saying it will probably get me taken for a babbler and driven away. Who could believe that a country doumana who'd only been off her commune for mating and one other time could find her way to Chimbalay?

Snow begins to fall, swirling around my legs. I pull my cloak tight around me. The creator, in its wisdom, made us smooth, without hair, fur, or feathers to come between us and the touch of the world. The beasts and birds are luckier. They are warmer during Barren Season.

The corenta at my back makes me nervous. My emotion spots flare blue-red, showing how I feel to any who might see me, though no one does. The corenta gate begins to open. I bang my fist harder against Chimbalay's massive gate, calling, "Let me in! Let me in!"

Metal hinges squeal gently as the two halves of the huge

gate glide apart. I shove my body through the opening to get inside and am driven back by dozens of doumanas shoving their way out. They push against me, seeming more irritated than alarmed at the sight of a ragged female standing in the gateway.

My neck feels alternately hot and cold. My emotion spots flare gray-brown, showing my horror. The doumanas' emotion spots can't be seen at all. Each wears a stiff, high-necked collar that, except for a slim V in the front, completely conceals her throat. The collars hang down below the hollow at the base of their throats and extend at the sides out over their shoulders.

The creator gave us emotion spots so that all who see us would know the truth of our hearts. To cover your spots is anathema. What manner of place have I come to?

The place of the orindles, I remind myself. I fight my way against the flood of doumanas and into the kler.

Are any of these doumanas orindles? Does this one passing me now hold the knowledge for my salvation? Is that one pushing her way through the throng she who can return my life? Are the orindles the best among us, as Simanca said, or evil, as the babbler claimed?

Am I as mad as a babbler myself to have come to Chimbalay? A sharp loneliness stabs my chest. I miss Lunge commune, where my sisters still rise each morning and go to the fields. The place I ran from, and yearn for.

The place to which I can never return.

CHAPTER TWO

$\mathcal{L}$UNGE COMMUNE
PAST

"IN LIFE there are two great tasks—serving one's community and mating during Resonance, thus ensuring the continuation of our kind."

—*Simanca, in her lessons to the hatchlings*

THE SUN WAS hot and my back was sore. My fingers were stained green and yellow from picking the long oval leaves of tiko that filled row after row of the field. When I was standing, the tiko's thick brown stalks reached chest-high, but their valuable leaves grew low, never more than knee-high up the stems. I crouched among the plants, my back toe pressed flat against the soil, taking care to remove the leaves close to the stalk.

A quiet grunt and the *whe-shosh* of a harvest basket being

dragged across the dirt gave away Thedra's location in the row next to mine.

"I'll finish first," she said cheerfully. "Again."

"Good for you," I said without looking up. I pulled my basket close to my knees and went back to pulling the fragile but stubborn leaves from their stalks and laying the leaves gently into my basket.

"Someone should invent a mechanical harvester for tiko leaves," Thedra said. "We have them for every other crop."

"Keep complaining," I said. "Maybe you won't finish first after all."

Thedra pulled her back straight and sang,

"Who is she, the one called Khe?
Working with her sisters three?
Plucking tiko, sad to see
That Thedra gleans more leaves than she."

I picked up a small dirt clod and heaved it at her. It hit her arm harmlessly and broke apart.

Tiko gathering was always assigned to first-year doumanas precisely because it was a difficult, unpleasant job. Once you had successfully hand-harvested tiko, nothing else would seem too hard a task to accomplish. That's what Simanca had said. She was our commune leader. She knew about these things.

Simanca was good about providing life lessons like that and backing them up with a saying from *The Rules of a Good Life*. I admired her knowledge of the Rules and her skill at quickly calling up the one she wanted on the textbox she always carried—the small silver square tucked into a special holster on a leather belt strapped around her waist. The rule quoted with the tiko assignment was "The hand callused by hard work strokes a heart made glad by accomplishment." My heart must have felt absolutely elated, given how callused working the fields had made my hands.

I went back to plucking leaves. When one row ended, I took a new basket and started down another.

Finally the day-ending colors, red with stripes of pale green and deep yellow, filled the sky. All across the commune, my sisters in the fields would be putting down their work. I set the handful of just-plucked tiko leaves into my basket, wearily stood up, and stretched. Thedra was standing too. She was much further along her row than I was in mine. She waggled her fingers, just to make the point. She needn't have bothered. The bright-green pride colors on her neck already said everything.

Lunge was a medium-sized commune with seventeen fields, though not all of them were planted. With a population of only fifty-three field sisters, food preparers, hatchling tenders, and beast herders, there weren't enough of us to make use of all our fields. Our small number was Simanca's greatest sorrow. She prayed daily for a harvest bountiful enough to earn Lunge the credits needed to buy extra hatchlings. As yet, the creator had not granted her request.

Thedra wiped the sweat from her face with the back of her hand. Her skin was naturally a darker shade of red than mine, and the days in the field had darkened it further to a reddish brown. Except for our skin color, Thedra and I looked mostly alike, heads shaped smooth as eggs with ear holes on either side; medium foreheads; large dark eyes; flat, broad noses; wide thin-lipped mouths. She was taller than me, though, and her neck was longer. Her usually thin arms and her normally flat chest showed, as mine did, the effects of the extra food we'd been eating in preparation for Resonance.

Thedra rolled her shoulders to loosen the kinks, cleared her throat, and started to sing. She chose a fitting song, considering what day it was.

"First Warmth's at its end, the fruit's in the tree.

Resonance calls, my heart answers free.
Soon I will come, a good mate to find
At the end of the journey, in Resonance time."

Thedra had a beautiful voice and knew it. Sometimes I hated her for that.

Our unitmate Jit rushed up just as Thedra finished the first verse.

"Don't sing that song," she said, her arms pulled in close to her body as if she were cold. "I heard there was a doumana in Chimbalay who sang that song the day before Resonance started, and she didn't feel it."

"Didn't feel it," Thedra scoffed. "What does that mean?"

"Resonance," Jit said. "She didn't feel the tug. She didn't see her color. She couldn't mate."

Thedra tsked. "That's just a scare story, Jit. Everyone feels Resonance."

"No. It's true," Jit said.

Thedra and Jit could argue all day about nothing and forget it all in an instant.

"I'm starving," I said, to change the subject.

"Resonance hunger," Thedra said, as if she knew more about everything than anyone else.

"And my last chance to do something about it," Jit said.

A rush of heat whipped across my throat and the emotion spots on my neck lit bright-blue in excitement. Thedra and Jit had the same color glowing on their necks. I felt a rush of love for my sisters, seeing our harmony of feelings.

"Double portions for me tonight," Thedra said.

"I'll go triple after this day's hard work," Jit said.

I rubbed the knuckle of my right thumb over the place just above my left wrist, where two small blue dots were visible. Our first dot appeared at Emergence, the day we left our hatchling state behind and joined society as mature doumanas. A new dot appeared every year after that on Commemoration Day, which fell on the new moon of First Warmth Season. My unitmates and I now had two dots each and were old enough to experience Resonance.

"Where's Stoss?" I asked. We couldn't go to the communiteria until all the members of our unit were together.

Jit hitched up her shoulders in a shrug. "I thought she was right behind us."

Thedra tsked. "You know how Stoss is. She probably ate most of what she plucked and is trying to get at least one basket actually filled with leaves. Then she'll tell us how hard she worked today and have a very creative excuse to explain why she harvested less than the rest of us."

In spite of myself, my mouth crinkled in agreement.

"Stoss," Thedra called. "We're hungry."

In the corner of the field, Stoss's face, round as an orb and pink red, appeared over the green and yellow tiko leaves. She hastily wiped her mouth, stood up all the way, and looked toward us.

In the communiteria, I stared down at my plate and pushed the thick mélange around with my spoon to make it look like I'd eaten more. Jit and Stoss sat on either side of me, gobbling their meals like they hadn't eaten in days. Thedra was in line for another helping.

I glanced at Hwanta, sitting across the table. She was small for a doumana. With the extra layers of fat she'd put on in preparation for Resonance, she looked nearly as round as an awa fruit. Her skin was about the same shade of fire red, too, and her eyes were as small and black as awa seeds. I started to giggle. My spots flared red-purple.

Hwanta shook her head and muttered, "Resonance madness." She eyed my plate. "You must have eaten faster than the rest of us if you're finished already, Khe. I didn't see when you went back for seconds."

Thedra plopped back down in her chair. "I don't like mélange, but I can't stop eating it."

Hwanta reached across the table. "I'll just help you not waste the last of yours, Khe."

Stoss pulled her head up from the plate that had absorbed her attention until that moment. "It's hard to believe that tomorrow I won't feel hungry at all, but that's what they say." She pushed back her chair and went to stand in the slow-moving line of doumanas at the food stalls.

"Tell me about Resonance," I said to Hwanta, who was older and knew things.

"Didn't you pay attention during the visionstage presentation?"

"I did," I said, "but that orindle on the stage was so dry, she made Resonance sound almost boring."

Jit looked up. "How could anything about Resonance be boring?"

"Fttt," Thedra said. "Just listen."

Hwanta pulled her back straight and adopted that blind gaze and the listen-carefully-this-is-important tone that speakers on the visionstage have. All the first- and second-year doumanas at the table stopped eating and turned their eyes toward Hwanta.

"In response to changes in the planet's magnetic fields, a small gland housed where skull meets spine—the Resonance sac—secretes a chemical allowing us to perceive the Resonance force visually and follow it back to the place where we were hatched."

I clapped my thigh. Hwanta sounded exactly like the boring visionstage orindle. Hwanta beamed at her accomplishment.

"Simanca said that there were hundreds of nesting sites," I

said. "She said that we might share a site with some of our commune-sisters, but that if we did, we probably wouldn't see them there, the crowd would be so large."

I'd lived all my remembered life with the same fifty-two sisters. The thought of being among stranger doumanas and seeing a male for the first time excited me. My emotion spots felt suddenly warm.

Hwanta wiped her mouth and set down her spoon. "The force is there all the time—we just can't see or feel it. When the magnetic field of the planet changes, and that only happens every other year during the fifteen days of Resonance, our chemical and electrical levels change too. Then we can see the colors of the force and follow it back to the right nesting ground."

I leaned forward. "What is it like, feeling Resonance?"

Hwanta's lips crinkled. "Wonderful. Something that can't be described. You have to live it to know. The only thing better is mating."

Each doumana at the table had bright-blue excitement spots flaring on her neck. Males stayed in their own communities, living no differently than we but among their own kind, as was right and proper. Simanca said that if females and males lived together, they would always have the urge to mate. The creator had separated us so we wouldn't be distracted from our work.

In the same way, the creator had devised three types of communities—the country communes where food was produced or raw materials like ore or wood were gathered, the large klers where policy was made, and the corentas, nomadic trading communities that transported goods back and forth between commune and kler.

Hwanta pushed her chair back and stood up. "I'm ready for another bowl. How about you, Khe? More, now that you've sat for a while?"

I didn't want more, but I stood up and followed Hwanta anyway.

THE MORNING LIGHT cut through the window like a knife. The three cots where Thedra, Jit, and Stoss slept were empty. My stomach rumbled in hunger. I bolted up into a sit and threw off the thin blanket I'd slept under. This wasn't right, wasn't possible.

"Jit?" I called. "Stoss? Thedra?"

My voice was shaky. I'd never woken in an empty room before. My stomach rumbled again.

No one felt hungry once Resonance began. In the days before individual transportation vehicles, journeys to the nesting grounds were often long. Needing to stop for food was inefficient, and the creator had relieved us of the burden. When Resonance ended, hunger returned.

But my hunger had not gone. And I felt no crazier than I had yesterday, or the day before, or the day before that. Felt no lust surging in my blood, no egg quickening in my sac. Saw no colors in the air to guide me anywhere.

Broken.

Impossible, I told myself. Desire would come. My own special color would shimmer in the air.

I climbed off my cot, planted my feet on the warm stone floor, threw back my head, and held my arms wide, waiting to feel the pull.

Nothing.

Only hunger.

Broken. A drain on my species.

What good was I?

CHAPTER THREE

"*P*raise your sisters who soon will be dust.
From dust does rise the creator's breath*."
— *"The Expectation of Returning"*

THE WORLD HAD SWUNG ONCE around the sun since my commune-sisters had gone to Resonance and I had not. Everyone knew. They'd seen it in my emotion spots when they'd returned. No one spoke of it to me, not even Simanca.

No one spoke to me about Resonance, either. Of the tug, the journey, the joy. I heard plenty, though. Sisters in the field, on the commons—the first-year doumanas could hardly stop jabbering. Until they caught sight of me. Then they turned silent.

I tried to ask Thedra about it.

"There's no point, Khe," she said. "It would be like telling a grass eater what meat tastes like."

I asked Jit, too. She only crinkled her lips in a smile, hummed a bit, and said, "It's wonderful." Her eyes opened wide. "It's not all that grand," she said quickly. "You didn't miss anything." Then her eyes went all misty again.

I didn't bother asking Stoss.

THE FIRES WERE ALREADY LIT and the large cast-iron cauldrons set on when we crossed the pale-green brick threshold into Emergence House, all fifty-three doumanas of Lunge commune fitting easily into the large room. Sweat trickled down my sides. No one liked the long pale-green gowns that swaddled us throat to ankle and were too hot on a morning like this, but we didn't complain. Not on Commemoration Day, the day our hatchlings would have their downy outer skin peeled away, allowing the fully developed doumana within to emerge—a ceremony everyone loved. It was also the time we celebrated the Returning to the creator with the aged doumanas, which I didn't like so well.

In the windowless room, spice-scented water bubbled in the cauldrons, filling the air with steam to help soften the hatchlings' skins and make peeling easier. The scent made me woozy. I felt hot and prickly, as though I were a hatchling again, nervously waiting to withstand a rite everyone promised would be wonderful, but that I had my doubts about.

The hatchlings who would emerge today were off-Resonance young who hadn't hatched in the year they'd been laid, but had grown more slowly, needing extra time to develop enough strength to break free from the egg. Off-Resonance hatchlings tended to be weak and often died before they could emerge as doumanas. Of course, they cost less, too. That we'd brought these three through in complete health made the prospect of seeing them emerge even better.

"Praise now your second birth," we chanted. Simanca

seized a hatchling firmly, dug her bony fingers into the loose flesh behind the hatchling's neck, and began peeling away long strips of yellow skin. The hatchling wriggled beneath Simanca's hold, eyes wide, face set in a mix of excitement and fear.

"Be still," Simanca said, squeezing the hatchling's shoulder —which only made her wriggle more.

"Be still," Simanca insisted, and the hatchling settled down.

She had said the same thing to me on my Emergence Day and had pinched me hard enough to leave a mark. But peeling tickled. It had been hard to stand motionless, as we had been told to. I'd wanted to please Simanca and to make my sisters proud. Instead I'd hopped around like a bird with both feet on hot coals.

When Simanca finished with the hatchling, a much-changed being stood before us. Her body covering of yellow down was gone. Her skin glistened with sweat and moisture from the steam that nearly choked the air from the room. The newly emerged doumana stretched out one arm, admiring the lovely smoothness of her skin, her new light red color, the single blue dot on her wrist.

I sneaked another look at the new third dot that had appeared that morning on the inside of my left wrist. A thrill ran through me, as though my dot showed real accomplishment, not just the passage of time.

We weren't like the beasts, whose fur whitened with age, or the birds, whose feathers grew straggly over time. A doumana looked the same from the moment she left the hatchling state behind until she returned to the creator. To know how old a doumana was, you had to count the dots on her wrist.

"I present to you," Simanca said, "the doumana Denil. Welcome your new sister."

"To grow a happy heart," says *The Rules*, "till well the fields of celebration."

We stomped our feet and shouted welcomes and praises. Our commune and our kind would continue.

———

THE PAINT on the murals lining the walls of Community Hall was flaked, and the colors had turned dull. The painted doumana harvesting kiiku had lost most of one hand and parts of her shoulders. I don't know why I suddenly noticed; the mural must have looked the same all of my life.

Once Lunge commune had thrived. Then the commune's weather-prophet had failed to see the coming of a series of hailstorms that destroyed most of the harvest. That was in the days when each commune had its own weather-prophet, before the Powers started examinations and certification and centralized the prophets in the klers.

Food production went down at Lunge in each of the next three years. With each decline, fewer hatchlings were assigned, meaning fewer doumanas to work in the fields, which meant production went down—a cruel circle that our community seemed unable to break.

"Praise to the creator," Simanca said, drawing my attention back to where we were and why. She stood on a riser at the front of the hall—the textbox belt around her waist, the embroidered shawl of leadership over her shoulders, her arms held out as if she could enfold us all in her embrace. Her unitmates, Tav, Gintok, and Min, stood behind her.

We rose from our seats, calling, "Praise to the creator, who gives us life and plenty. Praise to the creator, who will soon receive our sisters into its soul."

From the back of the room, the four Returning doumanas walked in a single line down the center aisle toward where

Simanca and her unit stood. My unit sat in the front row. I couldn't see the coming doumanas' faces clearly over the heads of my commune-sisters sitting around us, but I knew who they were.

Hwanta and the three more Returning doumanas would be robed in scarlet, while the rest of us wore our pale-green Emergence gowns. Scarlet was the color of Returning, the color of the day-ending sky, the color of the creator. Only doumanas who had entered their thirty-fifth year were allowed to wear the color. It was a great honor, earned by survival. The life of a commune doumana was not an easy one.

Once the Returnees came into view, I kept my eyes on Hwanta. She'd been the only one to seek me out after Resonance, bringing me a small picture orb of Lunge that I knew she treasured. The orb showed Lunge as though seen from a cloud, looking down on the buildings and the full-blooming fields. It was beautiful.

"Put this where you can see it every night before sleep and every morning when you wake," she'd said. "Lunge is our heart. Some might even say you are blessed to never have to leave it."

I'd gazed at the orb every night and morning for a year now, but I'd never felt blessed.

"The riser looks lovely," Jit said, and sighed.

Thedra, who sat on the other side of me, nodded. "The flowers are nice. I'll bet the unit that made them gets a special mention."

I looked at the riser, where four bunches of red stenme, green yawo, and white snowcrown waited to be presented to the Returning doumanas. Each bunch had thirty-five flowers, one for each year we live.

The exact day of each doumana's Returning was unknown. It could be that day, the next day, or not until the year is nearly complete. The celebration on Commemoration Day was the only time the entire community could be certain of honoring them, and sharing our happiness at their good fortune. We would praise their accomplishments with songs composed especially for them. There would be speeches and a feast.

When the four scarlet-robed doumanas stepped up onto the riser, Simanca called out, "Stand and lift your voices for 'The Expectation of Returning.'"

"The Expectation of Returning" was one of my favorites —a cheerful song with a lively beat. As we sang, we clapped out the rhythm with cupped palms against our thighs, swaying in time to the music like rows of green saplings in a good wind. I wondered suddenly why we sang for Returning but chanted for Emergence? Was it habit, happenstance, or one of the Rules? It wasn't the kind of question I could ask Simanca without getting a lecture on unseemly curiosity— and there was plenty in *The Rules* about that. Maybe Hwanta would know.

When we'd finished, Simanca nodded to Thedra. The rest of us sat, but Thedra walked to the riser, chin in the air. She'd been working on a new song for the Returning doumanas. For days we'd heard her humming snatches of the lilting tune she'd composed, but no one knew what words she had put to the music. I'd asked her to make some kind lines especially for Hwanta, but with Thedra, you never knew.

She began to sing.
"O this, O this,
My Returning sister—
O this, may this
Be your Returning day."

"No," Hwanta screamed from her place on the riser—an anguished wail that seemed to pierce my skin all the way to the bone. "No." Hwanta swayed on her feet and then crumpled in a heap. Tav ran over and knelt next to her. Hwanta's back arched like a bridge. An awful gurgling sounded in her throat.

We all rushed forward, all of us near the front, crowding close around our injured sister. I knelt beside Tav to help hold Hwanta still so she wouldn't hurt herself.

After a while the convulsions stopped and Hwanta opened her eyes. She rolled onto her side and lay there, panting hard. I stroked her neck. Every one of her emotion spots was lit brown-black, the color of anger.

"Are you all right?" I whispered to her.

Hwanta's breathing slowed, but stayed harsh and ragged. Wide-eyed, she looked up at me. I didn't know if she recognized who I was. Slowly she pulled herself to her feet. I stood up beside her. Hwanta leaned against my shoulder and stared blindly toward her sisters gathered around her. I felt a long shudder shake her body head to toe.

"The creator is cruel," she said, so low that I was sure I was the only one who heard her. "It cheats us all."

"No," I whispered back. "The creator is kindness."

"The creator is jealous of our lives," she screamed. "Why should it take us back when we are still healthy and filled with the desire for life?"

My heart thudded in my chest. My emotion spots burned blue-red with anxiety for Hwanta's soul, in fear for my own soul that I'd even heard these words.

Someone said, "Hwanta's gone insane."

"No," some called out, but more said, "Yes. Hwanta's gone mad."

"Guilty of pride and punished before our eyes," Gintok said loudly from her spot next to Simanca on the riser. "Turned into a babbler."

I felt my hands shaking, my emotion spots flaring an ugly rainbow as fear, disgust, and sorrow raced through me. A babbler had wandered into Lunge commune once. Simanca had already warned us about them—that they were not only insane but vicious, and would hurt any doumana or hatchling they got ahold of. We drove that babbler away with sticks and stones, and shouted curses.

A swarm of angry doumanas rushed toward the riser, yelling, "Babblers must be banished." I stepped in front of Hwanta, wanting to protect her.

"Babbler," my sisters were shouting. "Send her out. Babblers must be banished."

"Stop," Simanca commanded the swarm. She didn't look or wait to see if her command was followed—she knew it would be. "Return to your dwellings. Now."

The rushing doumanas stopped as suddenly as if Simanca's words were a wall. Those who'd been standing by their seats sat down, only to rise again immediately to obey Simanca's order. The sound of bare feet tramping across the wooden floor filled the hall. No one spoke.

We filed out of Community Hall and headed toward our own dwellings. Jit walked with her head down and muttered under her breath. Colors blotched her neck—purple-gray concern, brown-black anger, soft-gray sorrow. I felt my spots fire with the orange-yellow of confusion and the dark-purple of grief.

The Rules says, "Value your sisters as you wish to be valued. Love as you wish to be loved." These doumanas, Hwanta's sisters—how could they do that to her?

CHAPTER FOUR

"The creator walks by day and night
Its will hidden from our sight."
—*Prayer Song*

ALL MY COMMUNE-SISTERS had gone to what should have been my second Resonance. They'd left me behind, cast off from their thoughts and concerns as if I didn't exist.

I dragged my toes through the soft dirt in front of our dwelling, looking around, hoping for something to catch my eye, something I could do. We had two hatchlings, but they were locked into Hatchling House for safety. I couldn't visit them. Something had gone wrong with the visionstage and it showed the same presentation over and over. There was no one to fix it. Everyone had gone to mate.

It wasn't fair that I was left behind. I worked hard, obeyed the Rules. It wasn't my fault that I was different.

I kicked a pile of dirt into the air and headed out to the fields, just to not be standing there like ... something useless.

I didn't know why I hadn't thought of this earlier, but

plants don't stop growing just because Resonance hits. Fruits that should have been picked when hand sized had grown as long as my arm. Water-loving vegetables shriveled from neglect. Roots grew hard and woody under the ground. "The sin of waste," Simanca often said, "is unforgivable." But that sin, at least, I could undo.

A cooling breeze blew as I crouched low, picking the tender new leaves of a glasme plant. The best leaves jutted like a collar of stiff fingers only a handsbreadth or so above the soil, around thick stalks. The leaves were used for everything from flavoring hard sweets to making insect bite balm. Harvesting them without machinery was muscle-cramping, backbreaking work. It was exactly what I wanted.

It felt strange to be in the fields without Jit, Stoss, and Thedra. Lonely. Too quiet. I longed for Jit's laughter, a remark from Stoss, one of Thedra's sudden bursts of song.

I stood and wiped the sweat off my forehead with the back of my hand. The harvest bag was nearly full again. The gathering I'd done pleased me, but I wasn't looking forward to dragging the large, heavy bag back to the silo a fourth time. If I'd known how to run the harvester, I could have stripped the field of its crop in no time.

If wishing made a thing so, I'd have gone to mating.

The sun was sinking toward the horizon. The sky blazed with wide strokes of scarlet, thin trails of cerulean, arching sweeps of chartreuse. The air had grown crisp, chilling my sweat-drenched skin. I rubbed my arms and shoulders to warm them.

Simanca would be pleased when she came back from Resonance and saw what I'd done. My unitmates and commune-sisters would be pleased because we'd all share in what the extra crops bought. Maybe Thedra would make up a song about what I'd done.

"A positive spirit lifts even the heaviest burden," Simanca

often said Maybe. Grabbing the heavy harvest bag by the towrope, I lugged the sack down to the silo and emptied the crops into the deep wooden bin that had been empty when I began, but that I had nearly filled. *The Rules of a Good Life* says, "Hard work well done makes an easy heart." I'd recited those words all my life, but never truly understood them before. Sometimes, on dark days, I'd thought the saying was just a way to stop complaints. Standing in the silo, my legs, back, and arms sore but my sense of usefulness restored, I realized how much truth and wisdom were in those words.

Hard work made a doumana hungry, too. I headed toward another bin to grab some root crops for my supper.

"Can I have a root?"

I jumped and twisted toward the sound. Han—one of our two hatchlings—stood in the doorway.

"Please, doumana," Han said, stretching one downy yellow hand toward me. "We're lonely. No one has come to play with us. Will you come? We like it when you come."

"What are you doing out here?" My voice came out harsher than I'd meant it to be. "You could get hurt."

Han lowered her arm and her down-covered head. "The door wasn't locked."

Resonance madness. My sisters had been in such a hurry to mate, they hadn't secured the hatchlings. A wandering hatchling could break a leg or fall in the well and drown.

"Did I make a mistake?" Han asked. "You've got a lot of brown-black spots right here." She touched my throat.

I sighed. "You didn't do anything wrong. Someone left your door open and you might have gotten hurt. I was worried about you, that's all."

And jealous. I felt the muddy-green spots rise on my neck. I'd have given anything to feel the fine madness of Resonance, to have been in such a great rush to find a mate that I forgot to lock a door.

I ruffled the downy feathers on her head. She looked up at me and cooed.

"Are the feeders full in Hatchling House?" I asked. If my sisters had forgotten to lock the door, they could have forgotten to make sure the hatchlings had food while they were gone.

Han nodded, then grinned. "Treats, too. Kiiku squares. My favorite."

Usually the hatchlings ate with the doumanas. During Resonance, when no doumanas would be in the commune, food was provided in Hatchling House. Except that I was here. Next Resonance, I'd ask Simanca if the hatchlings could be left in my charge.

"And the water lines?" I asked. "Are they working?"

She nodded again. Then she hunkered down, thrust her butt out behind her, and shook it.

"Look!" Han said, and began dancing in an erratic circle. "I'm a preslet!"

I had to laugh. Preslets are stupid, quarrelsome birds, and I didn't much like them. Han had their dance down perfectly.

I bent my knees, shoved my butt out, and wriggled around with her.

Han giggled.

"Ack. Ack. Ack," I cried, still dancing.

"Ack," Han squawked back in her thin hatchling voice.

Han stopped dancing and sighed. "I wish you tended us instead of Gris and Freneel. They never laugh. Gris says Simanca won't let you because you're broken. I wish they'd fix you, so you could always be with us."

I turned away so Han wouldn't see how my spots had lit soft-gray with sorrow and brown-green with shame. To turn away was no different from lying, but I couldn't bear for Han to see my hurt.

When I felt my spots quiet, I turned back again toward Han. She was watching me with wide eyes.

"Come on," I said. "Let's gather those roots and I'll make us a feast."

When we walked outside, a soft rain was falling.

THE FIFTY-THREE MEMBERS of Lunge commune were gathered in Community Hall to hear the results of the season-end crop weighing. The doumana who'd left the door to Hatchling House open when she'd rushed off to Resonance stood alone, just inside the door, her head hung in shame, ignored even by her own unitmates. The planet would travel a full quarter around the sun before any of us would acknowledge her or speak with her again. Resonance had taught me the horror of solitude. As we filed in, I brushed my fingers across her neck, to say that she was not forgotten.

Stoss, Thedra, Jit, and I took our places near the front on the left side. I'd been assigned a row-end seat. Did that seat mean I'd be coming to the riser to receive an award of merit? Simanca had seemed pleased when I showed her the extra crops I'd gathered while the community had been gone. "Good work," she'd said, and touched my throat, which was a great show of approval and affection from her.

At Simanca's signal we stood and sang "Praises to the Creator" and then "The Song of Togetherness." Thedra's sweet, high voice sailed through the air. My own voice cracked, and once I started on the wrong verse. A jab from Thedra's sharp elbow told me my mistake. But singing helped soothe my nerves, and I felt calmer when we sat again.

But the calm didn't last. My eyes felt stuck on the small wooden awards box near Simanca's feet. The awards of merit

—small glass orbs with the winner's name, unit, and accomplishment on a continuous holographic loop inside—were handed out to individuals who'd made special contributions to the commune. Larger prizes—bolts of cloth, visionstages, artwork—went to outstanding units. It wasn't humble to want, but I'd worked hard for more than four years and won nothing. I wanted to win.

"I am pleased to announce," Simanca said, her voice ringing out, "that for the first time in seven years, Lunge commune has surpassed the yearly quotas in the production of aromatic plants."

We all began stamping our feet. The sound welled in the hall, rising to a loud crescendo that almost hurt my ear holes. Simanca stood on the riser, her lips crinkled in a smile. She raised her hand to quiet us. Her emotion spots flared bright-blue with excitement. We stopped stamping to hear what news could bring out this color in her.

"Because of the fine efforts from all the doumanas of Lunge commune," Simanca said, "we will receive three extra hatchlings this year."

Three extra hatchlings. For Lunge to receive that meant we'd surpassed quota by almost five percent.

The stamping began again, a thunder of feet on wood. My extra effort was at least some of the reason we'd done so well. My stomach fluttered as if wild birds flew in it. The skin on my neck prickled. My spots flared greenish-blue from the hope zinging through me. I wanted to hide my spots, to not seem as anxious as I was, but no one seemed to be looking my way. Surely Simanca would mention my contribution. I bit my lip to hold back my excitement, my expectation.

"Doumanas of unit seven, come forward," Simanca called out.

The five doumanas of the unit charged with raising

aromatic plants rushed to the dais a little faster than was seemly, stepped up, and stood beside Simanca, grinning, their emotion spots flaring.

"It is my great pleasure to present these outstanding workers with a prize worthy of their contribution to the community," Simanca said.

The wide double doors to Community Hall were flung open. Gintok and Min stood just outside, next to a flatbed vehicle with a new visionstage strapped to it.

The foot stamping and cheering began again, the doumanas showing their approval of the reward.

I cheered with the rest, but a voice in the back of my mind grumbled. Our visionstage was old—we'd inherited it from the unit that had lived in our dwelling before us—and we could have used a new one. I fought the grumbling voice into silence.

Another unit had sewn new Barren Season cloaks for the entire commune, and for their efforts received an emotions painting—a thin, clear disc in which the pale-green of contentment and the bright-blue of excitement constantly swirled, forming changing patterns. The painting had been traded for in a corenta. Simanca hated the mobile trading communities. I was surprised that she'd spent any extra time in one seeking out an award.

I cheered each unit and individual as they came forward, truly pleased to see their efforts acknowledged, and waited, thinking, Simanca will call me next. When I wasn't next, or next after that, I thought, I'll be the last one called—the greatest honor of all.

"This season," Simanca said, her voice raised and ringing out, "there is one doumana whose work was so outstanding that it is only right and proper that she should be held up as an example for us all."

She paused. The silence felt like a sudden heat hitting my face.

"You will stand in honor of this doumana," Simanca said.

Feet scraped across the floor. Doumanas jostled each other, getting their balance, craning their necks toward the riser. Thedra looked at me, but her spots were quiet.

"Nosilon, come forward," Simanca called.

I heard a squeal from the back of the hall and turned to see Nosilon hurrying down the aisle toward the riser. Her entire neck was bright-blue with excitement.

Standing on the riser, Nosilon accepted her prize, a palm-sized award of merit. Her emotion spots flared bright-green with pride and crimson with happiness. Her mouth worked, trying to get words out that wouldn't come. She settled for grinning like some hatchling. Hugging her award to her chest, she hurried back down the aisle to her unit.

We all sang "We Will Tear Down the Mountain." I made myself sing with enthusiasm, ringing out loudly on the refrain.

"For the one can do nothing,
The work is too hard,
And the mountain reaches up to the sky.
But with my sisters,
We will tear down the mountain,
And a commune will stand on the site."

I sang, but dark thoughts scratched at the back of my mind. The song was a lie. One could make a difference. Nosilon proved it.

I proved it.

I wondered why I'd bothered.

CHAPTER FIVE

"*I*t is my constant prayer that Khe be made normal."
—*Communiqué from Simanca to the orindle Pradat*

THEDRA STOOD in the center of our receiving room, singing,
"Kiiku is green and I've had a dream,
I know where I'm going.
Will you come along? Singing this song?
Resonance wind is blowing."
"Stop, Thedra," Jit said, and gestured with her chin to where I stood in the prep room, plucking gray-and-blue preslet feathers for a quilt. A thin shell of wall pierced by a large arch separated the two rooms. I was in full view of my unitmates. My hand stopped in midair. Jit came and stood close to me—a show of solidarity, for which I was grateful.
"It's all right," I said.
In the almost four years since we'd reached maturity, I'd gone past resenting the others for their ability to know what I could not. I tilted back my head and sang the next verse.

"Fruit in the bough, do you wonder how
I know where I'm going?
Creator will give us to feel
When Resonance wind is blowing."

Thedra's laughter rang through our dwelling.

"Good for you," she said. "I wondered when you'd get over that sickening self-pity you'd wrapped around yourself."

Jit remained angry, pleating the faded blue fabric of her hip wrap between her hands. "If Khe wants to feel bad, I think she's entitled. Leave her be."

"I don't feel bad," I said. "Just curious. I'd like to know how Resonance feels, what the males are like. Every time I ask ..." My words faded away.

Thedra and Jit looked at me a long, silent moment.

"What it feels like," Thedra said, "is wonderful. When Resonance starts your body is flooded with pleasure. There's lightness to your being. Your skin tingles and your eyes sharpen so that you can see the tiniest details in the grass or sky or water. And the energy! You feel you'll never need to rest or eat or drink again. Then the color comes, shimmering in the air, and the pull begins. And you know you must, just must go where the color is leading you. You want to go more than anything. There's such joy in it."

Setting down the half-plucked preslet, I leaned against the table listening.

"Go on," I said. "Tell me everything."

"Mating," Thedra said, "is slow and lovely. The males have long claws on one hand that they use to rout out the nest. All around, pairs are digging and singing. Not singing like we do here, but something else, something raw. I've tried to do it outside of Resonance, but can't."

Thedra looked away, as though hearing again the music that I would never know. She drew a deep breath and turned her attention back to me.

"At the right moment, the male reaches inside you and bursts your egg sac, not with the claw hand, which might damage the egg, but with his other. Then he scoops out the egg."

She stopped talking. A long, slow shiver shook down her body. Colors flared on her neck—bright-blue of excitement and the light-blue-red of blissful memories.

Thedra cleared her throat. "Then exhaustion hits. You lie down with your mate and sleep. Contented. When you wake, you go back to your commune."

I'd almost stopped breathing, listening to her. I glanced at Jit. Her eyes had closed. Her spots glowed light-blue-red, remembering. I sighed. It sounded lovely.

Jit opened her dark eyes and looked at me. "It had to hurt to hear it, Khe. Why did you ask?"

I shrugged. "I wanted to know what it was like, even if secondhand."

The front door banged open and Stoss burst in.

"Turn on the visionstage," she gasped. "Oh, Khe. Turn it on."

The "listen carefully" voice of the holographic news-reader filled the room. A written transcription of the words hung in the air above the stage. The print caught my attention before the speech:

... *announced today partial success in an experimental procedure that stimulates hormone release from previously nonfunctional Resonance sacs.*

My heart thumped. My hands and scalp began to sweat. I closed my eyes and concentrated on the spoken words.

Orindles at Morvat Research Center report they've successfully restored Resonance feeling in three patients. While calling it a breakthrough destined to change the lives of doumanas unable to reproduce due to dysfunctional Resonance sacs, doumanas are warned that the procedure is not yet ready for mass usage and that it is not always successful.

I turned my back to the visionstage and ran to my sleep quarters.

Experimental procedure. Not always successful. Then why talk about it?

THE EVENING of the following day I sat in our receiving room, repairing a hand plow that I'd broken that morning. I'd cracked the elbow-to-wrist-length metal blade against a stubborn rock. "Because you were too lazy to dig the rock free from the furrow," Thedra had said. Trust her to have a nasty comment, and you'd never be disappointed.

Stoss sat next to me on the floor, engrossed in a vision-stage presentation about composting methods. Thedra sprawled over several floor pillows and watched the presentation with half an eye. Jit dozed, her head on what bit of pillow Thedra hadn't taken over. A knock came at the door. Jit roused with a little yelp.

"Khe," Tav said from the doorway, "Simanca wants to talk to you."

I've often wondered why doumanas knocked to let you know someone was there, when they were just going to open the door and start talking anyway.

"Come to our dwelling when you've finished your evening chores," Tav said, and was gone.

Thedra hissed a long stream of air through her brown lips. "My, my," she said. "My, my, my."

Jit and Stoss said nothing, but their eyes spoke it all. We lived as a community. Individuals, yes, but units. Reward, condemnation, and conversation were all handled publicly. I had been summoned for a private meeting.

I searched my memory, wondering what I had done wrong, but could think of nothing. I tried to concentrate on fixing the hand plow, but my palms were wet and the handle kept slipping from my fingers.

Thedra tsked. "I'll finish that. Go see what Simanca wants."

"I wish I could go with you," Jit said.

"I wish you could, too."

My stomach heaving, my emotion spots blazing blue-red with anxiety, I shut the door behind me and walked the short distance to where Tav, Simanca, and their unitmates lived.

I knocked on the door and pushed it open.

I'd never been inside Simanca's dwelling before. It was much grander than ours. Bigger, with plastered walls painted pale-green—not like our plain wood ones—and softly padded chairs—not like our slat-backed ones—set around a large table of polished glass-stone.

"Sit down," Simanca said.

I sat in a heavily padded chair that felt to me now like it was made of rocks. My eyes fell to Simanca's left wrist, to the twenty-four blue dots that marked the years since she'd emerged. It was my duty to respect the wisdom of my elders and to obey their commands.

"I will come right to the point," Simanca said, and settled into a chair to my right side. Tav and the others remained standing behind her like leafless trees in Barren Season.

"I have been in touch with the orindle Pradat, at Morvat Research Center One," Simanca said. "She has agreed to accept you as a volunteer in the Resonance restoration trials. Tomorrow a guided vehicle will arrive to transport you there."

I stared at her. I knew that Simanca hadn't arranged this because she thought I wanted it. She'd done what was best for the commune and the species, and expected that I would do my duty. That she'd given me the thing I most desired, the chance to mate and lay my egg, was not the point for her. Still, I wished, just for a moment, that she'd asked if I wanted to join these trials.

"You may return to your dwelling now," she said.

I nodded and stood to go. At the door, Tav put her bony hand at the small of my back.

"Don't hope too much, Khe. The procedure doesn't always work."

The skin on my throat tingled. My spots glowed bright-blue with excitement. Tav's warning had come much too late.

THE ORINDLE, Pradat, had explained what to expect so many times, always in the same cold, unemotional way, that I'd begun to find it funny and had to stop myself from mouthing the words along with her. In the white room I shared with five other doumanas, I whispered the words to myself like a prayer.

Resonance begins in four days. The success or failure of the procedure will be immediately apparent. You will either respond to Resonance, or you will not. If you do not, the procedure is not repeatable. You will return immediately to your community. If you do respond, due to your years of deprivation, you may experience Resonance more intensely than other doumanas. If you wish, medication to lessen the symptoms is available. An individual transportation vehicle will be provided by Morvat Research Center so that you may travel to your mating site.

I tried not to pick at the healing wound where skull and spine joined, and watched the post-surgery drugs and food solutions designed to fatten me up drip through tubes inserted into my belly.

Resonance began in four days.

Three days.
Two days.
Tomorrow.

I AWOKE SCREAMING. The pristine white room, absent of any stimulant that might jar a recovering patient, shook with color. Swirls of emerald, vermilion, amber, cerulean, and brilliant orange merged and flowed out in the air above my cot. The colors vibrated in concert with a high-pitched wail that came from everywhere and nowhere. My head throbbed. My back arched in pain. A helphand rushed in and plunged a needle into my neck, and all went black.

When I woke again, the colors still floated above me but the wailing had gone, replaced by a low and pleasant hum. A round-faced helphand wearing a yellow hip wrap sat next to the bed. She lifted my hand and held it between both of her own.

"How're you feeling?" she asked.

I wasn't sure the helphand really cared about the answer. She didn't look at me when she spoke. She kept her eyes on the machines monitoring my well-being.

"Confused," I answered truthfully. "Scared."

"Congratulations," she said, and finally looked my way. "The procedure's a success. It's Resonance you feel."

I'd seen Resonance reaction. First-day Resonance made doumanas silly and full of themselves. Thedra had described exquisite pleasure. No one at Lunge commune ever screamed.

"No," I said. "It's something else. Something horrible."

"Sometimes it is frightening at first," the helphand said. "Your body, so long denied a natural sense, overreacts to the onslaught. But believe me, it is nothing but Resonance. The symptoms will lessen as you adjust."

I closed my eyes. The colors disappeared but still reflected inside me somehow, deep in my nerves, bones, and muscles. The hum continued. I began to like the sound, to love it.

My voice quivered. "What happens next?"

"You'll be overtaken with the urge to return to your nesting site." She sighed. "Are you seeing colors yet?"

"Yes," I answered, but kept my eyes shut.

"One stronger than the others?"

"I don't know."

She pressed my hand gently. "You'll have to look. Open your eyes and tell me what you see."

I didn't want to—didn't want the crush of colors. The helphand squeezed my hand, tightening her grip until it hurt. I knew she wouldn't stop until my hand was broken if I didn't open my eyes, so I did.

The colors no longer flowed over and into one another, but ran in orderly lines the width of an arm, except for the emerald that was maybe four times as broad and still shimmered where the others had gone dull.

"Green," I said.

The helphand nodded. She turned her eyes back to the machines and spoke to herself as much as to me. "Green is your directional color. Follow it to your site."

"How?" I asked.

"In an individual transport vehicle, of course. The research center will provide one."

"No, I meant, how will I follow the color? Does it run like a path or a river? Will it be on the ground or in the air?"

The helphand's mouth pinched tight. "Didn't they explain this to you? You need only to follow your directional color. Green, is it? Follow the green to your nesting site."

She kept talking, but her words were nothing but an annoying buzz. A tremendous energy rushed through my every cell and fiber. Joy filled me. And a desperate need to move. I jumped halfway off the cot, only to be pushed back down by the helphand.

She waved her hand over a depression in the wall. "The orindle will decide if you're ready or not."

Ready? My pulse pounded against my temple like a fist. Hot blood roared in my veins. I drummed the fingers of both hands against the soft white sheets. It seemed to take days and days before anyone came.

My feet tapped together nervously as the orindle Pradat poked me with her instruments and fiddled with her machinery. I made myself focus on the orindle, noting how the pale-red shade of her skin made her dark-brown eyes look almost too big for her small face. I watched her jaw flex and relax as she performed the tests. The discomfort of the examination was nothing compared to the horrible confinement.

At last Pradat pronounced me fit to leave and walked me to the vehicle lot. She seemed distracted, unable to concentrate. She couldn't find the start switch to make my vehicle run. I had to point it out, and for me, it was just a guess.

Resonance had her in thrall, too, I realized, and the helphand as well. Amazing that they could work at all.

Green. Beautiful green. Emeralds scattered in the air for me to follow.

I'd forgotten to thank the orindle and had to guide my vehicle back to where she stood.

"Be fruitful," Pradat said. "That's thanks enough."

THE EMERALD BAND SHIMMERED, growing wider as I plowed

over hills, past klers, and across fields, hardly noticing my surroundings. The day grew old, became night, became day again, and still I drove on. I had no hunger, thirst, or need for sleep. Steering the vehicle with the guidance stick, I never doubted the rightness of my direction. I followed the emerald light until it led me to a small valley filled with hundreds of doumanas and males. When the light winked out, I knew I was where I had longed to be.

Wild plants dotted the brown soil, a stand of tall, thin trees with flat blue-green leaves here, a sudden burst of sun-yellow from bushes there. Off to the side, a wave of dark-red-purple flowers rippled and bent as anxious doumanas and males pushed through them to reach each other.

I joined a group of doumanas watching thirty or so males dancing. They'd woven large grass hoops that they jumped in and out of as they danced, to show us how strong and lithe they were.

I'd expected the males to look different from us, but not as different as they did. They had the same hairless, furless, featherless skin as we, in the same various shades of red. The same dark eyes, thin or broad noses, and small or wide mouths, but their arms, shoulders, and chests were slimmer and their hands more delicate, like two tiny birds—one bird with hard talons, the digger claws, for routing out the nest, the other as soft as hatchling's down.

Most of the males wore hip wraps—some brightly colored, probably from the klers, and some plain, like the sort commune doumanas wore—but some wore nothing. I couldn't help but stare at those. They didn't have the protective skin flap covering the egg channel like we did. Well, why would they?

The males were beautiful. Exotic. Exciting. My neck was nearly humming with all the colors playing there—joyous crimson, the bright-blue of excitement, the dark-blue-red of curiosity gone crazy. At Lunge, a doumana who had dark-blue-red that shade on her neck would surely get a talking to from Simanca. I didn't care about Simanca. The colors could swirl on my skin for all to see.

As the males danced, they scanned the doumanas ringing them, just as we scanned them. When one saw someone he liked, he'd pass his hoop over her head in invitation. If the doumana was attracted back, she'd take hold of his hoop and they'd leave together. Sometimes a bold doumana would wade in among the dancers and, finding one she liked, sway her hips until the male either offered his hoop or turned away.

Three hoops passed over my head. I didn't take any of them. But there was something I liked in the fourth male who approached. His neck was splotched blue-purple with desire. He sang a wild song to me, like branches whipped by a storm, like worlds cracking apart.

I took firm hold of his hoop, threw back my head, and joined my wordless song with his, note and timbre of long-ing, of desire and fear, and of hope. Side by side, we went away from the dancing, to where other pairs were mating. I watched as my mate dug a shallow nest with his long claw. He settled himself in the hollow and reached up to me. I lay down beside him and felt my egg move, swelling, sliding through the channel. I felt his hand move slowly, carefully, tenderly down my side. His skin tasted spicy. He smelled of fresh loam and leaves. If I weren't already crazy from Reso-nance, I'd surely have gone mad from the sweetness of his touch.

Then, in the moment when I thought I would die of delight and didn't care if I did, my mate slipped his soft hand up the channel, burst my egg sac, and scooped out my egg. My body shook, quivering with pleasure. With dim aware-ness, I saw the male lift my fist-sized egg and cradle it in his arms. His digger claw swelled to twice its size and opened at the end. My mate screamed as his essence dripped over the soft shell and was absorbed through the egg for the new being that we were making together. I sat up—frightened he was hurt. But his mouth crinkled and he fell on his knees beside me, panting hard. I knew that it wasn't pain that had made him scream.

He lay beside me again. I stroked his neck. We'd said nothing. To feel your mate and know his soul needed no words. We closed our eyes and slept.

I left my egg there in that valley, and felt finally whole.

CHAPTER SIX

"*S*inging over the bones of the land, our hearts become glad."
— *"The Song of Growing"*

PLANTING ALWAYS FOLLOWED RESONANCE. Our unit was assigned to grow kiiku, thick-rinded gourds whose seeds were ground for flour. Several units grew kiiku since it was not only a staple for the commune, but also our major trading crop. The units competed fiercely to produce the most poundage each season and to secure the prizes that abundance won. Jit, Thedra, Stoss, and I made up our minds that this season we would win.

Most big chores on the commune were done by group— either the whole commune together, or unitmates. But not crop growing. I would plant, water, weed, and care for my own area within my unit's field. No one could tell me why we did it this way. Simanca didn't have a handy phrase from *The Rules of a Good Life* to explain it. It just was.

Jit, Stoss, Thedra, and I went to the fields together, but

spread out to begin planting our assigned areas. With each planted seed I thought of my egg cocooned in its warm nest, the new life within it growing, soon to hatch. I pretended each seed was my egg, that I was the life force itself, giving growth and vitality to the tiny waiting thing in my hand.

It was silly, this fantasy. Kiiku was only a plant, and I was only Khe. Still, I enjoyed my pretense with only a touch of shame. "Imagination and fancy distract us from our work in the true world," Simanca had said, but I could see no harm in it, and it made the work seem easier.

THEDRA'S SEEDS SPROUTED FIRST, their thin white stems backing slowly from the dirt as if hesitant to leave the warm soil for the uncertainties of life above ground. Small green, pointed first-leaves appeared, followed days later by true leaves—thick and leathery, red as a blood-rich heart, expert at capturing nutrients from the air and converting them into plant fuel.

My seeds sprouted, as did Jit's and Stoss's—row after row of perfection. We bent our backs under the furious heat of the sun, and dug our fingers into the rich soil to thin the seedlings. Insects we removed by hand, dropping the hungry little beasts into tightly woven bags slung across our shoulders. At night we sorted through the bugs, selecting the most delicious to go into the meal pot. We saved the ones that didn't taste good to feed the preslets. Those that weren't suitable for food we killed in the field, leaving their smashed bodies to nourish the soil.

We watered, hoed, and nurtured our kiiku with dedication, telling each other the extra work would be worth it when we won our prizes. At harvest we watched the crop being weighed and cheered when our poundage topped the next closest unit's by almost a quarter.

"It's all your doing," Thedra said after we'd returned to our dwelling.

Three of my spots lit bright-green with pride, but I said, "We're a unit. We all contributed equally."

"That's not true," Thedra said. "Your section had huge gourds. Bigger than anything the rest of us grew."

"Don't be silly," I said. But it was true. The smallest of my gourds easily outweighed the largest anyone else had grown. "My soil was probably prepared better by the doumanas doing the fertilizing. Maybe they should share our prize."

Thedra tsked. "Fertilizer." She glanced at me strangely then, as though a revelation skittered through her mind but left before she could properly catch hold of it.

I SAT on my cot alone, my left arm turned up, and stared at the inside of my wrist. The rising moon threw its thick light into the darkening room. The sounds from the visionstage leaked under the door. My neck prickled, hot and itchy. A sixth dot dot showed on my wrist, but I was only five.

I pulled myself to my feet and went into the receiving room. My unitmates lay sprawled on the floor, watching the presentation on the visionstage.

Jit looked up. "Khe! What's wrong? Your throat is practically all blue-red."

"This." I turned my arm so that she could see.

"What?" Thedra said, levering herself up. Jit and Stoss were already coming across the room toward me.

"There's an extra age dot," I said.

Jit sucked in a breath of air, then put her hand over her mouth, as if afraid of the words that might fly out. She didn't need words. The colors on her neck said everything. Stoss's neck was the same as Jit's, covered in the dark-gray of worry.

Thedra had come over to look, too. She put her hand on her hip and peered closely at the dot. No color showed on her neck. "How did that happen?"

I half shrugged. "I don't know. I noticed just a little bit ago. It could have been there a while."

"You have to tell Simanca," Thedra said.

Jit said, "It's probably nothing."

Thedra reached out to touch the spot, then drew her hand back as if she were burned. "It's something, all right. You have to tell. A secret is no different from a lie."

"I know," I said. "I'm going now."

As the door closed behind me, I thought I heard Thedra say, "Freak," but I must have heard wrong.

I KNOCKED on Simanca's door and walked in. Tav was so surprised at my unexpected appearance that three of her spots flared dark-yellow-green.

"Please excuse my coming uninvited," I said, looking down at my feet. "I need to speak with Simanca, if she will see me."

Tav nodded and called to Simanca.

Simanca strode immediately out from the back of the dwelling into the receiving room. She didn't look pleased.

"What is it, Khe?" she said. Her two unitmates, Min and Gintok, were seated in front of the visionstage. Like Tav's, their emotion spots showed their surprise at seeing me. Simanca's neck showed nothing.

I glanced nervously across the room. I didn't mind speaking in front of Tav, but I wished Min and Gintok, cold-necked doumanas both, weren't there. My heart beat against my ribs. Turning my left arm palm up, I held it out for Simanca to see. My pulse was jumping, making my dots rise and fall.

Simanca held my arm tightly and peered closely at my wrist for what felt like a long time.

"Insect bite," she said, and dropped my arm. "Nothing to worry about. Not worth mentioning to anyone."

"My unitmates know," I said. "And yours know, too. I have an extra age dot."

Simanca drew herself up as tall as she could be.

"This is an insect bite, Khe, not an age spot, and doubtless will disappear as suddenly as it came." She inhaled a breath. A faint, forced smile crinkled her lips. "You did right by coming to me. Say no more about this. You may return to your dwelling."

I trudged back across the commons. If the dot meant nothing, why was I ordered to silence?

―――――――

AS A REWARD—OR punishment—for doing so well with the kiiku, we were assigned awa trees next. Awa is not as highly valued as kiiku, and it's misery to tend. Thedra acted like the assignment was my fault and made little screeching noises every time she had to climb up the long ladder to hand-pollinate the awa flowers. But we did well with the stingy trees— so well that Simanca called us onto the stage at the season-end weighing and gave us a special award of merit.

The following season, we were assigned preslets. Preslets could be bitingly bad tempered, and usually were, or sweetness itself. No one liked tending them, but the birds were useful, providing meat for food and feathers for stuffing quilts and pillows and lining the insides of the warmest Barren Season cloaks. Their usefulness alone was reason to treat them well, but I thought the creator had its own good reasons for making preslets the way they were, that maybe they were a lesson of sorts—a way to see that good and bad were entwined, and that one had to learn to appreciate the whole.

Sometimes, when a preslet felt like it, the bird would crawl into your lap, roll over on its back, and make soft little yelping noises in sign that it wanted to be petted. Once I sat in the yard for most of a morning with a preslet on my lap, stroking the soft down on its belly, listening to it coo, lost in a world where thought had no place, where all was touch and sound and contentment. I heard footsteps and looked up to find Stoss staring at me. When our eyes met, she giggled. I looked at her, confused, and then realized that I'd been cooing just like the preslet. I didn't mind Stoss's laughter, but the bird took offense. It leaped down from my lap, scratching me with its sharp claws. It stalked around in a circle in front of us, fluffing its tiny, useless wings and screeching, "Ack, ack."

"You need to apologize," I told Stoss.

"To a preslet?" she asked. "Have you lost your mind?"

"Apologize," I insisted.

Stoss sighed and turned to the bird. "Sorry."

I couldn't prove it, but I'd swear that preslet was bigger the next day.

I SET about tending my flock with the same determination I'd given the kiiku and the awa. I tried a little experiment as well.

I don't know why I did it. Probably because Thedra was always going on about how it was my touch that made the kiiku and awa do so well, and I half wondered if it might be true.

I went to an old awa tree that hadn't produced fruit in years. I leaned my head against the smooth-barked trunk and thought how beautiful the tree would be in blossom, how happy everyone would be if the blooms turned to fruit. I felt a little silly but wished the tree well, and a long, productive life.

At season's end, not only were my preslets bigger and meatier than anyone else's, but the old tree bore fruit.

No one knew what I had done. The doumanas assigned awa were happy enough to count in fruit from the old tree with their poundage. No one seemed to think it strange that a tree that had hardly even leafed for as long as most of us could remember had suddenly fruited.

It scared me, thinking that maybe I'd truly had some hand in it.

WHEN I AWOKE the next day, a new dot had appeared on my wrists—small as the iris of my eye and as dark blue as the speckles on a preslet egg. Now there were eight, scattered like stars on my skin. It wasn't Commemoration Day. This shouldn't be possible.

I slipped out before my unitmates awoke, went to Simanca's dwelling, and showed her. She didn't take my arm and examine the dots like she had last time. She turned her back and strode away, taking Min and Gintok with her. I didn't know what I had done wrong, to make Simanca shun me like that.

Tav stayed behind. She stroked my neck and said, "Don't blame Simanca for her anger, Khe. She already told you the marks are unimportant. You were wrong to come again over the same matter."

I hung my head. "No one else has marks like mine."

"You know you're not like your sisters," Tav said softly. "Comparing yourself to them will only make you unhappy."

I looked up, straight into her eyes. "I'm not unhappy. I'm frightened."

I needed to say the words, even though the mass of muddy-brown spots on my neck already showed my fear.

"Oh, Khe," Tav said. "You're worried over nothing. The marks are just something … unique to you. What does *The Rules of a Good Life* tell us?"

Hadn't she heard me? Didn't it matter to her at all that I was so scared I could hardly stand there before her without shrieking? Did she not see the colors on my neck? I sighed and gave her the answer she wanted. "Only the obedient heart knows peace."

Tav smiled. "Exactly. Go now. Your unitmates will be up, and there's work to be done."

———

"I SAW YOU," Thedra whispered, standing next to me in the morning meal line in the communiteria.

"Saw me what?" I asked in a normal tone.

Thedra still whispered. "What you did to the old tree. I know you made it bloom and fruit."

My throat went dry. I dropped my voice. "Lots of trees that don't set fruit one year make up for it in the next."

"Not that tree," she said. "First the kiiku, then the awa, now the preslets and that dried-up tree. Khe, it's not natural."

Behind me, Simanca's unitmate, Gintok, grumbled and said to get a move on—we were holding up the line, and she was hungry.

I moved forward."We'll talk later," I told Thedra.

"Too late for talk," Thedra said. "I have to tell Simanca. I can't hold this a secret. You know that."

I knew. The commune had no tolerance for private knowledge. For the good of the group, all things must be public.

"There's nothing to tell," I whispered furiously. I felt my spots brown-green with shame at the lie. I knew Thedra saw it.

Gintok gave me a small shove. I bit back my irritation and stepped forward again.

CHAPTER SEVEN

"*B*eware the secret heart that holds the hidden lie."
—*The Rules of a Good Life*

I WAS MENDING a torn hip wrap when a knock at the door was followed by Tav walking into our receiving room. She glanced around the room.

"Are you here alone?" she asked.

I nodded. "Stoss wanted a walk. Jit and Thedra went with her."

"Just as well," Tav said. There was a strained coolness to her voice. "You are to come to us, but first, Simanca wants you to wrap a bandage around your left wrist. If anyone asks, you are to say that you cut yourself slightly."

"Why?" I asked, meaning both why was I summoned and why was I binding a nonexistent wound.

Tav shrugged. "Because that is what Simanca wants."

Which answered both questions at once.

THE ORINDLE PRADAT, wearing the green hip wrap that marked her official medical researcher status, was sitting with Simanca and Tav when I arrived at Simanca's dwelling. Her almost-too-large dark-brown eyes that I remembered from Morvat Research Center widened when she saw me.

"Hello," I said, surprised to see her at Lunge commune, and even more surprised that Min and Gintok were absent from this meeting. But I understood why Simanca had me cover my wrist; she didn't want the orindle to see the additional dots. But if my "blemishes" meant nothing, why did she want them hidden?

"Hello, Khe."

Pradat didn't fumble for my name. I hoped she actually remembered me, though almost a year had passed since I'd left Morvat Research Center.

She looked at the cloth wrapped around my wrist. "You've injured yourself. Shall I take a look?"

Simanca's plan seemed to have backfired on her. Of course, an orindle would look at a wound. What had Simanca been thinking?

I quickly turned to Simanca, to deflect the orindle's question and get straight to my own. "Is this about—" My voice cracked and failed. "About what Thedra told you?"

Simanca nodded. "We contacted the orindle after Thedra spoke out. Pradat suspects your ability is a result of opening your Resonance sac. A few of her other patients have also manifested changes."

"They can make things grow?"

"That's a first," Pradat said in a voice as bland as water. "I have three patients who see what they describe as new colors. Another swears she hears the future in the wind."

My heart thudded against my ribs. New colors and predicting the future? Did the surgery make patients go mad? Was I doomed to become a babbler?

"What we suspect," Pradat said, "is that nature sealed your Resonance sac for a reason. We surmise that in some cases the Resonance sac also houses a mutated sense or Talent. By opening the sac, we released the ability."

I hunched into myself. All I wanted was to be like everyone else.

Pradat reached into a large beige bag lying at her feet and drew out three small clear, shallow bowls covered by clear domes. Each bowl had some sort of colored liquid in it. The orindle got up and walked over to a small table and chair that had been set up in the receiving room. She motioned that I should sit there.

"Of all my patients manifesting what seem to be new abilities," she said, "only yours is verifiable. The one who hears the future hears nothing that will come to be in our lifetimes. We have no instruments capable of detecting the colors the other patients describe but no one else can see. Organism growth, however, can be easily predicted and measured."

Sweat prickled my skin. My neck itched. I licked my lips twice, trying to work up the nerve to speak. "What do you want me to do?"

Pradat handed me a bowl filled with a thin green liquid. "There are organisms in here that grow at a set rate. We want to see if you can accelerate it."

I took the bowl and turned it in my hands. The others watched me—Tav with concern on her face, Simanca with expectation. Pradat seemed merely curious.

Curiosity filled me as well. As I stared at the small bowl, a fascination grew in me that I might truly possess an ability no one else had. I'd longed to be the same as my sisters, as good as they were. Now I wondered if different might also mean better.

I held the bowl and thought of the little animals or plants that were in the liquid. Did they have consciousness? Were they quarrelsome like preslets or serene in their floating lives? Whatever they were, I wished them success in their goals.

The liquid turned cloudy, but I couldn't know if that was normal or not. I handed the dish to Pradat. She set it on the table without a word. She took a thin, clear tube from her bag, extracted the liquid from the dish, and squirted it onto a small board marked with tiny squares. Then she took out a device with a palm-sized circle of black glass and straps that fitted over her hand. She slowly waved the black glass over the wet squares and turned her hand over to look at the glass.

"Seven percent over expectation," she said in her maddeningly neutral voice. "Enough to warrant further study."

I stared at her neck, looking for color to tell me her feelings. Her heart must have been as dull as her voice. Nothing showed on her spots.

We repeated the experiment twice more. Each time the clear liquid turned cloudy. Pradat calculated and noted the results without showing any sign of what the results meant.

Simanca's mouth crinkled. "You've done well, Khe. Go back to your dwelling."

"I'd like her again in the morning," Pradat said, still staring into her device. "I want to run the trials at least twice more, with an examination of Khe before and after to determine if the phenomenon has an effect on her as well."

Simanca said, "Khe will report here immediately after morning meal."

No one asked me if I wanted to come back. Simanca led the commune, and all decisions regarding anyone at Lunge were hers to make. Still, they could have asked me.

GOSSAMER FILAMENTS RADIATED from almost every inch of my body. Circles of colored light dotted my skin. My skin itched beneath the bandage Simanca had once again told me to wear around my wrist. She stood nearby, her thin arms folded calmly across her gaunt, flat chest. Tav bit her bottom lip. She looked ready to leap to my defense, if need be.

"Nervous?" Pradat asked.

I nodded. Who wouldn't be nervous, hooked to fourteen machines designed to test, calibrate, and analyze the very essence of her being? Expected to perform what Thedra had begun calling "the Lunge commune miracle"? Plenty nervous was how I felt.

"Afraid you won't be able to do as well as you did yesterday?" Pradat asked as she twirled a lever on one of her machines. The machine answered her touch with a string of blips and snarls that made my skin crawl.

"No," I said, staring down at fingers that rubbed against each other as though they had lives of their own. I wasn't afraid that I wouldn't do as well. My fear came from knowing I could duplicate yesterday's results. And do better. The proof of the kiiku, the preslets, and the awa trees had convinced me. Knowledge of my power surged through my blood, tissue, muscle, and bone.

I felt two of my emotion spots flare bright-green with pride, and another glow muddy-brown with fear. I looked up, worried that the others would see my feelings, but no one paid attention to me. Not even Tav, whose eyes were stuck on the motions of Pradat's hands on the machines. My emotions quieted enough for the spots to vanish, but dread still crept through me like ice spreading in my belly.

So much was unknown—how the community would react, what the ability might mean to my future. Was I to become a traveling freak, transported from research center to research center, performing my miracles on demand?

It wasn't *not* being able to perform that frightened me.

"Ready?" Pradat asked.

I drew a deep breath, straightened my back, and answered, "Yes."

The machinery on the floor and tables surrounding my chair glowed red, yellow, and blue. The blips and snarls quieted to a high-pitched hum that tickled the insides of my ear holes, making them itch. Pradat handed me the first covered bowl.

Bowing my head, I swirled the cerulean liquid in gentle currents, wondering what sort of little plants or beasts lived in the water, what they wanted from their lives. No more than I wanted—a pleasant place to live, food, companionship, and to leave their mark by reproducing.

I put my full concentration to the task. Remembering the joy and glory of mating during Resonance, in my mind I told the little organisms how lucky they were to have the chance to live and reproduce. I told them that if they wanted, I would help them with their task if I could. I told them how happy helping them made me.

When I felt I'd done all that I could, I handed the bowl back to Pradat.

"Seventeen percent above normal," Pradat said when she finished the count. Her voice held no excitement or disappointment to help me know her expectations. She tapped the information into a thin device on her wrist. While I'd been holding the bowl, Pradat had watched the machines, noting the blips, gains, and dips of my physiological changes while I'd worked. She recorded this information as well, but said nothing about what the machines told her.

I spent most of the day in that room, endlessly repeating the same act with various organisms. As I tired out, the rates of increase dropped, but never so low as normal. Finally, seeing that I was exhausted, Pradat sent me back to my dwelling.

At the door, Tav squeezed my shoulder. Her dark eyes gleamed.

"Oh, Khe," she said. "Think of the good you can do for Lunge commune."

CHAPTER EIGHT

"*C*lear water washes the bones of the land.
Hard work washes the sins from our souls."
—*"The Song of Growing"*

MY MOUTH FELL OPEN, seeing Simanca stepping carefully as she crossed the newly turned field. I slung my seed bag over my shoulder and walked toward her.

"Good day, Khe," she said when we met, as though her being here was an everyday experience.

"Good day," I said back. "Is something wrong?"

I glanced around. Thedra, Jit, and Stoss were watching us. Doumanas in the fields on either side were staring.

"Something is very right," Simanca said. "I wanted to speak with you here in the fields, the place where you will be privileged to make Lunge the most successful, highly regarded commune in the region."

I shifted my weight from foot to foot, waiting for her to go on. I could feel my sisters' eyes on us.

Simanca leaned close to me. "I've thought this over carefully. You have a wonderful ability, Khe. You can accelerate growth. I want you to try it with the kiiku. If you can produce an extra seventeen percent, we'll have that much more to sell."

She didn't say it, but I knew that if we produced that much kiiku, Lunge would easily win the annual production competition against the fifteen other communes in our region. I guessed that Simanca wouldn't mind that.

"Seventeen percent is a lot," I said.

Simanca's lips crinkled in a smile. "A goal, Khe. A number to reach for."

"What will Lunge do with the extra credits?"

"Bring in hatchlings, of course. Not only those we're allotted, but more. An extra seventeen percent in production will give us an allotment of six hatchlings, plus enough credits to buy two more." Simanca's emotion spots flared bright-blue with excitement.

I stared in surprise. Hardly anything meant enough to Simanca to show on her skin.

"Perhaps," she continued, "once our production has improved, you might work in the new hatchlings' wing."

Oh, now she wanted a whole new wing. Not just a few extra hatchlings to build up our population slowly, but many, and quickly. I'd never thought of her as ambitious, but now I saw how full her dreams measured. Simanca knew I wanted to tend the hatchlings. She was trying to bribe me—and succeeding.

I ran my fingers lightly over my skull. The work with the orindle Pradat, had tired me to the point that I'd taken to my sleep quarters and stayed the entire next day on my cot. Simanca had allowed the unheard-of luxury even though I couldn't really say I was sick. I was still tired today, but didn't want to complain again. Clasping my hands together in front of my belly, I looked down at my feet and said, "I'll try."

Simanca beamed. "Good. Begin now."

THE GOLDEN DAYS of First Warmth passed one after another into Bounty Season, then Cooling and Barren, and to First Warmth again. Commemoration Day arrived.

Thedra stood in the doorway to our sleep quarters, her hand on her hip.

"You going to sleep all day, Khe? The hatchlings have already emerged. You missed it."

I groaned and sat up. "I'll be right there."

I'd gone to Simanca when I'd first noticed how tired I was becoming. I'd overslept morning meal so many times that Jit started bringing me food—not only in the morning, but sometimes at night when I felt too tired to stand in line at the communiteria, or when chewing and swallowing seemed more effort than they were worth. Simanca had waved off my concerns. Pulling the textbox from the holster on her hip, she'd quickly found the verse from *The Rules of a Good Life* she wanted.

"The callused hand is soothed, the tired heart refreshed with the balm of work for the community," she said, showing me the same words on the box. "Take joy in your fatigue, Khe. It's a blessing from the creator."

I'd fought down a terrible urge to laugh. Instead I'd lowered my eyes and said, "Yes, Simanca," and walked away.

Thedra stayed standing in the doorway, her eyes wide and locked on me.

"We're just about to honor the Returning doumanas," she said.

And after that, I knew, we'd hear the crop weighing results.

"I'll be right there," I snapped, and then regretted my tone.

It wasn't Thedra's fault I felt like there was a little beast inside my skull, banging it with a hammer.

Thedra shrugged. "We'll see you there, then."

I heard the front door slam as she left.

Clouds hid the sun, making the day gray and dismal as I hurried across the commons to Community Hall. Blue drymoss was in bloom. My feet crushed their tiny white flowers as I ran.

The door to Community Hall had been left open. I slipped inside and stood at the back for a moment to catch my breath. I scanned the room, looking for my unitmates so I could sit with them.

I'd arrived too late to join in honoring our Returning doumanas. They were already seated in the front row, a line of crimson in a lake of bright green. I wished I could see their faces. Since the day that Hwanta had gone mad while being honored, I was afraid another of my sisters would blaspheme the creator as Hwanta had. But since then, no Returning doumana had been anything but anxious to join with the great soul.

Simanca stood on the dais, dressed in a green gown. The awards box lay near her feet. Tav stood to her left; Gintok and Min stood behind her. Soothing warmth spread across my neck. My emotion spots flashed pale-green with contentment. I loved my commune and my sisters, relished the comfort of seeing my leader and her unitmates on the riser as I'd seen them so many times before, as I would see them again every year until my own Returning came.

I spotted Jit craning her head toward the back of the hall. Catching her eye, I made my way down to the second row, where my unit sat.

"Twenty-four percent over last weighing," Simanca called out as I slid into a chair between Jit and Thedra. The room erupted into cheers. The stamping of feet made my ear holes hurt.

"What crop is she talking about?" I asked Jit, practically shouting to be heard over the clamor.

"Kiiku, of course," Thedra, not Jit, answered. "Increased by twenty-four percent. Can you believe it?" She leaned over and stroked my neck. I froze in surprise. Thedra had never touched me before that I could remember, much less favored me with a neck stroke.

"Twenty-four percent," I whispered, amazed myself.

Jit took my hand. "You've done so much for Lunge commune. Maybe now you can rest awhile."

Thedra snorted a laugh. "Maybe she can spend some time with us now, instead of sleeping away every free minute."

"I'm sorry," I muttered. I gave Thedra a small smile. "Believe me, I'd like to spend more evening time with you and Jit and Stoss. I'm so tired all the time, I don't even go to see the hatchlings anymore."

Thedra shook her head. "How can I be mad at the doumana who'll make ours the most famous, most honored commune on the planet?" Her mouth tightened. "You do sleep solidly, my sister. You've even started to snore. Maybe we can spend some of our extra credits from the kiiku on a new cot for you, something more comfortable."

I was so happy; it was easy to forgive Thedra. I didn't fool myself, though. We were unitmates, sharing equally in the honors and extras my work had brought. She wanted to make sure that glory splashed on her as much as me.

"I am very pleased," Simanca said when the shouts and stamps had died down, "to honor a doumana who has worked hard this season for our community." Her eyes focused on me. "Khe, come and take your reward."

My neck tickled. I knew my spots glowed bright-green, showing the pride I felt as I walked to the riser. The moment was worth all the effort, worth the fatigue. The tickle on my neck intensified and grew warm as more spots lit with the crimson of happiness.

I stepped up onto the riser and faced my sisters.

"It is I who am honored to have been able to give to my commune."

Simanca reached into the box near her feet and drew out the largest award of merit I had ever seen. On the loop inside, kiiku went from seedling to full vine, with huge black gourds. On the loop, too, was my name. Not the unit's, only mine.

As I looked out over my community, the spots on my neck tingled, turning orange with a pleased embarrassment.

"Next season," I said, making a promise I hoped I could keep, "thirty percent over last weighing."

I saw Simanca's mouth crinkle, her lips stretching out over her teeth.

***

SIMANCA TURNED UP THE PRESSURE.

"You have a duty to the commune." Her voice was flat and insistent. Her neck showed the colors of annoyance and impatience.

We stood up to our knees in kiiku. Pale-green stems, as thick as my wrist, twisted everywhere on the ground. Spiny red leaves and heavy black gourds hemmed in our legs. Jit was working nearby, but not close enough to hear. Stoss and Thedra were far across the field, harvesting the last of the Cooling Season crop.

"I have done my duty for twelve years since I first emerged as an adult," I replied evenly. "In the six years since my ability came forward, I have done all that was asked of me, despite exhaustion."

"You have compensation. All eighth-day work has been lifted from you to allow you to rest."

As if that made a difference. Fatigue and frustration made me bold. And the knowledge that Simanca needed me to realize her great ambitions. Her need kept me safe from punishment.

"I ask every season," I said, "but you still haven't kept your promise."

"Don't start that again," Simanca said. "I've told you why you can't work with the hatchlings."

"Because I'm needed in the fields. Yes, I know."

"You barely keep up with the kiiku. If you added hatchlings to your obligations, you'd fall apart. I'm looking out for your welfare."

"Perhaps if you cultivated fewer fields, I wouldn't be so worn out."

Her dark eyes narrowed to thin black slits. Spots flared on her neck. "Your job is to increase crop output, not to question my decisions. Are you unhappy that Lunge commune has prospered and grown? We have seven new fields ready for kiiku seeds. Old orchards are blooming again. Our population has doubled, and twenty-two hatchlings emerged here this year. We are the most respected and honored of all communes. Do you find these to be bad things?"

I sighed and changed my tactics. "I'm tired. I feel used up. Please, I need a change of assignment. I need rest."

"Yes, well, hard work exhausts us all," Simanca said. "Your duty is to serve the commune. Not as you wish, but in the way that best benefits your community." She took a step toward me. "I am surprised, Khe, that your neck is not awash in the colors of shame. Your sisters have worked hard harvesting and preparing the food you eat, sewing the garments you wear, keeping your dwelling in good repair for your comfort. The creator has given you a great gift—the ability to make things grow. Are you too tired to be of service to those who have labored for you without complaint?"

I lowered my eyes and said nothing.

Simanca leaned back, rocking slightly on her back toe. "We're nearing the end of the tenth-year competition. You know how important this harvest is for us. With your help, our production has increased again, but Grunewald commune is larger than we are, and pushing hard to win. To beat them, we must not only excel this season, but the next as well."

Simanca stopped rocking and leaned toward me, her face barely a breathing space from mine. She dropped her voice to a near whisper. "Do you want to see your community humiliated, filled with failure? If we lose the tenth-year competition, we will drop in hatchling assignments as well. Do you wish Lunge commune to lose this honor?"

I hunched my shoulders. "No."

"Then you must return to the fields tomorrow and continue your work without further complaints."

"But—"

"But what?" Simanca's voice was as hard as kiiku rind. "Khe, will you serve your commune or won't you?"

The voice of a lifetime of training whispered in my ear: "Contribution to the community gives joy to our lives. To serve is to find happiness." Words I had believed and lived by.

Simanca heaved her shoulders, making her look bigger than she was. "You must answer, Khe. Will you help your community or not?"

I spit out the words like rotten food. "Yes. Yes, of course."

Simanca lowered her shoulders back to their normal position. "None of what we've accomplished would have been possible without you. The entire commune gives you their thanks." She leaned forward and touched my neck. "Go now. Rest. Come to the fields tomorrow with a cheerful heart, ready to work."

I trudged back to my dwelling. In my sleep quarters, I sat on the narrow cot. Resting my hands in my lap, I looked at the insides of my wrist. Again. As I had so many times since I'd first noticed.

The inside of my left wrist now showed thirty-four small blue dots. Thirty-four reminders of the years I'd lived as an adult. Except I was only twelve. No. Thedra, Jit, and Stoss, who emerged when I did, were twelve. Simanca could pretend that the dots meant nothing, but I knew I aged one year for each crop I accelerated, growing older faster than my sisters. Pushing the crops was killing me.

Simanca knew it, too. My neck itched and burned; my spots lit with too many colors. Simanca knew. I was not Khe, a living doumana, to her, but a sort of wonderful machine. A machine that she had pushed to its limits, even while knowing that overwork would destroy it. I had gladly given prosperity to my community, but I would not give my life. How were we different from the preslets or food beasts if we existed for nothing more than sacrifice?

And what of my sisters? Whether we spoke of it or not, they couldn't have missed the number of dots on my wrist. Had they, too, decided that kiiku had more value than my life? Or did they worry and fret about me in silence, obeying some edict from our leader?

An anger as sharp as teeth roared through me. My neck burned. My life was worth more than what a few extra loads of kiiku could buy. What did I want that was so unthinkable? Nothing more than my due, the natural span of my life. Wanted it for myself, not for what I could give my community.

Contemptible—the thing I'd decided to do.

I clutched anger to my heart and made my plans. I

couldn't take a transportation vehicle. I had no experience as a pilot. I'd have to travel by foot. I would need clothing for Barren Season, tools, some food, but only the strictly necessary, to keep light the weight I carried.

The moon had turned its face from the world, leaving only the stars to light my way. In the fields, shadow-washed plants rustled in the breeze. Tenth-year competition was on and the fields had been mostly stripped, but here and there I found food still on the bough, vine, or bush. I took what I could carry—stuffing it into the small harvesting bag I'd stolen. I set my mouth in a hard line and did not look back when I crossed the border of Lunge commune.

CHAPTER NINE

UTSIDE

"WITH THE EXCEPTION of occasional mild fatigue, Khe's health remains excellent. She shows no ill effects from the Resonance sac surgery or her newfound abilities."
—*Ninth communiqué from Simanca to the orindle Pradat*

I LAY on my belly on a weedy hilltop. I could smell the green scent of the weeds where my body had crushed the seed heads. In the field below, twenty or so doumanas worked at harvest. The failing sun threw long shadows across the land. The air was growing chill.

For five days I'd walked south, moving away from the land that had nurtured me, and from the commune-sisters I loved. For five days the thrill of independence had fueled me, keeping legs unused to travel moving forward, a mind unused to solitude from falling into fear and loneliness.

Yesterday I'd run out of supplies. I'd thought I'd find food on the way, but each commune I'd crossed had been stripped of everything edible. It was the tenth-year competition, of course. Not a leaf, seed, stem, or root had been left that could be harvested and put on the scale to be weighed. My stomach twisted and groaned. My thoughts crawled slowly and always turned to food, no matter how hard I tried to concentrate. I had to find something to eat.

On the flat fields below the hillside, four doumanas piloted large harvesting machines, great silvery-gray crafts with high, smooth sides and a whirling metal string on the bottom. Doumanas on foot followed the machine—their backs bent in what I knew quickly became a painful position —gleaning the usable crops the harvesting machine missed.

Based on the size of the three neat rectangular fields spreading out below the rise, I figured that this commune was larger than Lunge. As far as I knew, all communes were built on the same model. I couldn't see any dwellings from my perch—only a few machinery sheds and outbuildings. If, like on Lunge, the main structures lay at the heart of the commune, this was probably a community of three hundred or more.

With a communiteria full of hot food and soothing drinks. And sleep quarters with fine cots and warm blankets.

Several doumanas stood on the beds of each vehicle, metal tridents in hand, pushing straw mulch onto the harvested ground. The faint strains of their work song rode on the cool breeze.

We'd sung the same song at Lunge. The doumanas in every commune probably sang it. Tav had said that even the males sang the same songs, spoke the same language, and adored the same creator we did. Thedra said that was because our species didn't have enough imagination to make up anything different. When I was young, I sometimes feared the creator would strike Thedra down for the blasphemous things she said, and sometimes I wished it would, but nothing ever happened. And what did that mean?

I sighed and watched the workers. I couldn't let them see me. No sane doumana traveled alone except during Resonance, and even then, none traveled on foot. If they caught me, they'd want to know my community. They'd send me back. What would Simanca do then? Order me shunned, and to the fields. Kill me in a season instead of a year.

My neck burned. My spots lit blue-red. What did I, who'd lived all my life as part of an entwined community, know of survival alone? I rubbed my neck for comfort. I didn't need self-pity. I needed to learn how to survive.

A second group of workers arrived, hauling tents and torches in a large open-back vehicle, and made their way to the field nearest me. I swore under my breath. This crew would harvest into the night.

I didn't have a choice. I was going to have to cross those fields. If I could get past the doumanas, I could grab some of the crops off the vine to eat. I drummed my fingers against the ground. The light would be completely gone soon. I had to go now.

I gathered my small bundle of belongings and started down the hill, hunched into myself, hoping to be inconspicuous, but one of the doumanas spotted me. She nudged her companions and pointed my way, then leaned over and called to the vehicle's pilot. The vehicle came to a stop. My neck burned. If they got close, they'd see the colors of my fear. Five or six doumanas jumped down from the machine and ran toward me, waving their tridents and shouting.

I stood as still as a rock, my mind spinning. Had word been sent out to look for me?

The other two vehicles stopped. The doumanas on them jumped down and followed their sisters in the race.

If word had been sent out, it was Khe the Grower they would be looking for, not some wandering babbler.

I twisted my back into the bent posture I'd seen in the babbler we'd once driven from Lunge, and let my face go slack, the way hers had been. Moving slowly, I pulled my cloak around my throat to hide the colors there.

"Pretty day," I said when the fastest doumana came close enough to hear. I hoped my voice didn't betray the fear pounding inside me.

The doumana's face screwed up with confusion. Her emotion spots flared brown-green.

I made my voice high, like a hatchling's. "I'm very hungry." I held out my hand. There was always a chance that they'd give me something to eat.

The doumana jabbed her trident toward my stomach. "Be gone," she said. The sharpened tips stopped no more than a finger's width from my skin. "Go on. Get out."

I hobbled slowly, hoping she'd let me go and none of her sisters would come to help her.

But her sisters kept running toward us until a crowd nearly surrounded me. They shook their tridents and their fists, yelling.

"Get out, babbler."

"She stinks like a dung pile."

One of them picked up a stone and hurled it. Pain exploded through my thigh. I grunted, and forced my face to go slack again. Babblers, it was said, didn't feel pain.

"Move," a doumana said, her lips pulled back over her teeth. "Filthy babbler."

Another doumana picked up a rock and held it high, squinting as she took aim and threw.

I ducked and ran.

I could hear them running after me. My heart pounded. A rock zinged past my head.

"Come this way again and it'll be more than rocks we aim at you," a doumana yelled.

These fields were well tended. There wouldn't be too many rocks for them to find. What if they threw their tridents instead?

"She's heading for the wilderness," a running doumana called.

"Over the hills and into death," another said.

"Let her go," a third said. "Let the wilderness have her. She'll make a good meal for some wild beast tomorrow or the next day."

Several of them laughed, but they stopped giving chase.

I kept running. My chest tightened.

The last commune.

The end of the world.

CHAPTER TEN

HE WILDERNESS

"THE WILDERNESS IS A WASTELAND, useless for commune or kler. The fearsome beasts there live by preying one upon the other."
—*Narration from a visionstage presentation*

HILLS GREW up beyond the last commune, sloping gently at first, and then turning mean. Fear had kept my legs moving, my hands scrabbling to push myself back up when I fell. If the doumanas came after me in vehicles—I couldn't outrun that.

The land was rocky at the top of the hill. Rough-edged stones, some as large as my fist, littered the ground. Scrubby gray bushes sprouted here and there, keeping their distance from each other. In the valley beyond, large red rocks, twisted into strange shapes, jutted from the ground. Panting, exhausted, I looked back across where I'd come.

The commune's fields stretched out, looking as brown and flat as a blanket in the failing light. I heard the soft whir of harvesters in the far distance, but nothing else. No one was chasing me. Beyond the fields, lost in the gloom, lay the low, rolling hills that sheltered Lunge.

My sisters were there, snug in their dwellings, their bellies full. Their world was so small. My belly was empty, but already my world was larger than any they would know.

Pradat knew a larger world. She'd come to Lunge. Maybe she went to communes and klers all over. The doumanas with me in Morvat Research Center were from klers and communes I'd never heard of. They'd never heard of Lunge.

How had Pradat known where Lunge was and how to get there? If she didn't know, if her vehicle had been preprogrammed, who set its course?

Simanca had said that she'd contacted Morvat Research Center about me. How had she contacted them? The visionstage only received, it couldn't send. Maybe Simanca had given a message to a corenta and the doumanas there had taken it to Morvat. How did a corenta know where to go?

How had Simanca arranged to buy land and fields adjoining Lunge when I knew she'd not stepped foot off the commune during the negotiations, and no strangers had come to us?

Somewhere, in the klers maybe, someone knew the answers to these questions and kept the information secret. Why weren't we told? The point of the visionstage was to keep us informed and educated. "Everything one needs to know" was the motto that spread across the stage between presentations. I'd been comforted by those words, felt smug and intelligent, knowing that eventually I'd learn everything if I paid attention long and well enough.

"Everything one needs to know." Who decided what our needs were? The same doumanas who decreed what crops we would grow?

My neck burned. I'd felt safe, had thought that distance from Lunge was all I needed. I'd been as naïve as a hatchling. If Simanca wanted the Grower of Lunge Commune back, or if those-who-knew-more-than-they-said wanted me, there were surely ways.

I DREAMED I pulled a sled piled high with ripe kiiku, slogging my way through thick, slushy snow. The kiiku was due at Community Hall for weighing, but it kept falling off the sled into the snow. Each time I stopped to pick up what had fallen, more tumbled off. I grabbed at the kiiku. My hands were freezing and my fingers wouldn't bend around the gourds.

I awoke in the morning shaken and depressed. *The Rules of a Good Life* says, "Give attention to dreams, for in the dark of sleep come truths hidden in the light." That dream was the last thing I wanted to think about, but I was too well trained to the Rules. I sat up and made myself consider what the dream could tell me.

Another of the Rules was "Seek always for the positive."

I laughed. It was so obvious. I should make a sled to carry my pack, any food that I found, and firewood. A compact sled, maybe the length from my fingertips to my shoulder, large enough to carry my things, but small enough to easily pull and maneuver.

Among the things I'd stolen from Lunge were two strong, sharp knives. I was lucky that this hillside was rich with rhantan trees—"runt" trees we called them because of their stunted height and slim trunks. I chose one and began sawing through the trunk. Back and forth, back and forth, leaning into the blade, rasp, rasp, rasp.

Most of the morning had gone by the time I'd carved three-quarters of the way through the rhantan. I put my foot against the trunk and gave it a shove. The trunk cracked, splintered, and fell over. I clapped my hands against my thighs in glee.

"Good work, Khe," I said, needing to hear the praise out loud.

A double reward came from my efforts. The rhantan was infested with blitters. I used the cap from my canteen to scoop out the tiny insects. I'd always hated the sour flavor and slimy texture of blitters, but these tasted wonderful. When I'd eaten them all, I still felt hungry, but not as ravenous as I'd been.

I attacked a second tree. My arms and hands ached. The knife's blade had gone dull and the work went slowly. I was as stupid as a babbler. I'd taken knives, but no whetstone. *Rasp. Rasp. Rasp.* Were simple mistakes like forgetting a whetstone going to be my undoing?

The sun had dipped behind the hill and long shadows were creeping across the land by the time I shoved over the second trunk with my shoulder. The second rhantan held no blitters. I needed food.

I hauled myself back up to the hilltop and peered over. No one was tending the fields, which seemed odd. They were working so hard yesterday, into the night.

Then I saw why—a corenta was perched on the open land behind me, to the north. The walls and buildings of the trading community hadn't been there yesterday. It must have arrived in the night. Simanca always said corentas were dangerous, the buildings, beasts, and doumanas in them without faith, and evil. That was why only she and Tav went to them. I gazed at the corenta, wishing I could see more than just rooftops beyond the high mud walls. The forbidden was always tantalizing.

"Another time," I told myself, and even as I said it, knew I would never see inside one.

THE RUNNERS for the sled lay next to where I sat cross-legged, peeling gooey, resinous fibers from the back of bark carefully stripped from the rhantan and braiding them into rope to tie the runners to the sled. I never would have thought of this on my own. I'd seen it on a presentation on the visionstage about life in the old days. It'd looked easy in the presentation. My fingers fumbled at teasing the fibers from the bark. Most broke, but some came away long.

Sweat prickled my scalp. My fingers, covered in rhantan sap, stuck to the fibers. The canteen sat next to me, empty. I put aside the work and hiked to a small spring I'd found some distance from my hillside camp.

Next to the spring, a stand of purple-leafed bushes with brown-husked fruit grew. I'd seen birds peck away the fruit's outer covering and eat the flesh and seeds inside, but was afraid to try them myself. Just because one species can eat something doesn't mean it won't hurt another. But I'd found nothing since the small, slimy blitters I'd eaten yesterday. My stomach rumbled. I had to give the fruit a try.

I picked several and sliced through the outer shell with a dulled knife. The fruit came apart in two neat halves. Inside, the flesh was bluish pink and creamy. Five small white seeds lay in a dead-center star pattern. I cut a chunk with the knife, lifted it to my mouth, and chewed. It tasted sweet.

I swallowed the bite, then slipped into the cool, running waters of the stream for a bath while I waited to see how my body took the food. After what seemed a reasonable time had passed and I didn't get sick, I took another bite. I waited again. Nothing happened. I chuckled under my breath and cut a larger hunk, popped it into my mouth, chewed, and swallowed. I felt a tingle in my ear holes and heard a ringing that grew louder and louder.

A sharp pain stabbed through my belly. My stomach heaved. I retched and retched but nothing came out. Sweat covered the parts of my body not underwater. My temperature soared, then plunged. I crawled from the stream and lay on the dirt, shivering head to foot.

My stomach heaved, but again nothing came up. The ringing inside my ear holes vibrated through my whole body. The air shimmered. A small green-furred beastlet crawled onto my bare foot and stared at me with huge yellow eyes. I tried to shake it off—but there was no beastlet. My stomach heaved again.

I began singing "The Expectation of Returning," the song for the dying. The words stuck in my throat, but I made myself go on.

"Sweet and merciful creator, too long have I been gone from you.

My heart cries out in longing to join again with the soul."

The words floated from my mouth, hanging in the air like text on the visionstage. My words came out in colors—blues, greens, yellows, and oranges. The wind picked them up like dry leaves, spun them around, and carried them away.

"Sweet and merciful creator ..."

The sounds from my mouth were not my words, but the sizzle of lightning, the crackling of fire, the wail of a hurt hatchling. My heart beat against my ribs.

This is death, I thought.

And I did not want it. Not here. Not like this. I'd given up so much to live my last year under my own command—I'd not let life slip so easily from me now.

Long blue ribbons of scream streamed from my mouth, the ribbons stretching on and on, floating upward and reaching for the sky.

If I run fast, I thought, death can't catch me.

The ground felt mushy under my feet, like wet wood pulp, though I knew the soil was dry and hard. Trees rose up on either side of the path, chanting "The Expectation," mocking me.

I covered my ear holes and ran until I reached my camp. The sled was there, chuckling low.

"Just a little more," the sled said.

I stopped and stared.

"A little more of what?" I asked.

"Sweat and blood. Hope and dreams."

I knelt by it and stroked its rough sides. "I know you now. I see how you want to be built."

"Build me strong," the sled said. "We have a long ways to go."

Even as I saw myself working, twining the ropes, lashing the runners, I knew I wasn't there, but back beside the poisonous bushes. My fingers bled. I mixed my blood with the rhantan sap that bound the sled together.

On and on I worked, the sled encouraging me, saying, "Yes. This is good."

At last, exhausted, I sat back. "Done."

"I am finished," the sled agreed.

I closed my eyes, and when I opened them again, I lay face down in the dirt by the stream and bushes. A hand's span away, a pool of vomit darkened the ground.

CHAPTER ELEVEN

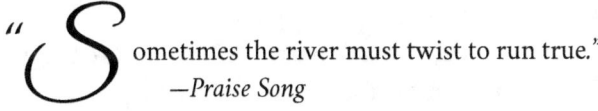

"*S*ometimes the river must twist to run true."
—*Praise Song*

I MUST HAVE SLEPT. Night had fallen. The moon and stars gleamed too brightly in an oily sky. I could hardly bear to look at them. I closed my eyes and lay still—one arm flung over my face. My skin felt clammy and ill-fitting over my bones. A chill wind blew.

After a while, I opened my eyes, slowly wriggled my toes, moved my legs, and stretched my arms. My shoulders and arms ached. My hands were smeared with dark blood where I'd somehow cut them, but everything seemed to work. I pushed myself up to a sit. The canteen lay a short distance away. Its silvery side glittered in the star-cast light. I reached over, grabbed it without getting up, and drained the last few drops of water into my dry throat.

It was slow going back to camp on legs that weren't quite stable. The wind grew mean and icy, whipping the leaves and bending the branches of trees and bushes. The ground was cold under my bare feet. I hugged my arms over my chest and walked bent forward, shrunk into myself for warmth.

The trees that in my delirium seemed to be chanting mockeries were simply trees now. I wanted to touch one, to feel the familiar roughness of bark against my hands, but was afraid that if I stopped, I wouldn't be able to start moving again.

At the hedge of thick bushes that protected the clearing of my camp, I did stop. My neck tingled. The sled was completed.

I stood still—afraid to move toward the sled, afraid it would speak to me again. I stood a long time, taking in shallow gulps of air, trying to work up my courage.

"Go around the sled. It can't hurt you," I murmured, not really believing my own words.

I walked toward my kit, keeping my eyes on the sled as I bent down to gather my cloak and put it on. I felt safer behind the fabric barrier, and foolish. There had to be an ordinary explanation for the sled's completion.

"Think, Khe," I said aloud, and made myself remember everything that seemed to have happened after the fruit made me sick. Most of it must have been hallucination, the chanting trees and the talking sled, but some of it must have been real.

Maybe something in the fruit gave me extra endurance. There were plenty of substances that did that. We used some of them at Lunge during planting and harvest. I must have returned to the camp and finished the sled while I was delirious, and then made my way back to the spring.

There must be something in the fruit that tricked my mind and made me think I'd heard the sled speaking. We'd learned about plants like that from the visionstage— madness-causing villisity, and sticker brump that could work its way through the soles of your foot to set in its dreamer's poison.

I felt better having figured a logical explanation. I wrapped up in my cloak and blanket, hoping I wouldn't dream of chanting trees or talking sleds.

IN THE MORNING I piled my few goods onto the sled and hiked down the hill. The valley floor was hard-packed red dirt, with red stones scattered around, as though the tall, twisted scarlet rocks had leaked all over. A light snow started to fall, dusting the red stones with white. Tufts of tan, weedy grass grew around the feet of the knobby rocks. Here and there something that looked like denish, a bulb crop we'd grown at Lunge, thrust brown stems out of the ground. I pulled the knife from my pack and made for the denish-looking plants.

The dulled blade wasn't much help in digging through the compacted soil, but I worked my way down and found the bulb. Like the denish we'd cultivated, the bulb was white with thin orange bands running top to bottom, oblong, but pinched in the middle—a wild cousin of the denish I knew, and smaller, about the size of my fist. I held it in my hand a long moment. What if it was poisonous too?

A long, low growl cut through the air. I jerked my head up and tried to work out where the sound had come from. It seemed to come from everywhere, bouncing off the tall stones. My heart beat against my ribs.

"A good meal for some beast"—that's what the doumana at the last commune had said. I squeezed the bulb in my hand. My neck burned muddy-brown. I had nothing to defend myself with but my two short, dull knives. I grabbed the sled's towrope and leaped to my feet.

What good would running do? If I looked like food sitting there, I'd look and smell the same moving, maybe more so.

I needed food. I couldn't fight or flee as hungry as I was. I bit into the bulb. It had the same sweet-tart flavor, the same juiciness as denish, but with a slightly bitter edge. I swallowed the first bite and took another, then another, all the time scanning for sight of the beast and listening for its sounds.

The beast called again—not a growl, but a series of sharp whistles. Another answered. Two beasts at least. I needed a weapon. The defenders at Lunge used stunners against predators, but I'd never held, much less fired a stunner. It'd never crossed my mind to steal one. Stupid. Stupid.

Sharp rocks lay all around. If I could fasten one to a handle, I'd have a spear. I dug through the brush I'd brought from the hill and found a straight piece that would do for a shaft. I needed a long, thin stone. I found two that seemed promising, picking them up with the hem of my cloak to protect my fingers. A beast called again, closer now.

My neck was on fire, my heart hammering. I made myself sit and carve a notch in the branch to fit the stone. At least three beasts were out there. I heard them coming closer. I ripped a thin strip off my hip wrap and used it to bind the stone to the shaft. I stood and looked, but couldn't see anything moving. Which was better—going deeper into the valley or holding still? Staying put, I decided. Better to save my energy.

A beast whistled, but its voice sounded fainter now, moving away from me. Another answered. I cocked my head and listened. The sounds were definitely fainter.

Teeth came at me, as long as my hand, thick as a finger, barbs on the end for holding prey. Teeth, and foul breath, and a huge beaked head covered in shaggy red and white feathers. I jumped back, held my spear with both hands, and thrust it toward the beast's large, round black eyes. The beast lunged sideways, lithe and quick. Towering over me, it stood on two powerful legs. The feathered body was barrel shaped and almost neckless. Its long arms had thick pincher claws where hands might have been.

I jabbed the spear again. Again, the beast lunged away, then rushed toward me, swiping at me with its heavy pinchers. I ducked into a crouch and shoved the spear as hard as I could toward the beast's chest. And missed.

A series of whistles sounded behind me. I whirled and saw two more beasts running toward me. The one before me whistled and clicked to its companions. My neck burned like fire. I turned back, wielding the spear like a club. The razor-edged stone raked across the beast's arm. Blood spurted from under the feathers.

The wounded beast wailed in pain. Its companions were almost on me. I heard their claws clattering on the loose stones. Snow was falling harder.

The first line of "The Expectation of Returning" rumbled unbidden in my mind.

My furious scream joined the wailing of the wounded beast as I turned and ran.

The cries of the injured beast rose up, louder and louder. The insides of my ear holes ached at the sound. I ran without looking back, jumping from rock to rock, skittering down the far rock face. I saw in the hillside ahead a small opening, not even as high as I was tall. I couldn't see how deep it was —my angle was wrong. I headed for it. It was my one hope.

The beasts whistled behind me, closer now. I ran, the muscles in my legs burning, and reached the opening in the hillside. It was a cave, deep enough maybe to hide me. Low enough to keep out the beasts. I turned, jerking my body through the small, dark hole.

I backed up and squeezed myself tightly against the rock

wall. It was cold and wet. A beast whistled. It knew where I was, and swiped into the darkness with its pincher hands. The cave wasn't deep, but it was enough. The beast couldn't reach me.

More beasts came. More feathered arms reached into the cave. I pressed against the rock wall. The snow was falling harder. Beasts wailed in frustration. My heart beat against my chest.

At last they gave up and left me.

I stood in the darkness a long time, panting.

When my heart and breathing slowed, I looked around. I wasn't at the back of the cave, but on the side. I walked carefully toward the back and saw there was a second, larger cave behind it. I eased in, worried that something smaller than the beasts but just as deadly might live there.

The larger cave was empty. My eyes adjusted to the dark and I looked around. There were no bones or scat to show that anything lived there at all. I'd left the sled when I ran. I'd have to go get it. All my food, blankets, tools, and brush for a fire were on it. I spotted something pushed behind a stone. A scrap of fabric. A hip wrap.

CHAPTER TWELVE

"*B*abblers have no idea what they are doing. They have no malice in their hearts when they strike you dead."
    —*Simanca*

A WHIMPERING SOUND startled me awake. I sat up hurriedly and stared into the near blackness of the cave. A dying fire gave the only light. A doumana sat cross-legged, stirring the fire's embers with a stick. The smoldering wood leaped into flame.

The doumana was filthy, with dirt splattered and streaked over her head, face, and body. One ear hole was caked with mud. The roundness of her face seemed out of place with her twig-thin body. I couldn't tell what shade of red her skin was under the dirt, or see the small blue dots to know her age.

She glared at me. "Who are you?" she demanded.

In the flickering light, her dark eyes looked like twin holes.

"Who are you?" I asked in return.

The doumana laughed, a low, throaty sound. "La, la. I have no name, only Babbler."

An icy burn streamed across my throat. The babbler scooted next to me and leaned close to my face. I tried to lean away, but my back was against the cave wall. Spittle ran down her chin and dripped onto my cloak.

"You're not a babbler," she said. "What are you? Some doumana lost coming back from Resonance?"

She looked away. "Yes. This was a Resonance year. I do so miss feeling Resonance. They didn't think I'd lose that, but I did. Made them angry, but it was their fault."

The babbler looked back at me. "Who are you?" she shouted. "What is your community?"

I swallowed and made myself look into her rheumy eyes. "I am Khe. Once of Lunge commune."

"Once of Lunge commune?" The babbler's high-pitched laughter echoed in the cave. Her breath felt hot on my skin. Her voice turned harsh. "You're no babbler. What are you, then? A reject? Another experiment gone wrong? Are you a mistake?"

I felt the colors glaring on my neck—blue-red, and muddy-brown—but the babbler didn't seem to notice. Her body stiffened and her eyes rolled. Her eyelids fluttered and closed. I was afraid to touch her.

I pulled my cloak tight, as though that could keep me safe if she awoke from her trance and grabbed for me. On my knees, moving slowly, I began to gather my few things. If the snow had stopped, I'd try to make it to the kler. Even that fearsome place seemed better than staying here with her. All I had to do was get past her to the cave opening.

The babbler sighed deeply. I swung my head around to look at her. My hands were clenched into fists. Her eyes were open and clear. She stared as if waiting for me to do something she both dreaded and expected.

"The storm is full-fledged," she said calmly. "It won't stop for three days. You head out into it now, you will freeze to death."

"I see mud on your foot casings. The snow probably turned to rain a while ago." I cocked my head and listened, but heard no telltale drip of water. "Has the rain stopped, too?"

The babbler picked at the mud on her casings. "I was hungry. The stream plants are delicious, but you get dirty fetching them out. I found that sled and those goods while I was out." She tilted her head back and stared at the rocky ceiling. "You do remember that I was a weather-prophet. Long, long ago. Before—" Her emotion spots erupted brown-black with anger.

As quickly as it had come, the color vanished from her neck. When she spoke again, her voice had the flat cadence of weather-prophets on the visionstage. "The storm will rage three days, then lessen. On the fifth day, it will rain slightly. On the sixth day, the sun will warm the land, and cloaks will not be needed."

The fire had nearly died out. I fed it more branches and sat back. I stared at the babbler, trying to judge how much of what she said was true, how much was madness speaking—and how frightened of her I should be. Had she really been a weather-prophet? Could she still do it?

"The storm will be at its height tomorrow at midday," she said. She waggled a long, pointed finger at me. "I wasn't just a prophet, you know. I was First. I could always taste the weather before anyone else—better than anyone else."

The emotion spots on her neck flared bright-green, the color of pride. If she hadn't really been a prophet, she certainly believed she had been.

Her mouth crinkled, spreading her lips over her teeth. "I'll tell you a secret. Coming snow doesn't taste cold at all."

Best to let her talk and stay on her good side. If she were right about the storm, I'd be stuck in our shared shelter for several days.

"What does snow taste like?" I asked.

"Like blood—what did you think?" She laughed and hugged herself. "I see by your clothes that you're a country doumana," the babbler said. "No doubt you stare up at the sky and watch the clouds, judge how the wind is blowing, see what colors circle the moon, and guess your weather that way. Then you consult the visionstage and let a weather-prophet tell you how close to right you've come. But if you've got the knowledge, you just open your mouth and taste. Rain is like sour fruit, makes my mouth pucker. Heat tastes like dirt." She patted my leg with her filthy hand. "There now, isn't that a good gift I've given?"

She'd given me nothing, but I said, "Yes. Thank you."

"Oh, the doumana thanks a babbler. That's a pretty bunch of manners they taught you at Lunge commune."

Before I could say more, her eyes rolled back in her head and she went rigid again. I couldn't know how long this fit would last. I crept past her, out the large chamber we shared and to the smaller front cave. Snow was falling hard and fast. I wasn't going anywhere for a while.

The babbler's voice came from behind me.

"What did you say your name was?"

I made my way back into the large chamber.

"Khe," I said, and suddenly very much wanted for her to have a name. When babblers were cast out from their communities, they left everything, even their names. Babblers didn't mind, so they said. Insanity robbed them of the will to care. They said babblers didn't even care about their own lives and died quickly once they'd departed. But the state of this babbler's clothes and body made me think she'd been away from her kler a long time.

"When did you leave your community?" I asked.

The babbler's full lips curled back from her teeth. "Long ago. Two years? I've forgotten." Her eyes lit with a sudden thought. "I was fourteen then. How old am I now?"

She licked her fingers to wet them, turned her left arm so the inside faced up, and smeared away the dirt covering her wrist. I leaned close to her arm, to see. We both stared at the cluster of small blue dots on her skin, two rows of seven and a third row with four.

"Eighteen." She seemed delighted with the discovery.

I blew out a breath. She'd survived four years on her own. Maybe I could survive Barren Season and into First Warmth.

"How old are you?" she asked.

My emotion spots flamed. I didn't know how to answer her. I turned over my arm so she could see the dots on my wrists, four rows of seven and a fifth row of six.

"Thirty-four," the babbler said and wiped her hands against her mud-splattered hip wrap. "One more year and you'll return to the creator." She stared at my neck. "Not too happy about that, are you?"

My heart clenched like a fist. To return to the creator was a joy, but not when almost two-thirds of my life had been stolen away, my span unnaturally shortened not by accident or illness, but by greed. A lifetime I wanted back.

I glanced away and took a deep breath, drawing the stale air of the cave into my lungs and holding it, then letting it out slowly, the way Tav had taught us to calm ourselves, back when we were hatchlings. Long before my defect was discovered. Before my abilities set Simanca's eyes aglow.

"Put some wood on the fire," the babbler said. "It's almost out again." She hugged her arms around her thin chest. "I haven't had a fire for … who knows how long? No firestarter. Lucky for me to have found this sled with so many useful things packed on it. I've been cold."

"It's my sled," I said. "I built it. Those are my things."

"Hmm," the babbler said. "Put some wood on the fire anyway."

I fed small sticks to the embers, glad for the warmth. When they caught and flared, I added a few broken branches. We'd have to conserve, though, if the storm was really going to last as long as the babbler predicted.

"You can stay," she said. "It never gets wet in here. And the wind doesn't blow through."

I rubbed my neck, comforted by the familiar touch of my own skin. "Thank you."

The babbler bit the tips of her dirty fingers. "Are you going to stay?"

"Until the storm stops."

"Are you going to pay?"

"What?" I asked.

"There's a cost for hospitality."

My stomach tightened and my neck itched.

The babbler hummed under her breath, a long low sound: *arrumm, arrumm.*

"I don't have food to offer." I said. "I only have what's on the sled."

Arrumm. Arrumm.

"I could maybe spare one of the knives."

The babbler stopped humming and pointed one dirty finger at me. "All this time I've been alone, without the sound of another's voice." She leaned close. "You must tell me your history as it happened, completely and in detail. Then you must listen to mine. Conversation and companionship is the price I ask."

CHAPTER THIRTEEN

"The trees all glitter with promises,
Broken, broken, and alone."
—*The babbler's song*

THE SUN'S rays stabbed through the cave's ragged opening, laying a too-bright line of white across the shadowed walls. I closed my eyes against the light and listened to the babbler moving about the cave.

I'd learned a great deal about her in the six days I'd been there. She often thought that what happened to others was directly linked to her.

I opened my eyes. The babbler was staring down at me.

"Is there more to your tale?" she asked.

I sat up in my makeshift bed. "There's always more, but I've told you everything that matters."

"Good." She stirred the dead ashes of the fire with a stick.

The snow had stopped falling on the third day. I could have left then, but I had promised to tell my complete story and didn't want to break my word. And in truth, the babbler's strange company was better than being always by myself.

"We should look for food while the weather's good," I said. Last night we'd finished the last of the babbler's stores. She'd been generous, sharing what she had and asking nothing in return but that I keep talking.

"Listen to this, Khe," the babbler said. She opened her mouth and sang in a voice as deep and pure as a river.

"Birds of the northern lands, a shadow on the rise
New as the leaves I once twined 'round my brow.
Where are you going,
Your sharp eyes turned blind?
Tossed by the traitor wind
On these barren grounds?
The trees all glitter with promises
Broken, broken, and alone.
Hear how the snow is mourning,
Broken, broken, and alone."

At Lunge we'd sung of Resonance, the joys of work, and praises to the creator. The babbler sang of herself, a song from the soul. I hadn't known that was possible.

She thumped her chest. "I am more than a babbler, more than a First in weather prophecy. I am a songmaker, too. Better than your Thedra, I'd wager. I used to be called to sing for—" Her face clouded and she looked down at her feet. "That was a long time ago. I'm surprised I remember."

I braced my elbows on my knees and asked, "Will you tell me your story now? How you came to be here?"

The babbler's lips crinkled. "I thought you were hungry."

I raised my shoulders in a small shrug.

"Sometimes, Khe, you act like a hatchling. Food and water always come first. Then shelter. Then fire. Stories can wait."

Outside the cave, the air smelled clean and wholesome. The heat from the sun warmed my head, neck, and hands, the only parts of me exposed outside my cloak. I heard the *schloosh, schloosh* of the babbler's steps through the slush. When she stopped, there was no sound at all. Was this what life was like inside the egg—white and silent?

The babbler disappeared around a small bend. I followed slowly, in thrall to the beauty of the land, the faint strains of a bird cheeping somewhere in the distance. Low-slung jipini bushes, their ripe yellow berries dusted with snow, grew nearby. In the leafless tree branches, drops of water hung from icicle tips as if holding their breaths, then fell. Water from the melting snow sheeted the canyon walls, darkening their natural pale-red color. The crystalline veins threading through the rocks acted as prisms, making tiny rainbows that slid across the stone.

The babbler's wail tore the silence. I ran through the slush, the muddy snow sucking at my foot casings. I came around the bend and saw the babbler on her knees, her back humped, her face in the dirt. I wanted to call her name, to get her attention, but had no name to call her. I bent over her and folded my arms around her waist and tried to lift.

She shoved me away. "Can't you see I'm eating?"

The babbler licked her mud-covered fingers, her eyes widening in concentration. Glancing around, she seemed to find what she was searching for and reached at something tucked between two stones. Grunting, she tugged and pulled and finally fell back, grinning, clutching feathery green stems.

"No," I cried, diving for her hand, which was full of lenrels, a plant so toxic that one bite would kill her before the shadows had moved. I shoved her hand away just before she put the lenrels in her mouth.

"Mine. Mine," she screamed, and tried to pull her hand free, but I had a firm grip and wouldn't let go.

"You've taken everything," she said. "I don't want to go. Please. Please."

Still holding tight to her one hand, I slipped my free arm over her shoulders.

"You don't have to go," I said, keeping my voice as soothing as possible. "You can come back to the cave with me."

The babbler stared at my face, but I could see she didn't know who I was. "Is it time for the presentation?"

"Yes," I said. "It's time. We have to go now or we'll be late."

"No," she screamed, and beat against my chest with her fists. I threw my arms up to protect my face and neck, and stumbled back. She kept coming at me, pounding my crossed arms with the sides of her fists. She pushed me hard. My heel hit a rock. I fell on the cold, hard ground, knocking the wind from my lungs.

The babbler turned and ran toward the cave.

I lay still, getting my breath back. My back hurt where I'd landed on it. When I could breathe again, I struggled to my feet and chased after her. I came through the entrance to the cave's rear chamber and found the babbler sitting with my opened pack on her lap. When she looked up, her eyes were clear and bright.

"There you are," she said cheerfully. "I was looking for the firestarter. We need warmth."

"The wood is gone," I said, keeping my voice conversational. "We used the end of it last night."

Her cheerfulness faded. "You'll have to go and find some."

I stared at her. If she saw the brown-black anger spots on my neck, they didn't concern her.

"You hit me," I said.

"Did I?"

"You knocked me into the snow and mud."

The babbler nodded. "Once, when I was newly insane, I

pushed an orindle out a window. The fall broke both of her legs." She shrugged as if all of this was of no consequence.

I sighed. There was no point in talking about what had happened. Crouching, I lifted the blanket holding my things from her lap and set it on the ground. I fumbled through, found the firestarter, and handed it to her. "I'll look for some wood."

"Good," she said. "And something for a meal. My last one was interrupted."

"Do you—" I began and stopped. I wasn't sure she could answer my question. "Do you remember what happens when a spell is on you?"

The babbler shook her head. "It's like being awake one moment and awake the next. In between, things happen that I know nothing about."

Another question nagged at me. "Do you remember your name?"

The babbler's sides shook with contained laughter. "I have no name. I never had a name. I hatched as a babbler."

I tsked my tongue on the roof of my mouth. "You said you were a weather-prophet. Was that a babbler's lie?"

"Of course I was a prophet. I was First in Chimbalay."

"I don't think so," I said. "Weather-prophets have names. I've seen them on the visionstage, and none was ever called Babbler."

The brown-black of anger flared on a few spots on her neck. She pulled herself to her feet. "I was a weather-prophet. I still am. Didn't I tell you about the snow and the rain and the warm day that would follow?"

I shrugged. "Luck."

"Skill!"

"Weather-prophets have names. Everybody has a name. Mine is Khe. What's yours?"

"Marnka." She spat the word at me, and fell silent. The spots on her neck glowed greenish-orange with amazement.

"Marnka," I said. "It's a good name."

"It is," she said.

"I think your story must be good, too. I'd like to hear it."

"Oh yes," she said. "It's quite the tale. Fetch us food and firewood and I will tell you what they did to me."

CHAPTER FOURTEEN

"To uphold your responsibility to the new generations, choose your mate for strength and beauty, and with great care."
—*The Rules of a Good Life*

THE FIRE WAS CRACKLING, the smoke drawn up and out fissures in the cave's ceiling. Marnka had made a mélange of the jipini berries, tano, and denish that I'd found. It was scant, but delicious, the way any food is to the truly hungry.

"I have been trying to remember all day," Marnka said, licking the last bit of mélange off her fingers. "All day trying and mostly failing. Some memories are there. I can recall my kler and how it looked—the walls and structures. Huge black buildings, rising into the sky." A shiver trembled across her shoulders. Her voice fell to a whisper. "There were needles and drugs. There was a dark room and a voice saying the same thing over and over. There was agony. I remember screaming."

A shiver ran through me as well. I remembered waking in

Morvat Research Center, the overwhelming brightness of the colors, the unbearable noise. But I received something I wanted for my pain. I didn't think it was the same for her.

Marnka drew her knees to her chest and laid her forehead on them. Her back rose and fell with labored breathing. Finally, she looked up.

"There were seven weather-prophets in Chimbalay," she said. "We shared a dwelling. From the window I could see all the way to the central commons. I would sit there and watch how the seasons changed the kler, the light glancing off the glass walls of the buildings in First Warmth, the rivulets of soft rain in Bounty Season, the way my breath would sometimes cloud the windows during Cooling, the quilt of snow over the streets in Barren Season."

She blinked rapidly and then rubbed her neck. "I remember this. I'm not making it up from madness." She pulled her spine straight and glared at me.

At Lunge, Simanca had warned us never to talk to babblers because they lied and didn't know it. Their disease made them do it, just as their disease took away their names and the will to live.

But Marnka was still alive. And she remembered her name. Or she'd made one up. Did it matter whether you called yourself the name you were given or one you chose yourself? A name was nothing but a sound other used to get your attention, or to mean you in their mind. Marnka served well for either purpose for us.

"I believe you," I said.

The rigid stiffness in her back relaxed.

"How much do you know about Chimbalay kler?" she asked.

"Chimbalay is the Region Seat, where the best orindles as well as the Powers, those who set the quotas for all the country communes, the lawmakers, and the price-setters live."

One spot on Marnka's neck lit ocher with impatience. "You think you know about Chimbalay, but you don't. Klers are walled for a reason. Walls keep the secrets inside. Do you know why all the weather-prophets live in klers?"

"To make sure they're qualified," I answered, glad that Tav had drilled us on this when we were hatchlings. "It used to be that each commune had its own prophet. When a commune's prophet returned to the creator, the available hatchlings were tested and the one showing the most ability was selected as the new foreteller. Some were good. Some weren't. A bad prophet could mean doom."

"At least you know a little something," Marnka said.

I cleared my throat. "After a disastrous year when several prophets hadn't seen a coming series of hailstorms that wiped out most of the crops in the Harvest Belt, the Powers decreed that all prophets had to come to the closest kler for testing and certification. The good ones stayed in the klers, where they could use the visionstage to reach all the communes in that section. The less able were assigned different work to do."

She nodded, much the way Tav used to when I'd gotten a lesson right. "When did this happen?"

I searched my memory. The hailstorms were before Simanca emerged. I made a guess. "Thirty years ago."

"Thirty-three," Marnka said.

Her tone made me feel that the number was supposed to mean something.

"Thirty-three years, Khe. We live for thirty-five. All the certified weather-prophets that haven't already returned to the creator are marching rapidly toward the end."

I still didn't see what that had to do with anything.

"Where are they going to get new prophets?" Marnka asked.

"Don't they still test the doumanas as they emerge, train the best prospects?"

"They do, but they have to test every newly emerged doumana to find just a few who show promise. It's very expensive and slow. No, the Powers have another plan. They want to breed what they need."

Shock made my spots flare gray-red. "That's impossible. You can't breed prophets."

Or maybe not so impossible. I'd wondered if my offspring might have gotten the growing abilities from me, the way the offspring of the preslets with the best feathers usually had good feathers too. If the Powers tracked the weather-prophets during Resonance and gathered their eggs, they'd have a good starting point for finding new foretellers. I told Marnka my idea, and she laughed.

"The Powers aren't leaving it that much to chance. They can't. The Powers realized long ago that they needed a reliable way of producing accurate foretellers. They set their best minds to the problem. Those thinkers declared that controlled breeding between certified prophets was the only solution."

My head swam. "Even if they controlled the doumanas, how could they get the males to agree? The Powers don't have authority over them, do they?"

Marnka chuckled. "The males were happy enough to do it. They thought it was a good idea. At first we all thought it was a good idea."

"What changed your mind?" I asked.

"Don't rush the teller through her tale, Khe." Her voice turned bitter. "Guardians came to collect me and three of my prophet-sisters the day before Resonance was to begin. At the research center, the orindles said we were fortunate—

we'd been blessed with special abilities, and now we could concentrate our Talents in the new generation by selective breeding. They said they'd done it before, and there were no bad effects." Marnka looked away. "It wasn't true."

I held my breath.

Marnka said, "The orindles made me what I am."

One of my spots lit blue-red with anxiety. Simanca had said that the creator made babblers insane, as punishment for their sins.

"You don't believe me," Marnka said. "You think no doumana would do this to another. You think that even if one might, it is not possible. But it can be done. Hush, I have remembered all day and I've got it right. I'd forgotten, they made sure of that, but they couldn't keep my memories dark forever."

I touched her neck gently. "I'm listening."

Marnka brushed my hand away. "I don't need encouragement. I've remembered now. I'd shout my tale to the rocks if you weren't here." She stopped and hung her head, a too-heavy flower on the thin stem of her neck. When she looked up, her spots showed the orange of embarrassment.

"It was my name, you see. I'd found bits and pieces of my history over the years, but when I discovered I had a name—when you gave me back my name—when I remembered, that was everything. Now I see backward in time. Oh, it's not all pretty to know."

I sat quietly until she was ready to go on.

"A vehicle waited for us," Marnka said, "even though the center wasn't far and we could have walked. When we arrived, the orindle Seldid—she was First there—was standing outside on the white stone steps. Those stones gleamed so brightly. The air smelled like spice. Seldid didn't say much to us, just greetings, and then brought us inside.

"My prophet-sisters and I followed her to a community

room. When we'd all settled into our seats, Seldid explained the breeding project. She told us that one hundred weather-prophets, both doumana and male, had been gathered at the center. When Resonance began, we'd stay at the center instead of going to our nesting sites. Each prophet could choose her own mate, as usual. Orindles and their helphands would note the pairings, watch the mating, and tag each egg to track which pairs bred the most skilled foretellers. Those pairs would mate again in future Resonances. She thanked us all for volunteering."

Marnka's tale nearly stopped my breath. This program went against nature, against all that was right. We were free to pick any mate we wanted, limited only to the choices available at the mating site. It was the one true choice we had in our lives.

"But how could this make you a babbler?" I asked.

"The drugs," she said, as if this were something I should have known.

Knowledge tickled at the back of my mind—drugs and babblers. Then I had it. "Did they use villisity?"

Marnka nodded. "Imagine how we felt. Our offspring would be more talented than we were, make fewer mistakes. They would free us all from hunger caused by unexpected drought or too much rain or unpredicted storms. We were proud to do this for all who would come after us. We gobbled our villisity and waited to feel the tug of Resonance."

She fell silent. Her head dropped to her chest again. It seemed a terrible effort for her to drag it back up.

"One of my sisters started showing the effects first," Marnka said. "She grew restless, pacing the large room where we were housed, touching things. She picked up a cup of water and set it down without drinking. She picked it up again and threw it against the wall. The water ran down in a rush. She touched her face, arms, head, and neck, over and over. She ran her fingers over the edges of chairs, cots, and windows.

"Another doumana, from a different kler—I didn't know her name—joined my sister on her uneasy walk. I felt unsettled too, needing to move. I thought it was the start of Resonance, but I was so angry. I wanted to strike out at something, anything. It took all the control I could gather not to. I joined the pacing doumanas.

"My sister started screaming. Other doumanas began to scream and howl like beasts. Doumanas were banging on the door, calling for help. No one came. Some of us began to push and shove the others. Fights broke out. Vicious battles. Someone was killed, I think. She looked dead, her head smashed against a wall and her brains leaking out."

Marnka said this in the same unconcerned way that she'd told me about breaking the orindle's legs, as if nothing that happened during a spell mattered.

"I suspect," Marnka said, "that the orindles watched us through hidden eyes or emotion paintings that weren't what they seemed. I was angry that they wouldn't come. I picked up a chair and hurled it against the wall. A doumana was in the way and she was hit. Blood pounded in my head. The pain was … I thought I would split in two. I heard myself laughing. The room filled with the scent of dead leaves and a harsh green fog."

NIGHT HAD FALLEN, and Marnka kept talking. The fire threw thin shadows on the walls of the cave. The air smelled overly sweet from the burning jipini branches. I wanted to cover my ear holes and block out the rest of this tale.

"I woke up fine," Marnka said cheerfully. "The green fog was medicinal. I was cured of that madness. All of us were.

Seldid came to apologize for our discomfort. She told me that while I'd been in that altered state, I'd picked a mate and laid my egg. I went back to my unit and back to work, no differently than before."

I rubbed my neck. "Then how did you wind up here? Why do you have spells?"

Marnka shrugged. "The season passed. During Cooling of that year, my prophet-sister who'd been at the research center with me started acting strangely. She would be tasting for upcoming weather or talking or singing, and suddenly stop as if turned to stone. A few moments later, she would pick up where she'd left off. One day a guardian came and said my sister had been assigned elsewhere. Rumors started that she'd turned into a babbler."

Marnka shifted position, folding her legs under herself. "By Barren Season, rumor was that six weather-prophets in other klers had turned into babblers. In Chimbalay, another prophet-sister started acting strangely. Suddenly she was gone too. Then it was my turn.

"I awoke in a blackened room." Marnka's voice was quiet. She stared at a spot above my head. "There were others there. I could hear them breathing in that slow way of the sleeping or the unconscious. I tried to move, but I'd been bound to the cot on my back. The bands were tight. I couldn't roll over. There was a voice in the room, a murmuring that never went away. I concentrated on the voice until I could make out the words. The voice said, 'Calm. Calm.' Sometimes it would say, 'We are not at fault. You are guilty. You have failed.' Sometimes it said, 'You hate Chimbalay. The sight of a doumana sickens you. You may go.'"

The fire was dying down. I put on more wood. The flames flared high, sending a sudden brilliance into the chamber.

"They took me to another room, a smaller one," Marnka

said. "The orindle Seldid was there. No one spoke, but I had become used to silence and this didn't bother me. My thoughts were on escape. I schemed for ways to overpower Seldid and her two helphands. I waited for my chance.

"Finally, Seldid spoke. She said, 'Reliable witnesses have seen you losing consciousness and being unaware that you have done so. You have been heard cursing the creator. You are guilty of insanity. All of your goods and your position as a weather-prophet are forfeit. You will be taken to the gate and will leave Chimbalay and never return. You will forget everything that happened here.'

"Her words brought my anger back, but I hid it well. The helphands undid the straps that held me. I pulled myself slowly to my feet, testing my legs, wondering if the helphands would let me stand on my own. They did, and they let me walk across the small room toward Seldid. I gathered every bit of strength I had and pushed her through the window. She landed in the hard dirt two levels down. When I saw the leg bones sticking through her torn flesh and heard her screams, I laughed."

My neck burned and my emotion spots burst into the color of fear. If the snow was still stopped tomorrow, I'd get away from Marnka before she hurt me like she had the orindle.

Marnka watched the color play across my neck, but said nothing.

"In some ways I was lucky," she said. "Chimbalay edges onto the wilderness. I didn't have to pass any communes or other klers to get here. The madness I'd felt in Chimbalay passed quickly. I was able to find food and water, to find this cave."

"Is Chimbalay the kler I saw across the plain?" My heart pounded. Chimbalay. Where the orindles who might save me lived.

Marnka nodded.

I leaned toward her. "You have to go back to the kler and tell the doumanas there what happened to you."

Her face hardened like a fist. "What good would that do? Would it make me normal? Chase away my spells? Would it stop the orindles from making more secret experiments?"

"If no one speaks out," I said, "the orindles can keep doing their awful work."

Marnka laughed under her breath. "Who would believe such a tale from a babbler?"

But I could see that she was thinking it over.

"No," she said. "They track me; they know where I am. I'd never get inside Chimbalay's gate."

"Marnka," I said softly, "did you never think that perhaps in Chimbalay they've found a cure?"

Her laughter turned as harsh as the Barren Season winds. "I told you, they know where I am. If they'd found a cure, they'd come for me. I am too valuable, my skills as a prophet too high, to let me rot in the wilderness if they could still use me."

That made sense, if they really knew where she was.

"How do they track you?"

She looked around and then whispered, "They come in my dreams."

I sighed. Was everything she'd told me only ravings after all?

Marnka's dark eyes sharpened. "Why haven't the Powers come for you? You have value—the Grower of Lunge Commune. I wonder why they let you go?"

"I don't think anyone knows I'm gone," I said. "Simanca was probably too ashamed to admit a doumana in her charge had run away. I doubt she told anyone."

"Maybe," Marnka said. "But I'd wager the orindle Pradat

told the Powers about you. You'd be a good candidate for breeding. Oh yes, they'd like to get ahold of you, I'm sure."

"Too late for that," I said with a bent sort of satisfaction. I might be forced to the fields or roosts for another season or two of growing, but the thirty-four dots on my wrist meant that my last Resonance was already past. Unless …

"Pftt," Marnka said. "You're a fool."

She jumped to her feet and stalked over to where I sat. She loomed above me, a dark shape. "Who are you?"

I shrunk away from her. "You know the answer. I am Khe."

"And what is that? A frightened runner? A timid doumana seeking only to cower in the hills until her time runs out? A sad soul longing for her commune and the comforts of ordinary life?"

I stared at her and then hung my head. "Yes. All of those things." I snapped my head up. "And no, none of those things. I left Lunge to find the orindles in Chimbalay. In hope that they might give me back my life."

I felt Marnka's breath on my skin. "The orindles have cures for many ills."

My spots flared greenish-blue, the color of hope.

"On the streets," Marnka said quietly, "doumanas talk. If you listen, you hear things, learn things you're not meant to know." She picked up my hand, pressed it to her mouth, and set it down gently. "You must go to Chimbalay. It is your only chance."

WHEN I WOKE in the morning, Marnka had gone. She'd fixed a meal of cold mélange for me. I could hardly eat it for the nervous twists and kinks in my stomach. She'd heated melted snow water, which I used to clean up my clothing and myself as best I could. When I was done, I didn't look nearly so raggedy.

I left my sled and most of my goods for her, keeping only the spear and one of the two dull knives. The rest I wouldn't need in the kler, and she could use them. I lay the firestarter on top—my special gift to her.

I was foolish to hang my hopes on Marnka's vague thought that the orindles could cure me. Still, I clutched her words to my heart as I walked the ice-patched wilderness toward Chimbalay. Perhaps I was mad as a babbler to believe her, but I'd convinced myself that she spoke the truth—the orindles could save my life. Believing is easy, if you want to badly enough.

A sharp whistle cut through the air and was answered by another a short distance away. My neck burned where my spots flared muddy-brown with fear. Beasts. I looked over my shoulder. A pack had caught my scent. Three. Four of them, judging by the whistles. Maybe more were hidden behind the low hills. The beasts were far enough behind that I might make it if I ran fast. If I didn't slip on the ice. If the gates of Chimbalay were open.

I ran as fast as I could, my eyes on Chimbalay's main gate. My heart pounded in my chest as if it might burst. I heard the beasts calling to each other, making their plans. One sped past me and turned, as if trying to drive me back toward its companions.

A sudden wind seemed to rise, tearing across the plain. My cloak was nearly torn from my shoulders. Fearful, I glanced back and saw the walls and buildings of a corenta sliding across the icy plain. My heart beat faster. Corenta or beasts—which was more deadly?

The sound of the raging wind grew louder. The whistles of the beast changed, coming faster. The calls came so quickly together that they were almost a continuous sound—

one voice springing from many points, fighting to be heard over the wail of the rising wind in the still air.

Anxiety made me slow and look. I had to know what the beasts were doing. One and then another beast stopped, staring at the corenta rushing across the plain. The mobile trading village hovered a handsbreadth above the land, streaming toward the open space between the kler and me, the way vehicles moved. It was close enough that I could make out the outer wall and some of the buildings behind it.

The beasts had stopped to stare at the corenta as well. Their whistles changed to fast, high-pitched clicks. One threw back its great shaggy-feathered head and howled. The beasts feared the corenta as much as I did.

I turned and ran.

The wind roared. The corenta slid across the plain. The beasts wailed and scattered. I would have run away from the corenta too, if the safety of Chimbalay were not at hand.

I ran and ran and reached the closed gate of Chimbalay before either the beasts or the corenta caught me. I pounded on the gate, and they swung open. A deluge of doumanas poured out, sweeping me away. I pushed and shoved and sidled and swore and made my way past them.

Into Chimbalay.

The place of the orindles.

CHAPTER FIFTEEN

 HIMBALAY KLER
PRESENT TIME

"THERE ARE secrets in the sky
And whispers underground."
—*Tales for Hatchlings*

THE BUILDINGS of Chimbalay rise in front of me—black glass towers reaching toward the sky. I stare transfixed. Chimbalay's doumanas swarm around me like water around a stone. One bumps into me and I am nearly knocked off balance, but she doesn't apologize. Around her neck she wears a thick white collar. They are heading for the corenta.

A hand seizes my shoulder from behind. I whirl and see a red-faced doumana in a fur-trimmed hooded cloak, a white collar on her neck too.

"Are you recently emerged, sister?" she asks. "If you're not heading for the corenta, you'd best get off the main path."

"Thank you," I say, and duck my chin and hurry off, making my way up a stretch of open dirt behind the backs of one- and two-level glass buildings. Now that I'm close, I see that the glass isn't truly black, but a very dark gray. True black wire, as thin as a single hair from a hard-furred beast, form a bottom-to-top grid through the walls. At Lunge, small panels like this glass captured the magnetic force of the planet and translated it into power for cookers, water and room heaters, and irrigation pumps. What is in the kler that it needs so much power to run?

The street is full of doumanas heading toward the gate. I cleaned up as best I could before leaving Marnka's cave, but feel conspicuous among these kler doumanas in their fine cloaks and foot casings. There is little room between the structures, but I squeeze between two of them and hide. After dark, it will be easier to move. Then I will find the research center.

I must have been mad to come to Chimbalay. What made me think the orindles that caused Marnka's insanity might be able or willing to help me? But I am here now, and every bit of me hopes the orindles will save my life. I huddle between the building and wait.

I wait all day. My stomach rumbles with hunger and my throat itches with thirst. My legs cramp from crouching so long in the tight space. Finally, the doumanas begin coming back. At first only a few straggle in. I wait until the streets are crowded before creeping from my hiding spot and joining them.

A sudden laugh behind me makes me turn. Three doumanas are walking, their heads bent together. They see me looking and glare. I drop my gaze to the ground and keep walking, trying to look like I know where I'm going.

I turn up a path that opens onto a wider street, Pale-Green Circle. The curving avenue is crowded with doumanas, most carrying sacks filled with food and goods. They have taken off their collars, the stiff fabric poking from the tops of sacks or hanging from curled fingers.

My stomach grumbles. There must be a communiteria, probably several for the large population. It's likely that this Pale-Green Circle has its own communiteria, and I will find it if I follow the street. I can't join the doumanas in line—they'd know me for an outsider at first glance—but perhaps I can break in after dark and steal something.

My neck prickles. I have fallen low. The sin of the collar is light compared to the ease with which I plan theft. I come to another path and almost without knowing I've turned, come into another street. A sign says Crimson Circle—the Place of Happiness. I follow the street, reasoning that a communiteria in one circle is likely just as good as one in another. And likely just as easy or hard to find. And break in to.

Fewer doumanas are out on Crimson Circle. I don't know if these tall buildings are dwellings, but if they are, it's hard for me to think how many doumanas must live in Chimbalay. I stop and rest against the smooth glass. A doumana wearing a purple cloak slung back from her shoulders and a purple hip wrap also stops. She looks into a window as if there is something of interest there, but I don't think she can really see anything. I start walking again. The purple-clad doumana starts too. My heart thuds. I quicken my step and the doumana quickens hers.

I pass four doumanas all dressed in blue. They stare at me. No one rushes here. They move slowly, as if the day will stretch out for them if they need more time. I hazard a look over my shoulder. I don't see a purple cloak.

Another pathway opens up, and I take it. It leads to Bright-Blue Circle—Excitement Street. The buildings here are seven to ten levels high and have arching white stone bridges connecting them at the fifth level. The wide spaces between the buildings are paved in blue stone. I stop and watch the doumanas coming up the same path behind me. They're well dressed and empty handed. Several give me curious stares, but none wears a purple cloak and hip wrap. I make myself walk slowly and tell myself I'm worried over nothing, that no one is following me.

In front of each building on Bright-Blue Circle, a tall, thin obelisk of translucent stone rises two levels in the air. In the darkness, the stones glow. Their soft pink light washes the kler, making the few doumanas still on the street look flushed. My head feels heavy from hunger and fatigue. I give up the idea of finding a communiteria. I'll settle for a sheltered corner where I can sleep unnoticed.

But not here in Bright-Blue. I'll go back to the edge of the kler, to be closer to the gate if trouble comes. I walk, turning away from the kler's heart until I am back at Pale-Green.

I find what would have been a mulch pile at Lunge, a place to turn food scraps into fertilizer for the crops. But this hill contains whole fruits, large chunks of meat, bits of cloth, and hunks of wood all thrown in together. The waste is astounding. This bounty is behind a fence and beneath a clear dome—to keep insects out and the smell in. There's a small door in the dome.

I glance around. No one is on the street, but still I am wary. I climb over the fence and pull on the door. It's unlocked and pulls open at my tug. I reach inside and push aside an old, worn cloth sack and a piece of wood to grab three denishes and a slice of meat. The denishes aren't the wild cousin I've grown used to, but the same tame variety we grew at Lunge. The meat is unidentifiable and moldy. I put it back. I pull out the worn sack. The bottom is still good. At Lunge we would have mended the holes near the top and kept using it. I put the denishes into the bag.

"Are you ill, sister?" a voice behind me says.

I whirl, holding tight to the sack. A doumana stands just outside the fence. Beneath her open purple cloak, she's wearing a purple hip wrap.

"My name is Larta," the doumana in purple says. She glances at the sack clutched to my chest and extends her hand. "If you like, I can hold that for you while you get over the fence."

My heart pounds. My neck spots flare brown-green in shame at being caught scavenging and muddy-brown in fear of who this doumana might be. Larta watches the colors play across my neck, seeming to note them.

I look hard at the kler doumana, memorizing her. Her skin is pale red and as smooth as still water. She's taller than I am and better fed, but probably no faster in a sprint. She leans gently into the fence with a studied indifference.

My mind whirls, running my options. The fence pens me in more than it protects me. On the other side, at least I'll have a chance to escape. I take the few steps needed to hand the sack over the fence. She takes my small hoard and sets it down. We keep our eyes on each other as I climb over the fence.

As soon as my feet touch the yellow paving stones, Larta takes hold of my wrist firmly enough to let me know there's no use trying to escape. Close to her now, I see the pin that closes her cloak at the base of her throat—a silver lattice-worked circle. A hand and part of an arm stretches down from near the top, extending toward another hand reaching up from the bottom. It must be a kler insignia of some sort, showing rank or importance. Larta sees where my eyes are focused.

"Yes, I'm a guardian," she says. "But you needn't fear me if you tell the truth."

My neck burns where my spots are lit with fear colors. It

was guardians, Marnka said, who held her down while a helphand drugged her, guardians who carried her to torture at Research Center One. I clamp my jaws shut, determined to say nothing.

Larta hitches up one shoulder in a shrug and says, "You're hungry. Come with me and I'll give you better than the garbage you've found here."

My stomach cramps. The offer is tempting. There are no shame colors on her neck, and I think that she's not lying. But her words could mean so many things—food at a safe haven, food in a cell. Hunger wins me over. I nod my head.

Larta keeps a hold on my wrist as we walk the dusky, emptied streets of Pale-Green, and tightens the hold when we turn into Crimson. There are more glowing obelisks on this street. The black buildings, yellow pavement, and Larta's red skin seem to blaze in the pink light. There are doumanas out here too, walking in groups. The night is cold. The doumanas all wear fur-trimmed hooded cloaks.

As we enter Bright-Blue Circle, Larta leans close and whispers, "I can't keep holding your wrist. We're too noticeable. I'm going to let go. If you run, you'll regret it."

I swallow and nod.

"We know what they've done to you," she whispers.

A chill shoots through me. Was Marnka right when she said the Powers tracked her location? Have they discovered me through her? Is Simanca looking for me after all?

We come into Bright-Blue Circle and turn, heading west, I think, but my sense of direction feels scrambled. Larta walks quickly, her hand cupped on my elbow to keep me next to her and moving at her speed. We come to a building that's dark except for lights shining on the third and fourth levels. I feel Larta stiffen as we approach and relax when we're past. There's a small metal plaque fixed to the front wall, but I can't read what it says.

Light-headed from hunger and fatigue, I stumble. Larta steadies me and says, "We're nearly there."

I almost don't care where she takes me, so long as I can rest.

"Do you remember how you got to Chimbalay?" she asks.

I shake my head.

"Do you remember anything?"

I shake my head again. Better that she assumes I've forgotten whatever she thinks I once knew, or that I'm simpleminded.

Larta squeezes my elbow gently. "Nothing to worry about. We have ways to help your memory."

Fear makes my spots flare. Do they use drugs here? Pain? To bring old memories to the surface. I don't trust her friendly manner.

We stop in front of a building that looks like all the others on the circle.

"Here we are," Larta says cheerfully, and waves her hand in front of a sensor that makes the rounded door dilate. I draw back in surprise. Doors at Lunge swung on hinges. This one opens like a mouth.

The bright light inside the building stabs my eyes. I want to squeeze my lids shut but force myself to look into the place I've been brought.

The entrance is wide and long. The floor is paved in white and green tiles arranged in a recurring V pattern. The walls are the same pale-green as contentment spots. Several closed green doors line the walls. At the end of the entry is what looks like a large receiving room. I hear laughter from the room—high-pitched, like hatchlings make. I can't see who might be in the room.

"Mees," Larta calls out. "It's Larta. I've brought a guest."

I hear many feet moving. I'm sure there are hatchlings here. One pokes her yellow, down-covered face from the doorway and peers at me. A short, round-bodied doumana with skin so dark red it is almost black sets her hand firmly on the hatchling's shoulders and pulls her back into the room. I hear a door whoosh open and what sounds like feet thumping up wooden stairs, then a door whoosh again.

Larta sighs. "Mees is supposed to be in charge, but I think the hatchlings rule here."

The doumana called Mees, the dark-skinned one, comes out the end room. She tugs at her blue and gold hip wrap, straightening it as she walks. She's smiling as though she'd been expecting me.

"You must be hungry," Mees says to Larta and me. "There's a big pot of mern bubbling in the cooker. Come have a bowl."

Larta takes my arm and we follow Mees down the entryway, through an arch into a room that is like a small communiteria. Five round cookers fill cubbyholes piercing one green wall. The cookers are like the ones at Lunge, but smaller. The room is so clean, it's as though no one had ever stepped foot into it before. Two long, clear tables are suspended from the ceiling on thin, nearly invisible wires. Thick cushions are arranged around the table, ten on each side and one at each end. I look at those cushions with longing. I could stretch out on them and sleep until the sun has risen and set a dozen times. The mern smells wonderful. My stomach rumbles, embarrassing me.

Larta motions for me to sit. I settle on one of the cushions. Its softness is a wonder to me. Larta slips off her cloak and settles herself next to me with a sigh. I notice that she wears a bracelet on either wrist with the same insignia she wore on her cloak.

Mees pulls a large pot from one of the cookers and sets it on a small, square wood table. This table is not suspended from the ceiling, but stands on four sturdy metal legs.

Tucked between the legs is a wood chest. Mees takes two bowls and spoons from the chest and ladles mern into the bowls until they are full nearly to the brim. She's standing sideways to us. I watch her check the pleats in the front of her hip wrap and adjust one slightly before bringing the bowls to the table. I am so far past vanity that it seems odd to see it in another.

I take a tentative spoonful of the mern. It's been a while since I've eaten this kind of food, and I'm not sure my stomach can take it.

From the corner of her eye, Larta watches me. Mees sits beside me.

"Is Inra around?" Larta asks between bites of mern.

"She's putting the hatchlings down for the night," Mees answers. "She'll join us soon."

A doumana comes into the room, dusting off her hands as she walks.

"We were saying your name, and here you are," Mees says in a merry voice.

Inra is taller than Mees, but shorter than Larta, about my height. She's thinner than the rounded Mees, more like the active-looking Larta. Her skin is medium red. Her eyes are as dark as a night without stars.

Inra takes a seat across the table from me. I glance at her, expecting the same warmth Larta and Mees seem to carry with them. Inra doesn't smile. She catches my glance and holds it. Her eyes are hypnotic. She's not looking at me, but into me, as though my skin is glass.

"Have you been suffering long?" she asks.

Her voice is as sweet and gentle as Jit's. A glaze of sweat breaks out on my skin. I want to answer that kindly voice.

Larta wipes her mouth with the back of her hand and says, "She hasn't said a word since I found her."

Inra nods slightly, still holding me in her black-eyed gaze.

"She can talk. She's frightened, but aware enough to know that silence is her best protection."

"Pfft," Mees says. "Larta was all dressed up in her guardian cloak. The doumana probably thinks she's about to be sent back to the research center. But if she can think that, she isn't completely mad, is she?"

"I haven't run across a babbler like her before," Larta says. "She understands everything we say. She doesn't seem diminished."

I stare into Inra's eyes and try to think. Marnka told me that after the procedures were performed, the weather-prophets went back to their communes or klers to work. Going insane didn't take the same amount of time for every-one. Some prophets lived several normal years until one by one, over time, they began showing the effects and were banished. Maybe these doumanas think that I'm one who hasn't been found out yet.

Inra looks away, releasing me from her hold. She rubs her hand lightly over her throat and gets up from the pillow. Mees gets up, too. Larta turns back to her bowl and eats as though she, like me, has been too long without food. Exhaus-tion washes over me. I make myself pay attention, to watch everything happening in the room, without seeming to.

Mees and Inra meet at the small wooden table. I see their heads bent together, but can't hear what they're whispering. I keep eating until Mees comes back and lays a hand on my shoulder.

"Inra trusts you," she says.

Surprised, I look up.

"Larta is right," she says. "You do understand. But not everything. You can't fathom why it's important that we trust you. You think it's the other way around. You'll stay here tonight. You'll be protected that long at least."

"Don't let your spots light too brightly," Larta says. "You'll be in a room with Mees, Inra, and Tanez, who you haven't met yet. I'll warn you now, Tanez sniffles in her sleep and Mees snores. You'd rest better in a beast-keep."

Larta gets up and pulls her cloak over her shoulders. She leans over and whispers, "When you decide to start talking, don't hold anything back from Inra. She's an empath. She doesn't need to see emotion spots to know your secret heart."

CHAPTER SIXTEEN

"Inra says she's found the one you've been seeking."
—*Larta, to Azlii the corentan*

MARNKA IS SINGING WITHOUT WORDS, *her voice playing up and down the notes like wind through leaves. Her voice alters, doubling, singing harmony with herself. That can't be. I must be singing with her. Marnka's voice splits again, letting her throat make three tones, and then four. I look around the bright, day-lit cave, but she is nowhere to be seen.*

"Marnka," *I call out.* "Why are you hiding?"

The cave goes black. I can't see the ground I'm sitting on.

"Marnka. Don't play tricks on me."

I FORCE my eyes open and blink in the bright light. I'm lying on a cot in a room painted pale-green. Inra—the one who's an empath—stands next to the cot.

"Where is Marnka?" she asks in her gentle, prodding voice.

Where is Marnka—not who. Inra leans over me. I can't look at her. I turn my face to the wall.

"I knew Marnka the weather-prophet," Inra says. "Is she the Marnka you called for, or another with the same name?"

I keep my head turned and say nothing.

"They told us Marnka the weather-prophet had died in an accident," Inra says. "The entire kler turned out to celebrate her unexpected Returning. I never believed it myself."

I wonder if Inra and Marnka were friends or if Inra's talk is a deceit meant to start my tongue moving. I lie still, as though I haven't heard her.

Inra sighs. "No matter. You and I have other things to worry about. First, a cleaning. You'll feel better after."

The blanket covering me is pulled away. Rolling over, I snatch it back and glare at her.

"We need to go while the hatchlings are on the upper levels at their lessons," Inra says. "We can't let them see you. They're too likely to let the wrong word slip if an inspector comes around."

I ease off the blanket. I must have slept like the Returned. My cloak, foot casings, and hip wrap have been taken from me, and I never knew it.

Inra's shod feet and my bare ones thud and pad as I follow her out and down a long hall to the cleaner. At Lunge we had a large room for cleaning that several units visited together, not a small chamber like this, only big enough for one. I lean against the smooth white stone while the sound waves do their work. I close my eyes and stay in the chamber long after I'm clean, until Inra's voice blares through the door.

"I've brought you a fresh wrap and foot casings."

I shoulder the door open, thinking I can't keep mute forever, wondering when and how to break my silence.

"We couldn't salvage your old clothing," Inra says as I step out from the chamber.

The fabric she holds out is beautiful—dark blue with a design of tiny gold fedephloc blooms and red seedpods. I wrap the soft fabric around my hips. It feels like wearing feathers.

Inra hands me a pair of foot casings in the same dark blue as the wrap. The thick, quilted winter casings are knee-high and hard soled. Guilt pricks at me. Someone has given up these fine things so that I might wear them. I wonder if they are Inra's, since we are about the same size.

"The clothing is assigned to Tanez," Inra says. "She wanted you to have them. Are you hungry? There's food waiting."

I nod, and we go down the hallway to the little communiteria.

The room is as spotless as before. I wonder if the hatchlings eat here or somewhere else. So much in Chimbalay is different from Lunge. I don't know the rules in this place.

Inra fills two bowls with kiiku porridge from a large pot, then hands me a bowl and spoon. I take them and sit at the table on the same pillow where I'd sat the night before. Inra takes her same place, across from me.

The room is quiet, as though the building is deserted except for the two of us. The quiet makes me nervous, like it's pressing on me. Inra seems content to eat her meal, but I know she's watching me, judging. I keep my head down, my eyes focused on the porridge, and eat. My bowl is nearly empty when Inra sets down her spoon and stares at me until I'm forced to acknowledge her attention.

"Larta tells me she followed you for a long while yesterday," she says.

I try not to show the small triumph I feel—the shadow was there. I didn't imagine it.

"Larta thought at first that you were from the corenta, one of Azlii's crew who'd lost her way or grown curious about the kler," she says. "Are you from the corenta?"

She waits for me to answer, as though she won't speak again until I do and doesn't mind if it takes days. My mind spins, wondering if this is the moment to break my silence. Wondering, too, if it's usual for doumanas from the corenta to come into the kler. Corentans never came to Lunge. Simanca kept us safe from that danger, at least.

Inra's spots glow dark-blue-red, the color of speculation, then fade. The silence stretches out, filling the room like smoke.

At last Inra says, "Larta changed her mind after she'd followed you awhile. She brought you here because she judged that you'd escaped from the research center."

Inra's hands rest on the table, her fingers stretched out flat. Her black eyes lock onto my own. I can almost feel her reaching into me, looking for the truth. I search back, for her truth. Why did Larta, thinking I'd come from a research center, bring me here?

"Would you like something to drink?" Inra asks.

I nod, and she gets up from the table, returning with a white clay pitcher and two glass cups. She fills both cups with a red liquid that I guess is awa juice, then slides one toward me. I lift my glass and sip. The light, sweet juice isn't awa or anything I can identify.

Inra takes a tiny sip and sets the glass down. "It must be hard, now that you've been silent for so long, to find the best moment to speak. Would you like to tell me what happened to you?"

I look down at the table. I don't want to tell these doumanas anything until I know more about them.

The sound of footsteps coming toward the room makes my muscles tense.

Larta, Mees, and a new doumana enter the room. The stranger is tall, much taller than I am—taller than Larta, who is taller than me. The hood of her cloak is drawn tightly around her face. Her neck is hidden. She loosens the drawstrings of the hood, slips it back, and settles onto a pillow next to Inra. She settles down with ease, but I think that she doesn't live in this dwelling. More like a guest who's come so often she feels at home. Her eyes are a light brown, almost yellow. She gazes at me like one might look over a newborn preslet to judge its quality. I don't like the way her lips draw back, as though I'm less than she expected.

Mees's voice comes from behind my shoulder. "Do you know her?"

The stranger tsks her tongue against the roof of her mouth.

"She hasn't spoken at all," Inra says.

"Can she speak?" the stranger asks. Her voice is deep and confident, like Simanca's.

"I believe so," Inra answers. "She chose silence as a shield when Larta found her. She's not ready to lay down her protection."

Mees sits on one side of me. Larta takes the pillow on the other. I feel penned in, hardly able to breathe. The stranger stares at me with a cold, sharp gaze. I reach for my glass and take a sip of the red liquid. Four sets of eyes follow my movements.

"Maybe she has good reason to protect herself," the stranger says. "Or maybe silence is what the Powers ordered."

"The Powers didn't send her," Inra says, so quietly that I hardly hear her.

The stranger doesn't seem to hear at all. She keeps her eyes on me. "I don't believe you've escaped from the research center," the stranger says, and watches for my reaction.

I look down at the bowl in front of me. Dried porridge sticks to its rim.

With a quick movement, the stranger sends the bowl flying off the table with the back of her hand. The bowl skitters across the floor, clangs against the wall, and shatters into pieces.

"Why were you wandering in Chimbalay?" the stranger demands.

I stare at the inquisitor.

"I think that you are a new kind of spy," she says. "A spy fixed in the research center so that the shame of lies doesn't show on your neck. Fixed so well that even an empath can't feel your treachery." She leans toward me. "Is that what you are—a new abomination?"

My mind whirls. Whose spy do they think I am? What are they doing that would bring them trouble if others knew about it? What would they do to ensure their safety?

The stranger leans back on the pillow, lacing her fingers together in front of her chest. Her voice has turned to the sound of one giving friendly advice. "If you have any hope of saving yourself, you'll start talking. And telling the truth."

I want to speak, but can't. My mind tumbles like a rock knocked loose on a hillside. I'm frightened, but I see that the stranger is frightened, too. What do these doumanas fear?

"Azlii," Inra says, "leave her be. She doesn't know what you're talking about."

Inra turns to me. "Sometimes corentans can seem harsh to outsiders."

If Azlii is an example of what corentans are like, no wonder Simanca hated to be among them.

Azlii pays no attention to the apology Inra's offered on her behalf. "She's not a babbler, is she?"

Inra draws in a breath. "She's not a babbler like any we've housed."

I see their secret. There are babblers who weren't sent from the kler. Some escaped. If these doumanas are hiding babblers here, it's no wonder they fear a silent stranger.

Azlii leans toward me. Her voice is as sharp as a knife's edge. "Who are you? Where do you come from?"

I stare back at her and manage to keep my voice calm. "My name is Khe. I come from Lunge commune."

Azlii glares at me, but Larta and Mees look to Inra.

"She's telling the truth," Inra says.

"Unless—" Azlii begins.

Inra tsks her tongue against the roof of her mouth. "I feel that she was in a research center, but long ago and not in Chimbalay."

"I was in Morvat," I say.

"When?" Azlii asks.

"Seven years back."

Her almost-yellow eyes widen. "For Resonance restoration?"

I nod. The orindles at Morvat were proud of their early success and hosted two visionstage presentations about them.

"Were you one of the ones with new Talents?" Azlii asks.

I don't know how Azlii knows about this; it wasn't part of the presentations. The orindles wanted to keep the side effects secret.

I don't know what to say. If I tell them about my ability, they might be more tempted to turn me over to the Powers or the orindles than if I'm ordinary. I'd come here seeking the orindles. Now I'd just as soon wait a while before meeting them. But if these doumanas hide babblers, my ability might make them more willing to hide me, too.

"I will answer your questions," I say. "Will you answer mine in return?"

Inra, Mees, and Larta turn to Azlii, which tells me it's the corentan who makes the final decisions among them.

"That depends on the questions," Azlii says evenly.

"Is this place a haven for babblers?" I ask.

"No," Larta says.

"Tell her," Azlii says.

Larta shoots Azlii a hard look. If there is something illegal happening in this house, Larta the guardian wouldn't want her participation known.

Azlii stares back calmly. Larta hitches up one shoulder in a shrug.

"From time to time a babbler wanders away from the research center. Once or twice I've come across them while making my rounds. Mees let the babblers stay here until someone came to retrieve them."

Retrieve. Spirited away, I think, though the guardian has tried to make it sound otherwise.

"How did a doumana from Lunge commune come to be in Chimbalay?" Azlii asks. All the doumanas in the room focus their attention on me, except Inra, who closes her eyes.

I tell them. They listen. The whole time I'm talking, Inra never opens her eyes.

When I finish, Inra keeps her eyes shut.

"I've told you my tale," I say. "I'd like to know the same about all of you."

Mees straightens an already-perfect pleat in her hip wrap. "We might as well tell her. She'll need to know some of it at least, and probably sooner rather than later."

"The less she knows, the better," Larta says. "She's a risk to us."

Inra opens her eyes but says nothing.

"Larta's right," Azlii says. "This wandering doumana is more a threat than a gift, I think. She knows enough already to be a danger to us. However, if she knows more, she may turn out to be an asset. If not ... Her shoulders hitch up.

CHAPTER SEVENTEEN

"To show respect to the creator, obey your leader."
—*The Rules of a Good Life*

SOUMYO IS a word hardly anyone uses. It names our species and means all the doumanas and males combined. Since male and female live apart, there's little reason to use a word meaning both, except when new laws come down that affect us all. But Azlii uses that word now.

"In the Before," Azlii says, leaning her back against the wall behind the bright-green pillow she sits on, "there were soumyo, no different in looks from us, but very different in their way of living. They didn't live their whole lives in one place, the way kler and commune dwellers do. They lived like corentans, in communities that traveled the planet freely. And like corentans now, the soumyo were in harmony with the walls that sheltered them, and the plants and beasts that fed and clothed them. They lived as part of a sentient whole."

The door to the receiving room yawns open and a new doumana comes into the room.

"This is Tanez," Inra says, "who gave you your hip wrap and foot casings."

If someone judged all doumanas by this new one and myself, they would think we came in only one size, shape, and color. Tanez's skin is the same shade of red as mine, and we have similar mouths, though her eyes are a slightly lighter shade of brown. She sits across from Azlii, next to me. The other doumanas make me nervous, but Tanez feels like an open door that lets in the breeze.

I turn my attention back to the corentan.

"When was this?" I ask.

"The Before stretches to the beginning of time," Azlii says. "It ends when the Powers came."

"Arose, you mean," I say. "The Powers arose from among us."

Azlii's mouth pulls taut. "The Powers arrived. And they aren't soumyo. They're … different."

I tsk my tongue on the roof of my mouth. "I've seen the Powers on the visionstage. Not often, but enough to know they look like you and me."

"What you've seen are kler doumanas who do the Powers' bidding," Azlii says, and shrugs. "Why not? No doubt you've carried out another's command."

"My commune leader's orders."

Azlii smiles as if I've just proved her point.

"Well then, how do these doumanas get their commands?" I ask her. "Do the Powers live in the klers?"

"No one knows where the Powers stay," Larta says, answering instead of Azlii. She fingers the guardian insignia on the bracelet encircling her left wrist. "The orders come as text on a small, special visionstage in Administration House."

These doumanas have quick answers for all my questions, quick enough that they sound worked out in advance.

"How do you know how the orders come?" I ask.

"Because I've seen it," Larta says. "I'm First of the guardians in Chimbalay. It's my duty to make sure the Powers' orders and policies are enforced. The Powers believe they should directly contact the doumana responsible for carrying out their edicts. That way no one can blame her failures on having heard an order secondhand."

Mees sighs in exasperation. "Let Azlii finish her tale. Khe needs to know the truth."

Azlii acts as through there has been no interruption.

"Everyone lived in corentas," she says. "Then the Powers came. Some reports say the Powers arrived in a globe of blue flames. Others say they tore open the air and entered our world in a crack of thunder. However they came, they were perceived by the soumyo and the other sentients as a presence that couldn't be seen or heard, yet was there—a disturbance. When the disturbance began, the corentas came together, linking so that communications could be immediate. That was almost a thousand years back. More than twenty-eight generations."

The time is so long, I can hardly conceive of it.

Azlii fills her glass from the pitcher but doesn't drink. "Shortly after the Powers arrived, things began disappearing. A plain that had been covered in grain would be suddenly bare. Beasts disappeared from the corentas. Whole buildings disappeared. And soumyo. One moment your sister or brother would be standing with you, and the next, she or he would be gone. Nothing that disappeared ever came back."

I try to imagine what that was like, but can't. It's too strange.

"Some thought the world was ending," Azlii says. "The beasts, plants, and structures demanded that the soumyo do something to stop the disappearances. Even in those days, soumyo were considered responsible for keeping the whole running smoothly. But there was nothing anyone could do. No one even knew how to start.

"The established order began to fall apart. Plants and beasts refused to be eaten. Buildings denied shelter." The corentan leans toward me. "Try to imagine what it was like to see your sisters and brothers vanishing before your eyes. To seek shelter and find that your dwelling won't let you in. To be starving with food all around that you could not eat."

"Terrifying," I say.

A small shiver runs across Azlii's shoulders, as if she remembers those dread-filled times firsthand.

"In the Before," she says, "doumanas and males lived together. But in the chaos, the partnership shattered as each sex blamed the other for the problems. That's when doumanas and males began to live apart, the way we do now."

My eyes ache from staring. Corentans are without faith, but I say what I know to be true. "The creator set the sexes apart. So we wouldn't be distracted from our work."

Mees touches my neck. "What we believe is not always the way things are."

"What good can it do the Powers to keep the sexes apart?" I ask, and hear the anger in my voice. Not anger that we are apart. Anger that these doumanas make everything I believe into a lie.

"In the Before," Azlii says calmly, "doumanas and males were like a body's two arms, working together to keep the world in harmony. When we began to live apart, we became a one-armed body, out of balance, less able to fight off an attacker. Can you think of a better way to control us than to push one half away from the other?"

I am quiet, thinking over what she said.

"Why did the Powers want to destroy our world?" I ask.

"They didn't," Azlii says. "The chaos was simply the effect of their presence. They came, so they said, only to observe."

I've caught Azlii in a contradiction. "You said the Powers couldn't be seen or heard. Then how did they make themselves known and speak with the sentients? Were there visionstages then?"

Azlii tsks her tongue on the roof of her mouth. "When they wanted to, they had ways of making themselves known. The Powers communicated the way all sentients spoke to a differing type, by directing pulses of thought-energy to the receiver. To the sentients, the Powers seemed to be directed energy. When they came to apologize for the chaos they'd caused, they were perceived as a shimmering in the air, something like a heat mirage. Their words weren't felt like the usual quiet whisperings between the minds of sentients, but like a great wind or a thunderclap."

My head aches from trying to understand these strange ideas. I rub my neck. Azlii keeps talking.

"The Powers told the sentients that they'd come to our world only to learn about it. They said they were sorry to have caused such disorder, but that what was done was done and could not be put back. The Powers said they would stay and observe what happened over the next few generations, and then leave. They promised to do their best to cause no more unforeseen changes. It was all lies, of course."

"Lies only seen now, looking back?" I ask.

Azlii shrugs. "I think that the sentients back then were so relieved to know what caused the chaos, and of more importance, to have order restored, that they likely would have granted the Powers anything they asked. To give the Powers their due, they upheld their promise for several generations. But over time, they began tinkering. Perhaps it was just their nature and they couldn't help but ask themselves what if, and put things in motion to find the answer. Perhaps they'd meant all along to turn our world into a place to carry out their experiments. Whichever it was, they deliberately began to change the way we lived."

"How?"

"They made deals with corenta guides, convincing them to give up the traveling life and live in klers or communes. In return, the guides gained total control over those living in their domain, became not guides but leaders.

I think of Simanca. She was neither guide nor leader, but a whip driving us toward her own goals.

Azlii lifts her glass and empties it in one swallow, tilting her head back to let the liquid drain down her throat. She sets the glass down gently, but her hand is squeezed tightly around it.

"The Powers also convinced the commune and kler leaders to forbid anyone telling the hatchlings about life in the Before," she says. "In one generation, all kler and commune dwellers lost the knowledge that they'd ever lived another way. In two generations, set-place life was accepted without question. This gave the Powers steady populations to study. They wanted their subjects to stay put during a life-span, not migrate across the planet, making them hard for the Powers to track."

"But there are still corentas," I say.

One spot on Azlii's neck lights bright-green with pride, then winks out. "Not everyone agreed to do the Powers' bidding. We are the offspring of those who refused to give up their freedom."

I glance at Mees, Tanez, and Inra, and then at Larta. They are kler dwellers, the offspring of those who agreed. As I am.

"Why did the Powers let some stay in the corentas?" I ask. "It seems it would have suited them better to have everyone in a kler or commune."

"Corentas are useful. Once most of the soumyo had

settled down, they needed a way for commune dwellers to get their goods to processing sites in the klers. Corentas provided the way. We became traders."

I think about all that Azlii has said. Thedra once said that most doumanas are like flocking birds—give us a leader and we'll follow. I can understand why so many went peacefully to the klers and communes when the Powers asked them to. And I think that really, the way things are now isn't so bad. If it wasn't for the discovery of my ability, I'd have lived my whole life at Lunge and been happy.

I tell Azlii this. She pulls herself up suddenly from her pillow and paces the room. Nervousness slides through my belly. I rub my neck and wait.

Azlii sits back down. "I told you that the Powers seem unable to stop tinkering with our world. Once they'd gotten a society that suited them, they began changing the soumyo, tinkering here and there, looking for perfection. You are one of the results of their curiosity."

Her words are like a blow.

"The Resonance restoration project?"

Azlii nods. "They seem fascinated with our way of reproducing. In the klers and communes, doumanas are taught that reproducing is the most important deed we do, but it wasn't always that way. In the Before, harmony of life was the goal. In the corentas, it still is. The Powers want more and more hatchlings—more victims for their tinkering."

"I wasn't a victim," I say. "I'm grateful to feel Resonance, however that happened."

"I can see why you would be," Azlii says coolly. "But ask a babbler if she's grateful for what was done to her."

I know the answer to that question.

"Azlii, how do you know all this about the Powers and things that supposedly took place a long time ago?"

She shrugs. "I'm corentan. We keep the history, passing

the stories from generation to generation. Except for these doumanas here and the few others like them across the planet, only corentans, all corentans, know the truth of what happened. My community is old. We have structures that existed in the Before."

She says this last as if it means something special, but I can't grasp the importance.

"Our wall," she says, "some of our buildings, were there, Khe. They witnessed it firsthand. Structures never forget anything."

Mees looks up. "Oh, dear me. I've been listening so hard that I forgot the hatchlings will be down soon for midday meal." She pulls herself up from the pillow and strides across the room toward the cooking area. Inra gets up to help her. Pots clang. Chests open and close. The rest of us sit in silence.

I turn to Azlii and fix her with a stare. "Who are you? You and the doumanas in this house? What are you after?"

Leaning forward, Azlii spreads her hands on the table. "We believe the Powers have been here too long. Our aim is to destroy their hold on our world. We want you to help."

CHAPTER EIGHTEEN

"To hear the creator's song, quiet the rebellion in your heart."
—*The Rules of a Good Life*

MY HEART THUMPS in my breast, the sound growing so loud that the room echoes with it. Then I realize the thumping is in the stairwell off the little communiteria.

"The hatchlings are coming down," Inra says over her shoulder. "Take Khe back to the sleep quarters. Mees and I will join you soon."

Larta, Azlii, and I thread down the green-and-white hall. My chest feels tight, as though I'm underwater. "We want you to help," Azlii said. They want me to drown with them.

"Did you follow everything I told you?" Azlii asks when the door to the sleep quarters closes behind us. The three of us stand just inside the door, as if each is waiting for another to go first.

"The history, yes," I say. "But I don't understand how

doumanas can use pulses of energy to communicate with plants and beasts."

"Sending is much like using a firestarter," Azlii says. She strides the short distance across the room and settles on the cot where I'd slept the night before. Larta remains standing just inside the doorway. "Instead of concentrating the electric energy of your body on the starter, you send the energy of your thoughts to another sentient. Learning to listen is harder. You have to accept the pulses being sent to you and know how to translate them. Plants and beasts don't use words the way structures or we do. They send and receive thought-energy as pictures. It can get a little confusing."

I sit on the other end of the cot. The sheet is dyed contentment-green. It's been a long time since I felt contented. "I don't understand the idea of communicating with walls and structures at all."

Azlii frowns. "You must stop thinking that just because something is made of wood or bricks or stones and mortar, it's not aware. Corentans learn to speak with all sentients almost as soon as we're assigned to a community. My dwelling and I worked together to get it built, so that we were both pleased with the outcome."

The soft-yellow-green of skepticism begins to light on my neck, but the memory of making the sled stops the color from blooming fully. I want to tell Azlii and Larta how the sled had seemed to talk, but worry if I do, they may decide I'm a babbler after all.

"Can anyone talk with the sentients, or only corentans?"

"I think any hatchling could learn to do it," the corentan says. "Once she emerges, it seems to be too late. Inra can communicate a bit, but I think that's because she's an empath. Mees and Larta have tried. They're useless."

I glance at Larta, who is still standing by the door. One of her spots fires orange, showing her embarrassment. I like and trust the guardian more for that emotion. She bends her knee and balances her foot against the wall.

"I think Azlii and Inra hear what they want to hear," Larta says. "They claim that everything in a corenta is sentient, but where's the proof?"

"Larta prides herself on doubting anything she can't see, hear, touch, or smell," Azlii says cheerfully, "though she believes in the creator and the Powers easily enough."

"Trah," Larta says. "I don't have to see them to see their effects, and that's enough for me."

"Can you talk to this structure?" I ask the corentan.

"I've tried," Azlii says, "but the kler structures don't respond. I hear them muttering to themselves, but I've never heard one speak to another. There seems to be something here that pains them. They grumble about being uncomfortable. I think that whatever hurts them also muddles their consciousness."

The more they talk, the more I feel at ease with these two. I want to trust them. Need to trust them.

"When I was in the wilderness," I say slowly, "I built a small sled to haul my goods. When it was about half done, I ate some wild fruit that made me sick. I fell into a delirium and dreamed the sled spoke to me, telling me how it wanted to be made. When I woke up, the sled was finished."

"What kind of fruit was it?" Larta asks.

Talking sleds don't seem to surprise her; it's the fruit she's interested in.

"I don't know what it's called," I say. "It was about the size of my fist, with an outer brown husk. The flesh was bluish pink and creamy looking. At the center were five small white seeds in a star pattern. The bush it grew on was about waist high and had purple leaves."

"Aruna," Larta says. "Aruna can have effects similar to villisity."

One of my spots flares an anxious blue-red. Marnka said it was villisity that made her lose her mind.

"You were lucky to get away with nothing more than a dream," Larta says. "Aruna can kill you."

I wipe my hands against the hip wrap Tanez provided and try not to look as frightened as I feel, though my neck spots betray me.

"Trees don't like to be cut down for nothing," Azlii says. "It would have wanted you to make the best sled of it that you could. Maybe the mind-changing qualities of aruna opened your internal ear to the sentients around you."

Azlii is quiet a moment and then says, "Inra says that you're an empath too, but don't know it. She says that if you let yourself, you'll realize you've always known things that others didn't."

My blood feels hot beneath my skin. "What kind of things?"

Azlii shrugs. "Inra said to ask you about the preslets."

"I don't like them very much."

Azlii says nothing. From the corner of my eye, I see Larta, her foot still braced against the wall behind her. She stares at nothing, as though not listening to Azlii and me. In the silence I remember the preslet that Stoss offended, and my insistence that she apologize. How could I have known the bird was offended and not merely surprised or frightened by Stoss's sudden appearance? But I did know, as clearly as if it were a commune sister.

I think about Azlii's description of how to talk with other species. It's not so different from how I did the growing. I spoke to the plants with thought-energy, and it did often seem that they spoke back to me, throwing a picture into my mind of how big and strong they would become.

"Are you an empath?" Azlii asks.

My head aches as though a rope is being twisted around

my forehead and pulled tight. I look at Azlii, but she seems far away and as though seen through a mist. My neck burns as all my spots flare greenish-blue with hope. Not my hope—Azlii's.

Blood pounds in my temples and my ear holes ache. It's enough to have my own emotions. I don't want to know what others feel. My temperature drops. I feel as cold as snow. My breath comes in short gasps. I try to breathe the way Tav taught me to calm myself, but can't.

The door whooshes open. Inra rushes to me, shoves Azlii aside, and wraps her arms around me.

I lean against her but can't slow my breath. The air feels like embers scalding my throat and lungs.

"Don't fight," Inra says. "Close your eyes. Put your heels flat on the floor and your arms over your head. Good. You're doing well. Now slowly blow out your breath."

I do as she tells me. My heart slows its frantic beating. When I open my eyes, I feel oddly refreshed.

Inra glares at Azlii. "You should have waited."

Azlii shrugs. "For what? The next Commemoration Day, for Khe to gain her thirty-fifth spot?"

"Until I could have been here with her," Inra says.

Azlii tsks. "Khe chose the moment, not me."

A tremendous energy rages in me, like the need to move that I'd felt at Morvat Research Center after my surgery. The air seems alive, electric. I have the crazy thought that if I concentrated, I could see through the walls. I jump to my feet and stalk the room. I feel Inra's concern for me, Azlii's confidence in herself, and Larta's interest, but knowing their emotions no longer hurts. I feel their deeper emotions as well, the forces that push them to rid the world of the Powers. Azlii feels like anger, Larta like humiliation, and Inra like grief. I feel their care about me, their desire for me to be safe and well.

"Sit down," Azlii says sharply.

I stop and stare at her, but I don't sit. How can I sit with this energy rushing through me?

"Please, Khe," Inra says. "You'll make yourself sick this way. You need to control what you're feeling."

"Sit down," Azlii says again, "and get your feet up from the floor."

I do sit then, pulling my feet up and sitting cross-legged. The careening energy in me seems to die down to a hum. I feel warm and strangely peaceful, given all that I've heard and experienced in this dwelling. My mind feels clear, my thoughts as sharp as broken glass.

I look at Azlii. "You think I have something you want."

Azlii rubs her chin, as if thinking before she speaks. "We've known for a while that some of the doumanas in the Resonance restoration project showed new Talents after their surgery."

I'd known this too. Pradat had told me.

"We'd hoped," Azlii says, "that one of these doumanas would come forward and tell her tale. But all the doumanas we'd heard about, the new Talents drove them mad."

Like the one Pradat said heard the future in the wind?

Like me, eventually? Is that what this sudden blast of energy means—that I'm becoming a babbler?

Inra takes my hands in hers. "You've passed the crisis time. If you were going to go insane, it would have happened years ago."

I let out the breath I've been holding. "Where are these changed doumanas now?"

"They were in the research centers at first," Azlii says. "Perhaps they are with the Powers now. We think that they are probably among the Returned."

My anger burns like a light through fog. Those doumanas

wanted what I did, to feel Resonance, to find a mate and lay their egg. And went mad in the pursuit.

"Khe," Azlii says, "we have the same enemy." She leans close and whispers, "Join us."

"And do what?"

Her mouth crinkles in a grin which disappears as fast as it came, as if satisfaction is not an emotion she allows herself to feel for long.

"We will tell your story across the planet. When the soumyo see what the Powers' tinkering has brought, they will rise up against them."

I blow out a breath. "Rise up how?"

"By refusal," Azlii says. "Once the truth is known, the orindles will refuse to continue torturing their sisters in the Powers' experiments. Commune and kler leaders will refuse to send their doumanas to the research centers. If the Powers try to take someone by force, all her sisters will stand with her and defend her. If the Powers ask for beasts or plants, we will refuse them that. We will reject them again and again, until they see their defeat and go."

Or the Powers destroy us all for our insolence, I think but don't say.

"Why should anyone believe me?" I ask.

"Why not?" Azlii says. "If you were telling an untruth, your emotion spots would give away your lie."

"Unless I was insane. Babblers can say anything and not be betrayed by their spots."

"Which is why only you can help us," Azlii says. "We've waited a long time for someone who's been changed by the Powers but kept her mind. When the doumanas see and hear you, they'll know you are sane and telling the truth."

"Even if they did believe me, why should my tale make the doumanas, and the males too, rise up?"

"Because of what we are, Khe," Azlii says. "As a species, we are loyal to our sisters or brothers above everything else. When the soumyo know for certain what the Powers are doing, when they see and hear you, their outrage will make them push the Powers out."

If I'd been loyal to my commune-sisters at Lunge, or they to me, I'd not be in Chimbalay. Yet I still cared for them, about them, missed them. I would do anything to keep them from harm.

"How would we tell my story?"

Larta, not Azlii answers. The guardian has been so quiet, I've nearly forgotten she's there. "We'll use the visionstage sending site to reach all the doumanas in the sections at once."

"They'll let us do that?"

Larta laughs without humor. "We'll use the site either without their knowledge or against their will."

My mind spins. Is it true that the orindles follow the Powers' orders? If the Powers are driven away, will the orindles be more or less likely to help me? I'm quiet, thinking. Azlii and Larta wait.

"All right," I say, surprised by the words I'm saying. "I'll do it."

Azlii's mouth draws tight. "You need to know that if we fail, it's likely the Powers will have us. We're not the first to have tried to overthrow them. The doumanas who tried before disappeared—all but one, who was sent back here when they'd finished with her."

Revulsion and pity sweep through me. I'm grateful I can't see Azlii's memory of that one doumana. Feeling Azlii's emotions is enough to turn my bones to water.

CHAPTER NINETEEN

"With my sisters I will tear down the mountain."
—*"The Song of Togetherness"*

"WHEN WILL we go to Presentation House?" I ask.

"Tonight," Azlii says.

I feel the muddy-brown of fear and the bright-blue of anticipation light on my neck.

Larta grins at me. "Fear is good. It will help keep you from doing something noble and stupid."

I glance at Tanez. Her neck is ablaze with bright-blue spots. I realize why her face feels familiar—she looks much like me. No, she looks like me mixed with the male of my second Resonance. I feel a sudden rush of affection for her, different from the warmth I felt for my sisters at Lunge. It's more like the satisfied pleasure of seeing seedlings I'd tended grow to mature and fruitful plants.

Larta catches Azlii's eye. "Who will be going with you and Khe?"

"Just Inra," the corentan answers. "To read the truth or lies of what any doumana we meet is saying."

"I'll go," Larta says.

Azlii shakes her head. "You're too valuable. As First of the guardians, you can go places and learn things no one else can. We can't risk your capture."

Larta's jaw clenches. She nods slowly and says, "Three is too few. Four would be better, in case you need to split up, leaving one or two behind as sentries while you and Khe breach the presentation room."

"We'll get a fourth from the corenta," Azlii says.

"I'll go," Tanez says. "I want to go."

I look at Tanez and then at Azlii, hoping she'll let Tanez come, then hoping she won't.

"Tanez will be number four," Azlii says.

The young doumana grins. Her spots are crimson with happiness.

A sudden thought strikes me. "Azlii, if the Powers watch the doumanas, how do we know they're not watching us right now and know everything we're planning?"

"Inra has been feeling for that," Azlii says. "The Powers watch this house often—they seem very interested in the hatchlings—but but they've had their attention elsewhere lately. We have to move quickly."

THE LIGHT from the obelisks makes the gently falling snow glow pink as Azlii, Inra, Tanez, and I leave Hatchling House behind. We look no different from any group of doumanas on the avenue, huddled against the cold in fur-trimmed cloaks and high-topped foot casings. Azlii is wearing Larta's cloak with its guardian's insignia pin, and both of Larta's bracelets. My nerves are strung as tight and thin as the black lines of a power grid.

I nudge Inra, who walks beside me. Azlii and Tanez walk side by side behind us.

"Why are there so many energy panels?" I ask in a low voice.

"It takes energy to run a kler," Inra answers, keeping her voice as low as mine. To anyone watching, we are just two doumanas chatting amicably. "Much of it is used to send presentations throughout the region and to run the research centers. Some is used to regulate building temperatures, run cookers, heat water, provide light."

The snow changes, becoming wetter, with bigger flakes.

"There's more energy being made here than a kler twice Chimbalay's size could use," Inra continues. "And the energy from every panel in the kler feeds into one building, then is routed out again. Azlii says that no other kler does it that way. Larta and I have tried to discover what it's used for." She turns her hands palms up in a gesture that says they've failed.

We stride down Bright-Blue Circle. The buildings look no different than when I walked this street only a day before, but feel more menacing. Each time we pass one of the wide blue brick paved spaces between buildings, I expect a guardian to stop us. Or for us to disappear, the way Azlii says the doumanas, beasts, and structures did when the Powers first arrived. Behind me I hear Tanez and Azlii talking together. Their voices are soft and conversational, muffled by the snow. I can't catch the words.

We come to the building that made Larta nervous when she and I passed it before.

"What is this place?" I ask.

Inra keeps her eyes focused straight ahead. "Chimbalay Research Center One. Where the babblers were made. Where they are now trying to change the energy levels in a fresh crop of victims."

And where the orindles are. I mark where the place is, so that I can come back later.

On Blue-Purple Avenue—Victory Street—the traffic thickens. We pass group after group of doumanas on their way to or from somewhere. Individual transportation vehicles stream past, stirring up soft wakes of snow. We walk in silence now. I feel the tension in Azlii, Inra, and Tanez. My neck prickles and burns from the dread rushing through me. I pull my cloak up to hide my neck.

Inra stops at a structure in a shadowed area between two obelisks. Tanez and Azlii stop as well.

"That's Presentation House," Inra says to me, and gestures toward it with her chin.

I tilt my head back to see the top of the tall building. It's fifteen levels at least. White stone bridges connect it with the buildings on either side at the fifth and tenth levels. Behind these buildings are even taller sites, rising twenty levels or more. Beyond them is a small forest of impossibly tall thin-trunked trees crowned with snow-crusted branches.

We follow Inra up the four black stone steps to the wide silver door of Presentation House. My heart beats like a fist against my ribs.

"Inspection," Azlii calls loudly.

A moment later the door dilates open.

"Now?" a nervous doumana says, her spots blinking on. She tugs at an orange hip wrap that contrasts badly with the purplish red of her skin. "It's mealtime. Only a few technicians are on duty."

"I am aware of what time it is," Azlii says, brushing a bit of snow off the shoulders of her cloak, drawing attention to the guardian insignia that clasps it closed. She sweeps through the doorway as if she makes inspections daily. I admire her sham of confidence.

We follow the orange-wrapped doumana down a long,

black-floored hall with walls painted a dazzling crimson. It's like walking through flames on charred logs. I stare at the back of the doumana's head and concentrate, trying to feel her emotions, to know if she accepts us for what we've said we are or if she's leading us to a trap. All I feel is my own anxiety, and Azlii's.

Halfway down the hall, the doumana stops and waves her hand over a nearly invisible depression in the wall. A well-disguised door irises open, but the doumana doesn't go through or invite us to.

"We were inspected only nine days ago." The doumana twists the hem of her wrap in her hand. "Were there any, erm, irregularities found during that visit?"

Azlii glares at her and says nothing. Following her lead, Inra, Tanez, and I harden our faces and stare at the doumana.

The doumana shifts from foot to foot. "I'll send for my First. She can better answer your questions."

"I'm sure you can answer well enough." Azlii pauses long enough that several of the doumana's spots flare dark-gray with worry, then asks, "How many technicians are on duty?"

"Only two," the doumana says quickly, more of her spots lighting. "Three were scheduled, but one is sick."

"I see," Azlii says as though she doesn't see at all and suspects that something is amiss.

The doumana stares at the floor. A few more of her spots flare blue-red with anxiety. I wish I knew what's making her so nervous. Something is wrong here, and this doumana is desperate that it not be discovered.

"We'll see the technicians now," Azlii says.

"Of course," the doumana says but doesn't move.

Azlii tilts her head to one side. "Perhaps you'd like to meet with my First?"

The doumana steps aside. "The third yellow door," she says as we sweep past her.

The hallway is as orange as the doumana's hip wrap. Orange floor, orange walls, orange ceiling fitted out with orange lights. We pass door after door, the colors—white, blue, black, purple, yellow—leaping out against the orange.

My heart thuds. Azlii doesn't knock on the third yellow door, but waves her hand in front of the wall, the way the doumana did. The door irises open. Two very surprised doumanas—an orindle in green and a technician in white—turn and gape at us.

"Equipment inspection," Azlii says. "You may leave."

The technician glances at a time measurer on a table and frowns. "How long will this take?"

Azlii shrugs and says nothing.

"Is this a full inspection or a partial?" the technician asks. Four of her spots light from nerves.

"Full," Azlii replies.

Both doumanas' emotion spots wink out. My hands begin to sweat. The doumanas should be more nervous over a full inspection. The technician looks again at the time measurer and motions with her head for the orindle to follow her. Their hurried movements worry me. I feel anxiety from Inra and Tanez as well. Azlii glances around the room, as if she's searching for something she doesn't seem to find.

When the doumanas leave, Tanez says, "All that's left is to set Khe down by the scan and let her talk."

"What's a scan?" I feel my spots prickling.

"This," Inra answers, and points to a small glass orb. "It will send your spoken and text words and your image to every visionstage in the region."

"Too easy," Azlii mutters, walking toward the door the doumanas have left open. Before she can touch it, the door squeezes shut and locks with a hard, metallic thud. The air smells suddenly of dead leaves. A brown fog fills the room.

CHAPTER TWENTY

"Learn first to surrender. All else follows with ease."
—*The Rules of a Good Life*

TWO ARE BREATHING in this darkened room. Me and ... can't see. Black in here. Groggy mind. Drugged? I remember ... a mist. Azlii and Inra crumpled on the floor. Tanez doubled over, gasping for breath. Are they with me? Only two here, from the breathing sounds. The other doumana wheezes, a rattle in her chest.

I remember ... a cold needle pricking my neck. Dreaming of Marnka. "Beware. Be strong," she said, and turned into a giant bird, flapping her great wings across the sky. Dreaming, Inra touched my mind. She said something. What was it?

I remember voices in the darkness. Too many questions. So tired.

Tanez? Where is Tanez?

Chair noises. Wood-on-tile squeak. The doumana rises. Air rasps in her lungs as she moves. Walking slow. Hard for her? No, she does it well—quiet walking. Knows how to move without sound, the way a helphand walks in a patient's room.

I breathe in, deep. Bad smell. Purifying chemicals. The smell of a research center. So tired.

———

THE HELPHAND KNOWS I'm feigning sleep. Three times she's come to check my pulse, and each time she lingers, watching, maybe wondering. In my mind, dark-blue-red and ocher swirl in a vortex—the colors of her curiosity and impatience.

They've stopped the drugs. I'm stronger now, and thinking well enough to know that I can't pretend to sleep forever. I make a quick prayer to the creator not to forsake me, and open my eyes. The room is nearly as dark as it was with my eyes shut. A shadowy figure moves.

"Awake at last," the shadowy doumana says, standing over me. "Good."

I try to move my arms and find I can. I move my legs and roll over halfway, then roll back. I'm not restrained, which must mean they're not worried that I might escape.

"Your body still works," the other says. "They took care with that."

Who are *they*? Orindles? Guardians? Why did they take such care?

"They must have found out something interesting during your conversations," the other says, sounding pleased with herself for knowing this information. "They say the Powers are sending new orders regarding you. Only you. Your companions are of much less interest."

My heart hammers. Do my spots light? I feel nothing on my neck.

"They'll want to know that you're conscious," the other says, and leaves me alone in the darkness.

The room is soundless. My throat feels as parched as the sides of a dry well. I sit up and fumble in the darkness, feeling for a table or chair that might have a pitcher of water on it, but there is nothing within arm's reach. I try to get up and walk. My head throbs at the effort. I lie back down.

When the door whooshes open again, no light comes in. The outside hall must be as dark as this room. Footsteps of two, maybe three doumanas tread across the floor.

"How are you feeling, Khe?" a new voice asks, a longer, heavier shadow than the one that wheezes.

They know my name. Did I tell them, or one of my companions?

"Where am I?" I won't refuse to speak—no point in that. No reason to answer their questions directly, either.

"You're in Chimbalay Research Center One," the long shadow says.

I don't remember being moved from Presentation House. The ache in my head grows worse. My arms and legs feel heavy.

"Could I have some water?"

"What is your commune?" the long shadow asks.

How do they know I'm a country doumana? "I'm very thirsty."

"Your sisters must be worried about you. Would you like us to contact them and tell them that you're well?"

"Some water?"

The long shadow taps her foot and leans close to me. I feel her breath. Her face is nothing but a deeper darkness in the gloom.

"We know you're not a Chimbalay doumana or a corentan." The shadow's voice sounds kind—an effort for her, I think. "The name of your commune can be found easily enough. You should tell us. It will go easier for you."

Do they ask because they don't know, or because they do and want to see if I'll tell the truth? I say nothing.

"Who planned this intrusion to Presentation House with you?" the shadow asks.

My voice cracks. "Some water, please."

"Just you four, then," she says. Her voice warms from kind to sympathetic. "You're not the first doumana taken in by Azlii the corentan's lies. She's led others astray and left them behind when her plans went wrong—just as she did to you."

A streak of brown-green erupts from the shadow's belly and arcs across the space between us. The doumana's emotion slams into my chest. My stomach heaves. I don't want to feel her shame.

I know now why the room is dark. I am not corentan, and this doumana won't insult me by wearing a collar. She needs the darkness to hide her emotion spots, the bodily proof of her lies.

The darkness hides my spots as well.

I lie on my side, panting from the onslaught of her emotion. My ribs feel bruised. Crossing my arms over my chest, I make myself breathe slowly.

"Please," I say. "I need water."

I listen as a set of feet moves toward the door. The door opens, then contracts shut. Almost immediately, the door opens again.

"The orders have come," someone new says, one with excitement in her high-pitched voice.

The one near me sighs and rises from the chair. A blindfold is slipped over my eyes, but I can tell that lights have been switched on. I hear the soft whir of a textbox.

One of them mutters and sucks air across her teeth.

My hands clench at my sides.

"We're to leave now," the long-shadow doumana says.

There's pity and fear in her. I see her colors behind my blind-folded eyes.

The lights go out again. I hear the door whoosh open and then close. I pull off the blindfold. The room is dark. I close my eyes, lie on the hard-as-stone cot, and wait.

Gradually I grow aware of a presence in the room, more than one presence—something hot, a disturbance in the air. I open my eyes, but see nothing.

"Who's there?" I ask.

"You know who we are."

The words are like a blow. My head snaps back as if hit by a large open hand. The room is empty.

No, not empty. Floating an arm's length in front of me are three faintly shimmering, insubstantial bands of light. They stretch almost floor to ceiling in a room twice my height. The vaporous bands, no thinner than my wrist, curve and twist as though blown by a soft breeze. The air in the room is still.

"We have a great interest in you, Khe."

The words come more gently now, like a sister's stroke on my neck. I hear them not with my ear holes but in my mind. Only one of the vaporous beings seems to communicate. The others hang back. I don't see emotion colors from any of them.

I know what they are. "Why are the Powers interested in me?"

The three streaks quiver, undulating like ropes flicked by a skilled hand.

"We forget that is what you call us. We call ourselves lumani."

My neck lights with the muddy-brown of fear.

Bracing my arms, I sit up and make my voice sound as calm as possible. "Why are the lumani interested in me?"

"I, in particular, am called Weast," the one speaking says.

Is it ignoring my question or did I interrupt the introduction and it continued on anyway? The other two lumani shimmer and then contract into small, hazy balls of almost-light. The balls sink down slowly and spread out until the entire floor glitters with tiny sparks. Weast remains shaped like a vaporous band.

My spots glow with fear colors. My voice sounds calmer than I feel. "Am I of interest to the lumani, or to Weast?"

A sound like the rumble of distant thunder vibrates through me. Laughter. The lumani thinks I've said something funny.

When the thunder dies away, Weast says, "To all, which includes, to a greater degree, I."

"Why you more than the others?"

The band vibrates. "We have decided that I am to be your donor."

Every muscle in my body tenses. My emotion spots flare blue-red with anxiety.

"Are you fatigued?" Weast asks. "You should be well rested first, to make a good decision."

A thousand years the lumani have been watching us, and they can't tell anxiety from exhaustion. They can't read the colors of our spots. The realization is comforting. What they don't know can maybe be used against them.

"I am well rested," I say, and don't flinch at the lie. My spots light, but it doesn't matter if I lie or tell the truth to these beings—they can't tell the difference.

The glittering band that is Weast expands to twice the width it was. "Good. We will talk now. Do you have more questions?"

I nod, and wonder how that gesture looks to the lumani, what it indicates to them—if anything. I wonder why the other two have spread out over the floor while Weast has not, and why Weast has suddenly doubled in size. Are these lumani gestures, filled with significance I can't read?

"What do you mean by being my donor?" I ask.

Weast undulates, the sides of its form swelling and shrinking in waves from top to bottom. I try to open my awareness to Weast and the others and grasp their emotions. All I feel is curiosity. But no, there is something else coming from them—desperation.

"There is an essence," Weast says, "a bit of chemical in every fiber of your being that makes you who you are, makes each doumana who she is, distinct from any others. All living things are what they are because of this essence, which they received from their progenitors. We too have this substance. Ours is different from yours, but not so different as you might think when looking at the ways we are made."

The vaporous band undulates faster. Is it excited?

"We will adjust your chemical and electrical levels," Weast continues. "In this way, we believe you will become enough like us to provide offspring. When you are more lumani, I will donate some of my essence to yours. My essence will find a place there and grow. Our species will continue."

My mouth drops open but I can't speak. My emotion spots riot: gray-green of disgust, muddy-brown of fear, pale-blue of despair.

"Why?" I manage to say.

Weast's form stops moving. Its outsides harden like a shell, so that thousands of tiny lights seem to be blinking inside a glass box.

"When we came to this world, we discovered that we aged more slowly. Perhaps something happened while we were not conscious during our traveling here. Perhaps it is something in the air, soil, or magnetic force of the planet. We have tried to discover the reason, but failed."

My mind spins. These, then, are the same lumani who

came originally to our world longer ago than I can imagine. Azlii was right when she said the Powers didn't seem to die.

"We have discovered, too, that on this world we cannot breed," Weast continues. "Unlike your race, we are complete in ourselves, being both what you call female and male. We do not mate within ourselves, however; we join with others for that. But here, when we join, our union bears no fruit."

I stare at the form that is Weast. I understand the lumani's longing, but don't grieve for their failures. I have no pity for those who've brought my world anguish.

The hard shell around Weast dissolves. The again-fluid band thins to a line no thicker than my finger.

"We are like your orindles," Weast says, its tone turning factual. "We find answers to questions. The answer to the question of when our lives will run out is very soon. The twenty-seven lumani here have perhaps another one hundred of your years left. Our thesstrin is destroyed. We cannot go back. Before our energies extinguish, we must pass our essence to a new generation who will call this world theirs. You will make that possible."

I don't know what a thesstrin is, but guess it must be what they used to come to our world. I do know that the lumani have no understanding of us, thinking that I would help make another generation of Powers ... lumani.

"You will be the first of a new race," Weast says. "No longer a simple doumana, groveling in the dirt for food to sustain you. Already you are superior to any other of your kind that we have found. We have probed your memory and know you are a Talent, but you did not go insane. You have eaten aruna and it increased your natural empathic abilities, again without making you insane or killing you. Your body and mind have unusual strength. No other has as good a chance of surviving the uniting and providing us offspring."

Sweat prickles my skin. My neck burns. I say nothing.

Weast straightens, the thin line growing tall, touching the ceiling.

"You too are aging," Weast says, "your natural span leaking away too quickly. We can give you what you want. We can give you back your life."

CHAPTER TWENTY-ONE

"*M*y heart cries out in longing."
—*"The Expectation of Returning"*

WEAST and its companions have gone, leaving me alone in the room. But not before Weast advised me to come to peace with the idea of the procedure and said that someone would come to prepare me. I wait in the darkness.

The door opens. Dim lights glow in the hall. A yellow-clad helphand pushes a waist-high rolling cot into the room.

The helphand sidles around from behind the cot, moving toward me in that efficient, almost silent way that helphands do. Her face shows her focus; she's thinking about what needs to be done, not what her patient might be planning. She leans over me.

I kick her belly, knocking her backward. She falls against the rolling cot with a thud. The cot rolls away and she falls to the floor. I leap on her, biting and clawing at her arms, face, neck, whatever I can reach. Her hands come up, defending herself. She rakes her nails across my face. I hardly notice. I press my shoulder into her belly and push up, trying to lever her onto the cot. Her hands flail, reaching for the instrument tray. I grab for her arms, but she's faster. An icy needle pricks my neck.

Against my will, my muscles begin to relax. My legs feel boneless and the floor rushes up. My arms won't move to break the fall. I hear a crash as I crumple onto the tiles. I feel nothing, though my mind whirls.

And feel nothing as the helphand grabs me, the muscles in her arms and shoulders tensed and bunched under her skin. Lifting me onto the cot, she grunts. There's no need for restraints, but she locks them around my wrists and ankles and fastens thick straps across my chest and upper arms, hips, and knees.

The lights are too bright. They pierce my eyes as I'm wheeled down one hallway and then another. The helphand walks with fast steps and then breaks into a trot, as though wanting to be rid of me as quickly as possible. Is the medication short acting? She takes a fast corner and my head lolls helplessly from side to side. I try to call out, but can't.

A door opens with a hiss and I am pushed into a new room. The helphand glares down at me and pinches my cheek between her thumb and first finger. Her teeth grit with the strain of how hard she's squeezing. It's horrifying to see, hear, smell, and know everything when my mind can only watch and record and my body can do nothing. Anger burns in me like a sun. The helphand pinches me again.

This room is well lit, the walls painted pale-yellow-blue, the color of acceptance. A bank of machinery stands in the middle of the room—dark orbs on long, spindly silver legs. Red, white, and yellow lights blink across their black faces. The helphand pushes the rolling cot to the machines and busies herself hooking me to them with wires and tubes. She focuses light beams from other machines on precise areas of my body—one on a spot in the middle of my forehead, one on my belly—on the place where, beneath the skin, the egg quickens during Resonance. She steps back to judge her work, then comes forward and makes adjustments until she's satisfied.

The helphand leans across me and twists a dial. A machine hums with a low-pitched sound. Greenish-black liquid seeps down a tube into my arm. My mouth tastes of brackish water. My muscles jump and begin to tingle.

She starts a second machine. Almost immediately I begin to feel drowsy and fight against it. The helphand flips another dial that starts a slow drip of red liquid leaking into me.

Another yellow-clad doumana slips into the room, all efficiency and bustle, a textbox clutched to her chest. She hands the box to the helphand, whose lips draw into a tight line as she reads. Contempt, but also fear, fills her eyes.

"Our orders are to leave you," the helphand says. "Someone will come."

I'm no longer drowsy and have gained back some command over my muscles. I turn my head to watch the doumanas leave. As soon as the door squeezes shut behind them, I try the restraints at my wrists and ankles, but it's no use. I'm too weak and they are too securely fastened.

I slump back on the cot. Greenish-black liquid trickles down the tube into my blood.

CHAPTER TWENTY-TWO

"*W*e hear the wind blowing,
            Generation to generation,
Carrying the seed."
—*The Song of Growing*

THE AIR in the room grows warm. A vaporous form takes shape between the rolling cot I'm strapped to and the closed round door. The thin hazy band twists slowly in the still air.

"Some time will pass before you are prepared properly by the machines to accept my essence," Weast says. "You will find your natural electrical energy magnified; your chemistry changed. Then we will bond."

Nausea makes my stomach heave—drugs or disgust? I clamp my jaws shut.

The whirring sound of one of the machines suddenly speeds up, its pitch rising.

A tremendous mental strength rushes through me. From the drugs. I am ... keenly aware. I realize that there are six separate chemicals mixed with the oxygen in the room. I don't know their names, but can tell each from the other by the subtle differences in their odors. I see suddenly how the haze of Weast is made of millions of tiny sparks, that each spark is made of three different elements, how two of the parts circle in a specific order around a central core. It seems natural that I should know these things, as though I have lived my life muffled in blankets, and now they have been lifted away.

"I, in particular, will monitor your progress," Weast says. It glimmers, then bends over me.

"Much time has passed since I've been this near to a soumyo," Weast says softly, as though speaking to itself. "To sense the slow rhythms of the electric fields, to study the hard container around the fields is a pleasure. But we must keep distance. To be among them invites familiarity. Familiarity invites dissent. Yes, we were right to stay away."

The vaporous band straightens and drifts off a short distance. My mouth is dry. I never got the water I asked for when I could still speak. Does Weast know that I can no longer speak? Does it matter to the lumani?

Weast drifts back to the cot. "But we are not common, you and I," it says, plainly talking to me now, and just as plainly knowing that I heard what it said before. "We should be companionable."

My mind is crowded with questions only a lumani can answer. I try to form words and speak, but no sound comes out. I'm tired of this one-way conversation. My teeth grind together in frustration. It sounds like a crash of boulders careening down a hillside. My heart thuds. What is happening to me?

I need to speak. I need my voice.

I think, maybe I can talk to Weast the way Azlii said sentients of differing species do. Like using a firestarter, Azlii said. Little different from asking the plants to grow. I form my question and concentrate on sending thought-energy to the lumani.

Weast has no reaction.

I concentrate harder and try again.

You can think-talk, Weast sends, its electrical bits whirling fast. *Did I not say that you were superior within your species? No other soumyo has communicated this way.*

I can't speak in words, I send. *My voice won't work.*

Because you would not come easily, you were given a relaxant. The speech areas return last.

Weast's thoughts come to me clearly, but it's different from when it spoke before. The lumani must have been sending all along, but now I hear its words not only in my mind, but also with my entire being. I catch emotions too— Weast's amazement and excitement. The emotions don't come as colors or feelings. More like a knowing. I worry that I might send thoughts I'd rather keep to myself, though Weast doesn't seem to know all that I'm thinking, only what I send.

I'm thirsty, I send. *Can I have some water?*

Weast doesn't react. Maybe it doesn't understand "thirst." I try a different tack.

Weast, what do you want to tell me?

So many things, it answers immediately. *Everything.*

Why?

The haze that is Weast shrinks to a line the width of my smallest finger. The line coils around itself, forming a spring-like shape. A moment passes, and then another.

There is a small chance, Weast sends, *that sharing essence with you will disrupt my energies until I cease to exist.*

If I could count on that, it almost would be worth going through the procedure.

Whether I disrupt or not, you will of course raise our offspring.

This is our way. Lumani offspring stay with the doumana half of any pairing.

You said lumani don't have doumana and male.

Indeed, we do not, Weast sends. *Not as you understand them. We are both. We can be growing an offspring within our form at the same moment we are providing what you call the male essence to another. It is of course efficient.*

Your offspring don't grow in an egg?

The distant thunder of Weast's laughter floats through the room. *No. Nor do our young have an in-between stage like your hatchlings. Our offspring are smaller but exact versions of ourselves.*

My shoulders shake and I feel cold. A dark pain starts behind my left temple.

On our world, Weast sends, *lumani pair-bonds are based on successful mating. If two lumani mate and no offspring results, the bond does not hold. Each looks for new mates. If the mating is successful, the two lumani set up a house-ring together. If the other is already in another pair-bond, the third lumani lives in the same ring. If the third is in a pair-bond, the fourth shares the same ring, and so on. The bond dissolves when the offspring are born. The "doumana" side then raises the offspring to maturity, in about twenty of your years.*

My breath catches in my throat. If Weast expects that I will see the half-breed abomination through to maturity, it is offering me at least that much more lifetime—twenty more of our years, a life nearly twice our normal span.

The machines thrum. The pain in my temple is gone. I feel my body changing inside, can hear the blood rushing, my electrical energy pulsing. I'm changing, but I'm not frightened. They must be feeding me a drug that makes me accept.

I will not accept this.

But … I am relaxed, happy almost. Twenty more years.

Weast glides around the rolling cot and shrinks its band

even more and begins to coil in on itself. The row of four brighter glowing spots that I think of as eyes are next to the machine. Its sparks flare, then drop back to what they were before.

There is no way of accurately predicting how quickly our offspring will mature, Weast sends. *Your species matures in a wisp of lumani time. The combining might not succeed, though our calculations indicate it will.*

But you might not survive. I need to keep my mind busy, focused. The relaxation drugs are stealing my resistance. If Weast returns in the combining … but what good is it to rid our world of only one?

Weast doesn't answer. I know it heard me. I can see our thoughts traveling back and forth like grains of sand in neat lines, rising and falling on crests of invisible waves. The gentle movements fascinate me.

Yes, Weast sends at last. *Which is why I must tell you everything that I want my lumanicate to know.*

I might as well be a textbox. Weast wants to fill me with information.

Is lumanicate the lumani word for offspring? I send. *Where are Azlii, Tanez, and Inra? If I can escape, how will I find them?*

Yes, of course, but no, Weast answers. *For us, the word lumanicate means not only the offspring of our bodies, but our hope for the future.*

For us also, I send. *Egg and hatchling are our futures.*

The coil of Weast contracts in. *You abandon your young. You cast them out and let strangers raise them. Not even your beasts or birds do such a thing.*

I feel the lumani's revulsion as clearly as if it were my own emotion. I feel anger rising up despite the relaxation drugs they've forced into me. My anger or Weast's? I can't tell.

We don't abandon our offspring, I send. *The gathers take them as soon as they leave the egg. The hatchlings are sent to the doumanas who have shown the best ability to raise them. We may not know which of our sisters raise our own offspring, but that doesn't matter. We don't know the doumana who laid the egg or the male who gave his essence to the hatchlings we raise, but we don't love or care for them any less because of it.*

Yet even as I argue, I think how I would like to know my own offspring. I think of Tanez, with her face so like mine, so like a male I once mated with, and how that familiarity warmed me to her. And perhaps it warmed her to me, so that she gave me her hip wrap and foot casings, and more—she asked to come to Presentation House with us.

My heart thumps. Whatever her reasons or mine, Tanez is now somewhere within the lumani's hold. Is it my fault?

All of this is of no importance, Weast sends impatiently. *You must listen and remember what I tell you. We will start with the history of the lumani on this world.*

The glittering haze uncoils and stretches again to touch from ceiling to floor.

Nearly twelve hundred of your years ago, we discovered the first sign of sentient life outside our planet—here on your world. Twenty-seven of our highest researchers were sent to this world. The trip was long. By time we arrived, those who had sent us were long dissipated. Nevertheless, we set about studying the native sentients and sending reports back, where others would interpret our findings and make practical uses of them.

Twenty-seven lumani. Only twenty-seven of them, and they've changed the lives of hundreds of thousands of us.

Energy pounds in my veins. I need to sit up, to move. I push against the straps holding my body to the cot.

You are in need? Weast sends.

Yes, I send back. *The straps hurt me. Could they be undone?*
Escape will be that much easier.

Weast gives no response. I pull my wrists against the straps. It's useless.

I'll remember more of what you tell me if I'm not thinking about how much my wrists hurt.

The vaporous band slides around the rolling cot, stopping to peer again at the gauges on the machines casting colored lights on my skin. Weast doesn't send words, but I know the lumani's pleasure at what the machines tell it. I think its pleasure should frighten me, but it doesn't. I want it to frighten me.

I cannot do what you've asked, Weast sends.

I clench my fists and turn my head away.

A helphand must do it, Weast sends. *I will call.*

The thin line of Weast contracts and grows thicker. Hundreds of sparks burst, glow bright, and then dim inside its form. Weast contracts further, then seems to wink out, and is gone.

I yank at the bonds at my wrists and ankles. They tighten, biting into my skin.

Finally, the door irises open and a different helphand bustles into the room, staring at me with wide eyes. She doesn't speak as she turns the dials on the machines or as she undoes the ties at my hands and feet and then undoes the broad straps across my body, but leaving in the chemical-carrying tubes. The moment I'm freed, she backs from the room almost at a run. Perhaps she's heard how I attacked her sister.

The air immediately warms again. I'm busy rubbing the circulation back into my arms and legs when Weast reappears.

You are happy? it sends.

Weast seems genuinely concerned. Likely my comfort has something to do with how well I can accept its essence. All the calming drugs in the world can't stop the shiver that thought sends through me.

Why did you call for a helphand?

The lumani laughs. *Can you not guess? Where are my bone and muscle tools to undo the straps that held you?*

I push myself up to a cross-legged sit. *Not having hands must be difficult,* I send, stalling for time. My body tingles from head to toe. Not from being bound, I think, but from the changes in my electrical energy. How long until Weast judges me ready?

Not difficult, but sometimes inconvenient. Not possessing hands became inconvenient when we realized we needed different tools from those we'd brought here to study the sentients. We could ask the question of what we need, and formulate the answer, but we could not build. We needed doumanas to build machines for us.

Why doumanas and not males? I send. *Or do both work with you?*

The haze of Weast glides around the rolling cot again. I swivel my head, watching.

Only the doumanas. By time the machines were necessary, the sexes had moved apart. We asked ourselves, which will be most useful? And answered, the doumanas, who have more vitality and endurance.

There were further problems, Weast continues. *There are always problems with your kind. You were nomadic. This was not optimal for us. We needed our builders in one place until the machines could be finished. We needed helpers trained in our methods and procedures to conduct our experiments. We made the klers as places to keep the trained helpers and the builders. We put research centers in some klers, to keep our subjects in one place while each experiment was conducted. We had Chimbalay built to meet our needs, which allows us to live in your world. We conceived of the communes to provide food and goods for those who work in the klers.*

Weast is bragging. My spots flare gray-green with

loathing at the lumani's pride and at its blindness that it can't read my spots and see how I feel. Now I know that Azlii was right when she said that the lumani, not the creator, made the three types of communities we live in.

But you left the corentas, I send, wanting a fight. The drugs have suppressed my fear, and what should have been fear is anger.

Some wanted to eradicate the corentas, yes, Weast replies. *Corentans are a great bit of trouble for us, but a necessity. We must have a control group—a way to view your natural changes.*

My spots riot on my neck, burning in fury. I've never felt this intensity before. It scares me. I breathe slowly, to calm myself.

What interests you most on our world? I send. Perhaps what interests the lumani can be turned to destroy them.

So many things, Weast sends. Its sparks are skating wildly inside its outline. *There are here a great variety of naturally occurring plants with medicinal effects. We are interested in the separation of the sexes. Lumani, being integrated, could never see the effects of that separation in our own kind.*

Weast breaks off communication. I try to send another question, wanting to fight with the only tool I have—words. Weast won't respond. It's like banging my fist against a wall.

I try again. *Don't you see that it's wrong to deprive the kler and commune dwellers of their natural way of living? You've made us into something we were never meant to be.*

It was necessary, Weast sends with a force that knocks against me like a fist. *How else are we to learn? We hunger for knowledge the way you hunger for food. Without learning, we wither.*

I feel the lumani's anger lessen, then drop away, replaced by pleasure.

The change in you is working, Weast sends. *Listen to how you ask questions and push for answers; you are becoming more lumani already. When you are as fully lumani as you can be, I will teach you the excitement of knowledge gathering. The joy of it. Only mating comes close to the feeling.*

I stare at my hands and legs, half expecting them to have faded into a lumani-like haze, but they are solid. One of the machines shining light onto my skin begins beeping. My neck feels suddenly cold. A shiver trembles across my shoulders.

The time is near, Weast sends. *One more dose and you will be ready. I will call an orindle to change the medication.*

Weast shimmers the way it did when calling the helphand before, then vanishes.

The door whooshes open immediately. I recognize the orindle, the pale-red shade of her skin, the dark-brown eyes that look too large for her small face.

Pradat.

CHAPTER TWENTY-THREE

"*R*ejoice! Rejoice! My sisters return weary from their work."
—Commune song

I KNOW PRADAT RECOGNIZES ME. She stops mid-step, plants her feet apart, knees bent, and yanks the textbox in her arms up in front of her like a shield. Her spots flare with the colors of surprise and fear.

"Khe," she whispers.

My neck tingles but my spots don't light. Is this from the drugs?

Pradat lowers the textbox. She lets her arms fall to her sides. "I often hoped to see you again at Lunge, but Simanca never invited me back."

It's good to hear spoken words again. I want to answer, to hear sounds coming from my throat and mouth. I try, but nothing comes out.

But Pradat is an orindle, a helphand to the lumani. She's here to adjust the machines and medications, to shove me over the ledge and make me into the thing Weast is creating as its mate. I should attack her now. My hands curl into soft fists, ready to harden.

"They used a drug to relax you," she says, her words slow and bland. "The effects should be almost gone. Keep trying to talk."

I look away and then back at her. I don't see Pradat, but her outline, and in that shape a swirl of colors pulsing slowly, brown-green mixing with pink. Blue-purple flows over the whole. A trickle of orange-yellow seeps down the sides of her shape. The colors confuse me. They aren't tied to what I feel of her emotions. Is this how the lumani see? I blink rapidly and see Pradat again as she has always looked. My breath comes in short, rapid bursts.

"How long have you been here?" she asks, walking toward me.

I shake my head. I must be patient, wait for the right moment to overcome her and escape this place.

Her jaw tenses. "Try, Khe. We have very little time before the Power will grow restless. There are things I need to know. You have to speak."

Do I trust her?

Pradat takes another step forward. "Did Simanca send you here?"

"No," I say. The word comes out rusty. I try for more. "I was caught at Presentation House."

Pradat nods in a way that tells me that she knew this and was only trying to get me to speak. She veers around the rolling cot, walks over to the machines beyond, and looks at each of them. She enters something into the textbox that must be more than a textbox, and frowns.

"Your natural energy pattern is completely altered," she says in the maddening noncommittal voice I remember from Lunge and Morvat. "It can't be undone."

A lump rises in my throat. I am no longer Khe. I'm something else now.

Pradat moves quickly, making adjustments to the machines. She concentrates on the two that cast the circles of colored light. I wonder where Weast is, if it is watching us. The textbox that Pradat has tucked against her ribs with one arm is hampering her work. She sets it on the rolling cart. The screen is filled with numbers that mean nothing to me.

The room begins to warm. Weast, or some other lumani, has slipped in. Pradat's mouth draws to a tight line as she begins turning the knobs on another machine, working faster. I feel dizzy and fevered.

I know it's Weast and not another lumani that has come in the room—though I can't say how I know. I know too that it won't become visible so long as Pradat is here.

Are you here? I send, and watch the thought-grains undulate through the air, seeking a destination.

Weast doesn't answer, but I track my thoughts across the room and see the spot where Weast absorbs them. The lumani is next to the machine from which the greenish-black liquid flows. I feel its excitement.

Pradat, too, seems to know that Weast is here. No spots are lit on her neck, but I feel a change in her, an anxiety, and determination. She makes more adjustments in the machines.

Weast, talk to me, I send.

This is the moment of our uniting, the lumani sends. *You do not feel the effect of my essence yet, but I feel it working.*

My heart beats wildly. My neck burns, but my spots don't light. I try to rip the tubes from my arms, but they are too well embedded.

Stop, Weast sends. *This will do damage. The tubes must be pried out easily, with two hands. You cannot remove them yourself.*

"Take the tubes out," I yell at Pradat. "Take them out."

Pradat doesn't answer. She twirls dials on the machines.

I slump back on the cot. There is no hope ... no hope.

We should speak together now, Weast sends. *To keep our minds from unpleasantness. You asked to speak with I.*

What do you feel? I send, but don't care about the answer. All I want is to sleep, and wake, and find myself back with Marnka, or in the kler with Inra and Tanez.

A draining, Weast replies. *More pain than the calculations predicted. Not normal.*

I'd laugh if I could. How could the lumani have expected something as unnatural as this to seem normal?

And you? Weast sends. *What is your experience?*

An egg is quickening in my sac. It feels like half-congealed blood. And hot, like the electric heat the lumani bring. My channel is expanding, to let the egg slide out. It feels like something clawing at me from the inside. I want to scream.

Nothing, I send. *I don't feel anything.*

Pradat leans over the machine where Weast is. Her bottom lip is caught between her teeth. I feel her concentrating as she makes more adjustments, working to get it right. I don't know whom I hate more, her or the lumani.

A wave of dizziness pours over me. The hum of Weast's whirring fragments changes pitch from a low, steady thrum to a higher, erratic sound.

You are fortunate to feel nothing, Weast sends.

I sense Weast wanting to say more, its nervous apprehension.

I want to talk too, to block my pain with words. The egg moving down my channel feels wrong. Too soft. Growing softer. Burning—a river of flame sliding through my core.

Pradat works at her dials and buttons. Nausea rocks my stomach. The hum of Weast's fragments grows shrill.

The orindle is mistaken, Weast sends. *Tell her to see the machine that tracks my changes. She must lower the energy.*

I clench my hands into fists and grit my teeth. I feel Weast's panic, its suspicion that Pradat is making the wrong adjustments on purpose, its failure to make that fit with its belief that orindles always follow orders exactly.

Make her stop, Weast sends. *Make her stop now.*

Sweat bathes my skin. I want her to stop as much as Weast does. The egg is wrong. Moving too quickly. Burning.

"You're doing it wrong," I tell Pradat. I can hardly force out the words.

Pradat's face screws up in anger. "You presume to tell an orindle how to do her job? My orders come from the Powers."

The textbox on the rolling cot begins whirring. I glance down and see words forming on the screen.

"Here." I try to point in Weast's direction, but am too weak. "Look at what the machine says. The Power wants you to stop."

I'm as desperate as Weast to end this.

"Please," I say.

Pradat gives the dials another twirl. Pain stabs through me. My stomach knots and my neck muscles tense, snapping my head back. I feel like I'm going to fly apart.

A deep gurgling sound comes from Weast.

The air turns suddenly cold—a shock against my burning skin. In the back of my mind, a dim awareness rises. Weast is gone.

"Quickly," Pradat says, hastily but carefully removing the tubes from my arms. "The Power may have sent messages to others."

She grabs my hand and pulls me from the cot. My legs are weak. I wobble, hardly able to stand. When I do, a thick, sparkling glob of something rolls down my leg and falls on the floor. My stomach clenches in disgust at the lifeless abomination splattered at my feet.

Pradat glares at me, pointedly ignoring the thing on the floor. Her voice is cold. "You'll have to walk. We'll go as slowly as we can. If the creator is kind, the Power hasn't called for help."

My head swims. How can Pradat expect me to walk when I can hardly stand? I must walk. I try a step and don't fall. Maybe I can make it.

Pradat presses a button on her textbox and the door dilates. She takes my elbow and drags me toward the door. When we step into the hall, there's no one there. She glances up and down the long passage.

"Is this a trick?" I ask, and mean a trick by the lumani, or by her, or both. It's hard to talk. I need all my energy and focus to stay on my feet and walk.

"Possibly. The Powers are fond of their tricks, though they don't see it that way. They see it as letting an incident run to its natural conclusion." I look at her neck. There's no color. She's being honest.

"That's how they caught you and your companions," Pradat says, and leads me down the hallway. "Azlii the corentan was spotted moving through the kler with three kler doumanas. The Powers watched your movements until they felt your destination could be predicted, arranged for gas in each room at Presentation House, and waited."

Her spots light with the brown-green of shame. I lean against the wall for support and wonder if Pradat helped in our capture.

"There never was any hope of success?" I ask.

"Not while you were with the corentan. The Powers know their enemies." Her mouth crinkles. "Most of them."

I open my mouth to speak, but Pradat hushes me. "We've no time to waste. Come."

She leads me down a hall painted the blue-purple of victory. I make my legs move one at a time, one foot after the other. We pass rows of doors, all shut, and another hall jutting off the one we are in. No lights are on, and I realize from the natural brightness that it must be day. Night would be better for escape.

"Where are we going?" I ask quietly.

"Out of Chimbalay."

"I won't go without the others."

Pradat gives me a hard glare. "I can maybe get one away from here, but not four."

"I won't leave them."

She stops and takes hold of my shoulders. "We are on the ground level, and near enough to the door that we stand a chance of escaping. Your companions are on the seventh level. If we try to rescue them, no one will get out. What good will that do?"

I let out a shaky sigh. She's right. I can barely walk; I'd never make it to the seventh level. And Weast will not stay silent for long. Our only hope is to go now and find help for the others. I slowly nod.

Pradat lets go of my shoulders. "We're going through the pink door."

Three doors and another passageway lie between the pink door and us. Pink, the color of nurturing. The door should be black-red, the color of my rage.

"Can you make it?" Pradat asks.

I nod again.

"Through the door is a foyer," she says. "A guardian and a few helphands will be there. You'll have to walk past them as though nothing is wrong."

My heart pounds against my ribs. I feel nothing on my neck.

"We're going to make you a helphand," Pradat says. "Wait here."

I slump against the wall and rest while Pradat walks to a

white door, opens it, and disappears. She reemerges a moment later with a yellow hip wrap and pair of brown foot casings in one hand and two collars in the other.

"Put these on," she says, holding the fabric and foot casings out to me.

I unknot the wrap I'm wearing—Tanez's—and Pradat helps me fold the yellow cloth around my hips the way helphands wear it. She steps back and appraises the results. Seeming satisfied, she hands me a collar. I don't tell her that I don't think I need it.

"We're on our way to the corenta for supplies," she says, and fastens a collar around her neck.

I do the same. Tanez's wrap lies on the floor. "We can't leave that."

Pradat picks up the wrap and tosses it into the room behind the white door.

"Ready?" she asks.

I nod and we head down the hall. She pulls open the pink door, showing a nerve I couldn't have managed. We walk through.

The foyer is painted the pale-green of contentment. Three helphands look up when we enter. They obviously recognize Pradat; deference is all over their faces. Two guardians, wearing cloaks held closed by the same type of insignia clasp Larta wears, stand near the door. Pradat pays them no notice. She strides to one side of the foyer, to a small nook that's filled with cloaks. She takes two and hands me one. My shaking fingers can barely manage the clasp.

"Oh," one of the guardians says. "Off to the corenta, I see."

Pradat nods.

"Something for your special cases?" The guardian's eyes widen and a slight smile stretches her lips.

Pradat strides to within inches of the guardian and glares

at her. "Not even within these walls are you to speak of what is none of your concern."

The guardian shrinks back. I think how clever Pradat is. Now the guardians and helphands will be thinking about Pradat's harsh words, the guardian's embarrassment. No one will be wondering who the unfamiliar doumana with her is.

Pradat glances over her shoulder and motions with her head that I am to follow her. The door irises open. We walk into daylight and see the doumanas of Chimbalay kler going about their everyday business.

CHAPTER TWENTY-FOUR

"*The* land is the deep song. The land is the creator's laughter."
—*The Song of Growing*

A CRUST of ice-snow sheets the ground, and a chill wind is blowing. The hem of my cloak flaps against my knees as we walk along Pale-Green Circle, two anonymous, collared doumanas heading for the corenta. The traffic in and out of Chimbalay is lighter than when I first came to the kler, but still busy enough that we don't stand out.

Pradat and I walk in silence. It takes all my will to move one foot in front of the other. No one seems to be pursuing us, but I don't trust anything that seems to be in this place. The lumani could be "letting the incident run to its natural conclusions."

Or Pradat could be leading me to a trap. Her emotion spots are hidden. When I look at her in an empath's way, the purple-black of guilt shines like a beacon. I wonder why she's in Chimbalay instead of at Morvat Research Center. I lean toward her and tap her arm.

"Where are we headed?" I whisper, even though no one walks near enough to overhear.

"The corenta," Pradat says.

"Not there. Sooner or later the lumani will come looking for us. They have Azlii. It's the first place they'll try."

Pradat's mouth thins to a narrow line as she thinks this over. I can see she knows I'm right.

"There's a cave in the wilderness," I say. "It's less than a day's walk. We'll be safe there."

Pradat sucks in a breath.

Probably the idea of the wilderness terrifies her. That almost makes me laugh. I have seen a different world than Pradat, even in all her travels.

Exhaling, she nods.

I'm not certain we'll be any safer in the wilderness than the corenta. I don't know how the lumani spy on us or what their abilities to track and find a specific doumana might be. It might make no difference where we go.

I have another reason for returning to the wilderness. I hope Pradat will know a way to help Marnka.

The wide-armed metal embrace of Chimbalay's main gate looms before us. My chest tightens and my neck burns. If the lumani want to stop us in the kler, now is their last chance. Several doumanas are close to us now, funneling from the streets into the passage between the gateposts We are squeezed together by the slow-moving vehicles passing on our left. None of the doumanas I see wears a guardian's insignia, but that doesn't mean anything. My shoulders tense. I expect someone to grab hold of me at any moment. We pass through the gate, carried along with the small crowd heading toward the corenta.

The corenta seems closer to the kler now than when I

came here. I blow out a breath. The corenta sits directly in our path. My eyes lock on the white mud walls that mark the corenta's boundary—the sentient walls. Do they take notice of us? I think I should ask them. The idea of communication with walls and buildings doesn't seem so strange anymore, not after Weast. If something like that can have consciousness, why not structures made of mud, or of bricks and mortar? I almost call out to the walls, but then change my mind. There could be empaths in this crowd who are not so kind as Inra.

The corenta's main gate is open. Empty-handed doumanas stream in, and doumanas bearing goods stream out. A group walking near us chatters happily about the trades they intend to make. A single vehicle makes its way past us, leaving little Vs of stirred-up snow in its wake.

I bend my head close to Pradat and whisper, "How did you make Weast sick?"

Pradat's mouth crinkles in a smile. "The Powers are made of tiny bits of matter held together by the attraction between positive and negative forces. I adjusted the machines to disrupt the balance."

An idea starts forming in my mind. It's vague, and I can't really get ahold of it.

"Could you have done it with any of the machines or only the one you used?"

Pradat takes my arm and casually walks us to the edge of the doumana stream—where fewer can possibly overhear our words.

"Just the one. The machine I used …" Pradat frowns. "This does get complicated, and you may not be happy to know exactly what was done to you."

Another slow-moving vehicle comes up beside us. We adjust our speed to match it, letting its low hum mask our words.

"For us," Pradat says, "fertility is triggered by changes in the planet's magnetic field. The machine created a temporary artificial matching field in the room. I used that field to make the Power's bits bounce back and forth until they overheated and began to scatter."

"I felt that," I say. "Like I was burning inside, and then as if I would fly apart. Did you feel it too?"

"No," Pradat says. "We are made up of the same kind of positive and negative elements as the Powers, but we are flesh, bone, blood, and muscle too. Your body has changed, Khe. My guess is that your bones are weakened, your blood thinned—some of the physical parts of you altered into pure energy. The Powers were more successful in making you what they wanted than I'd have thought possible."

My stomach churns. I want to be sick. My neck burns, but I don't feel my spots lighting.

"How?" I say. "How could I be changed that way?"

Pradat reaches out to touch my neck, but seems to think better of it. The last thing I want is for her to feel sorry for me.

"In the artificial magnetic field, your negatively charged elements were kicked into a faster energy orbit. You are no longer made of the stuff you were, but are now in some part made as the Powers are."

"A bird can't become a tree," I say.

I hadn't realized we'd slowed our pace until the vehicle hiding us suddenly moves on ahead. Four kler doumanas come alongside of us, chattering happily. We wait until they pass.

"Because, Khe, at times we are not so different from the Powers. During Resonance, the planet's natural magnetic force changes us, knocking our elements into an excited state that is not unlike the Powers' natural condition. Your elements are now in an even faster orbit than they would be during Resonance."

"Forever?"

"It's possible that your elements will quiet. It's just as possible…" Pradat does touch my neck now, but lightly, just brushing her fingers by. "It's more likely that your body will continue absorbing high energy levels from the planet's magnetic fields and making use of that energy."

Pale-blue is the color of despair. If my spots would light, that's what they'd show. I knew I'd been changed but had hoped that, away from the lumani's dreadful machines, I would go back to normal.

We walk a while, the corenta's walls growing closer, before Pradat says, "Khe, you are still yourself. The core of who and what you are hasn't changed."

I sigh and tell myself that body and soul are separate. That one part can change while the other stays true and immutable. I tell myself, but I don't believe it.

We're close enough to the corenta that I can see the corenta doumanas inside the open gate. In the kler, all the cloaks I saw were of a single color, like ours at the commune. The corentans' cloaks have dark-blue bodies with hoods in different colors and stripes of a third shade down either side in the front. Maybe the colors represent guilds or show what type of products they offer. Everyone I see is wearing a collar.

My collar feels suddenly tight; I don't like being this close to the corenta, but it lies directly in our path to the wilderness. It's unnatural, and it makes me nervous, until I think that no—the corenta is the most natural living arrangement on the planet. The only way it could be more natural was if males were there too.

I'm tiring and need to rest, but can't until we are safely away in the wilderness.

Pradat grabs my arm.

"Look, there at the gate," she says.

Two corentans have come out and are heading toward us.

Pradat's face tenses. "They hardly ever leave their community. Something's wrong."

"Move toward the plain now," I say. "Run if you have to."

We angle off, but the corentans adjust their course to match ours. They come slowly, as if they know where we are heading and are waiting until we get around the corner and out of the sight of Chimbalay's doumanas. I have the uncomfortable feeling that we are being herded where the corentans want us to go.

None of the kler doumanas seem to notice that we've turned and are walking alone now—Pradat and I—following the wall and heading away from the corenta's gate. The corentans still trail us.

We come to the corner and turn. Midway down the long wall, there's another gate, this one shut. I look around. The corentans have gone. As we come near the closed gate, I exhale a sigh. We've hit the halfway mark. Each step now takes us closer to putting the corenta behind us and reaching the wilderness.

When we're dead center of the gate when it bursts open, thumping against the wall. The sound makes my neck burn and my heart knock against my ribs. A collared corentan steps out, planting herself in front of us.

"A word, if you will, sisters," the corentan says. She's almost as tall as Azlii. Her skin is pale red, her eyes nearly as black and unfathomable as Inra's.

Two more corentans follow her out. Both have ruddy, red-brown skin. All three wear dark-blue cloaks with yellow hoods and white stripes down the front. All are collared, but I feel their anger as clearly as if I could see the brown-black of their spots. Behind us I hear the sound of foot casings crunching snow. I don't need to look to know that the two who were following us now stand at our backs.

"Of course, sister," Pradat says pleasantly. "How can we help you?"

The tallest corentan stares. "You are the orindle Pradat."

A shiver streams up my breastbone. Do they know her because she trades here, or has Azlii managed to send them word of our escape? Does Azlii know we've escaped? Are these doumanas in league with the lumani?

Pradat nods as if she's completely unconcerned. The two darker-skinned doumanas move to the outer sides of Pradat and me, hemming us in.

"The day is cold. Come inside," the tall one says.

The other corentans gently push us toward the open gate. I push back, but Pradat lays her hand on my arm and motions for me to go inside.

The gate slams behind us, though no one touches it. There are structures in the distance, but only open ground where we stand.

"Where are Azlii and the others?" the tall doumana demands.

Pradat spreads her hands, showing her palms. She looks calm, but I know the fear in her.

"Chimbalay Research Center One, so far as I know," Pradat says, then glances at me. "Except for Khe, who is here beside me."

The corentans pay me no mind.

"Are they alive?" the tall one asks.

Pradat shifts her weight. I feel her hesitancy and her fear click up a step.

"Two were this morning," she says. "Azlii was."

I turn and grab her wrists. My voice breaks. "Who has gone to the creator?"

Pradat sighs. "I'm sorry, Khe. It was Inra."

My neck burns as if a thousand fires roared inside it, but no spots light. I slump over. The lumani have destroyed Inra.

One of the dark-skinned doumanas takes my arm and helps me to stand straight. My bones are water. I lean against her for support.

Inra.

"Who is with Azlii in the research center?" the tall corentan asks.

"Tanez," I answer, the name coming out in a choked whisper. "From the hatchling house in Chimbalay."

The tall doumana looks at me for the first time. I don't like the way she stares down her broad nose at me. I pull myself up as tall as I can, though I'm still a handsbreadth shorter than she.

"You are Khe," she says. "Who Azlii thought was worth saving. And now you are with this … orindle?"

"She got me out," I say in Pradat's defense. "She saved me from the Powers." A long tremble shakes down my backbone. Once it starts, I can't stop shaking. Inra's dead, and I'd be worse than dead if it wasn't for Pradat. Perhaps I'm dead anyway—altered by Weast into something horrible. I'm afraid that Weast will give me what it promised, and I will go on a long, long time knowing that once I was a doumana, and now I'm not.

"Saved you from orindles like herself, you mean?" the tall one says. "Maybe saved you for herself, some little experiment she has in mind."

The harshness in her voice shocks me from my trembling.

"She saved me from the lumani," I say.

The tall doumana grabs my wrist. "Who told you to say lumani? Azlii? Only corentans know that word. Set-placers say Powers."

I pull my hand away; I hadn't realized I used the word. "The Power. It said that was what they call themselves."

"You have talked with one? How?"

"And seen three of them," I say. "In the research center. Azlii told me how corentans speak with other sentients. I tried it with the lumani. It worked."

All five corentans glare at me.

"Why would the lumani show themselves to you?" the tall one asks.

I hunch my shoulders and fall silent, too ashamed of what was done to me to speak of it. Ashamed and afraid. What would these doumanas—who hate the lumani—do if they knew what I've become?

Pradat takes a defiant step toward the tall corentan. "You'd do better and accomplish more if you asked me about Azlii. She was already damaged when I left her. I did what I could, but she and Tanez will likely be Returned soon if someone doesn't go after them."

There is a long silence.

"Can they be gotten out?" the tall one asks.

"If someone knew where they were, and knew some of the secrets of Research Center One," Pradat says.

"Secrets you're going to tell us?"

Pradat nods. "Do you have a stick, anything sharp?"

The doumana who helped me stand takes a few quick steps to a nearby tree. She sets her palms flat against the trunk, and I hear her think-talk, asking the tree if she may have a branch. If the tree answers, I don't hear it, but the corentan sends, *Thank you* and pulls off a thin, pointed branch that she hands to Pradat.

Pradat takes the stick and, hunkering down, begins to draw in the thin crust of snow as she explains how she thinks a rescue might, just might, be done and succeed.

CHAPTER TWENTY-FIVE

"*B*eware the deceiver. No good can come of her scheme."
—*The Rules of a Good Life*

PRADAT EXPLAINS her plan and rocks back on her heels, waiting for reactions. I close my eyes and hope for a moment's rest.

"I can see how that might work," the tall corentan says, "but I don't like it." She wipes her hand across her mouth. "There's violence and destruction in your scheme. That's not our way."

"It is harsh," Pradat agrees, "but it's quick and effective. If you want to save Azlii, you don't have much time left. You won't get a second chance."

The corentans eye each other.

"You need a diversion," Pradat continues. "Setting fire to the research center will force everyone inside to flee. Starting a fire won't be easy. The outside walls are made of glass and won't burn unless the temperature is very high. At least one of you would have to get inside and ignite the flames."

"Even if we manage to get a fire started," the tall one says, "what's to ensure that the doumanas inside will take Azlii and the kler doumana with them when they flee? They could leave them inside to burn."

"They might," Pradat says, "but I don't think they will. The orindles and helphands will be too afraid of angering the Powers by leaving them behind."

The tall corentan rubs the collar around her neck thoughtfully. "I can't agree to a fire that puts lives in danger. There has to be another way." The five corentans have all hunkered down beside Pradat. Now the tall one stands, followed by her sisters. "Come with us. Together, we'll look for a better solution."

I shake my head. "You know who we are. You must realize that we've escaped from the lumani. If you take us in, you'll put yourselves in danger."

The corentan laughs. "The lumani can't harm you here. They are helpless without someone to physically aid them. Who in the corenta do you think would do their will?"

The five corentans look at Pradat.

"She saved me," I say. "Not all of the Powers' enemies are obvious."

The tall one's mouth crinkles, but she doesn't smile. She draws her cloak closer around her body. "It's cold out here. We've a warm fire, food, and drink inside. Come."

The corentans start walking. Pradat looks at me. I shrug and follow the corentans. Behind us the gate closes without a touch or a word. It startles me to think that the wall likely shut its own door, and that it had been listening.

Fatigue is catching up with me. My legs feel weak, my mind dense. A voice behind me says, "I remember her," but when I glance over my shoulder, there is no one there.

The tall corentan doesn't hesitate in her step, but I see thought-grains floating from her and hear words in my mind: *What have you remembered, Wall?*

Where I saw her before. The medium-red one, as we were arriving, she ran across the plain, chased by beasts. She went into the kler.

The tall corentan's chin bobs in the smallest of nods. None of her sisters show that they've heard anything.

Good, she sends. *Thank you.*

A path stretches out from the gate, leading to the interior of the corenta. Most of the snow has been scraped from the path and piled in knee-high banks on either side. Pradat seems unsure of these new doumanas. I'm not afraid, but maybe fear is an effort I'm too tired to make.

The corenta isn't laid out in circular avenues the way Chimbalay is. The structures aren't bunched together in compounds like a commune. It's haphazard, as though things were set down any place that seemed good at the moment. The path we walk curves this way and that, but we walk fast, toward some specific place.

We take a branch path and head in a new direction. There are structures further down, made of mud, like the wall, and painted bright colors. The structures are unevenly spaced, as though they sprouted where they wanted, the way wild plants do in untended fields. I sense the structures watching our swift passage, and hear their soft whisperings as they wonder who the strangers are.

I tap the tall corentan on the shoulder. "Where are we headed?"

It's an effort to talk. I'm breathing hard and barely able to keep up with the pace she's set.

She glances over her shoulder but doesn't break stride. "My home. My dwelling," she adds, using the word that I know. I file the new word, home, into my memory.

We skirt the trading area filled with doumanas in kler- and corentan-style cloaks, each wearing a trader's collar. Long, buff brick structures with arched openings line its three sides. The trading area is far enough away that I shouldn't be able to make out details so clearly, but I can.

The path bends away toward where, in the back of the corenta and across the plain, the wilderness lies. Marnka is there. She's probably safe, at least. Azlii and Tanez are not. I feel my neck warm, but again don't feel my spots light. That bothers me, but not as much as I worry for Azlii and Tanez and fear that these corentans won't come up with a workable plan to save them.

My legs are about to give out when the tall corentan slows at a small one-level dwelling, steps up to a blue wooden door, and pushes it open. The door hangs on hinges, like doors in a commune. The tall doumana motions with her chin to two of the others, dismissing them. The two look disappointed. They nod, then turn and walk away without a look back.

Before the corentan goes inside she stops and presses her hand against the wall, just outside the doorjamb. I remember that Azlii said she and her dwelling—her home—worked together on its construction. I think maybe the tall corentan is greeting her home.

She steps aside and motions with her hand for us to enter first. I see the two even rows of seven blue dots that mark her wrist, and envy her.

Walking into the dwelling feels less like crossing into a structure, more like entering a living organism. I stop on the threshold. Pradat stops behind me. I feel the structure's awareness of us, its impatience at my hesitation. I step inside, half afraid that the home will swallow me up.

The door slams behind me, plunging me into darkness. I look around wildly, but I am alone in the room. Someone outside bangs on the door once. Lights come on in the room and the door opens again. The tall corentan comes inside, scowling. Pradat and the three other corentans follow her in. I wonder if they are a unit. Pradat's large eyes are bigger with fright.

Why did you do that? the tall corentan think-talks.

She needed a good scare, the home answers. *She was afraid of me. Now she'll be angry at my little jest and put fear behind her.*

She doesn't know you're aware, the corentan sends.

She knows, the home replies.

The corentan looks at me, and I give her a little shrug.

"Pftt," she says to no one in particular.

How did you know? she sends to the home.

The home chuckles. *Because she was afraid to come inside.*

The corentan wipes her hands on her cloak and sits down on a large pillow. The room is filled with them, each covered in fabric finer than anything I have ever seen. Some are solid colors and others have intricate designs in the weave.

"Well then, to business," she says. She unhooks the collar from her neck and sets it beside the pillow on the carpeted floor. A wooden chest painted blue-purple and a small visionstage are the only other things in the room. A firecave is cut into one wall. The room feels cold. I wish she'd light a fire.

The other two corentans take pillows and sit as well, forming a loose circle around Pradat and me. They remove their collars but leave on their cloaks in the chilly room. Pradat and I aren't invited to sit. We stand. The tall corentan leans back on her pillow and stretches her long legs out in front of her like spokes in a wheel.

"My name is Nool," she says. She doesn't name her companions.

"I'm Khe," I say, though Pradat has already told them my

name at the gate. I slip the collar from my neck. "You seem to know Pradat."

"You've come recently to Chimbalay," Nool says to Pradat. "I remember you from Morvat kler and the research center there."

I wonder what Nool was doing in Morvat Research Center.

Pradat bends her head slightly to the side, acknowledging that Nool is right. "I was brought to Chimbalay to work with the babblers."

My eyes fly to Pradat. I want to know about that, but this is not the moment to ask.

"But Khe is not a babbler, is she?" Nool asks. She turns her eyes toward me, but I don't feel that she expects an answer.

Nool knows something about me already, I'm sure—at least that I was with Azlii when she was captured. I put out a question of my own.

"Why were you waiting for us to pass at the gate?"

Nool's mouth crinkles as if she is amused. A soft chuckling vibrates through the room. The home is entertained by my question as well.

Nool rubs her chin thoughtfully. "Larta warned us that you were impatient. She came to the corenta soon after you left for Presentation House. She told us about the doumana who had been changed but had not gone insane, the one whose story she thought might begin to shake loose the lumani's hold on our world. Larta said that you'd gone to set the uprising in motion. We were at the gate waiting for word of your success or failure."

"How did you know I was the one who'd been with Azlii?"

"This corenta has traded with Chimbalay for a long time," Nool says. "A stranger is easy to spot."

"Forty thousand doumanas live in Chimbalay. You recognize all of them on sight?"

Shrugging, Nool says, "They don't all come to Kelroosh. Probably no more than a thousand have permission to trade. We know those doumanas by sight, yes."

Kelroosh is a word I haven't heard before, but I reason that it's the name of this corenta. One thousand doumanas still seems a large number to recognize, but there's no point in questioning her further on it.

"Would you like something to eat?" Nool asks, looking from me to Pradat and back again.

"I'd be grateful," Pradat says.

It's been two days since I've eaten. I don't feel hungry or thirsty. Still, I nod.

Nool jerks her head toward what I guess is the food prep area. A pinch-mouthed doumana gets up and heads in that direction.

I'd assumed these doumanas were a unit, but realize they can't be, not the way units are on the commune or in the kler, made up of hatchlings who've emerged in the same year. I've seen the dots on the wrists of Nool and the doumana still sitting with us. They're different ages. What binds them together, then?

"A fire would be nice," the third doumana says. I think of her as "Pinkling," for the light color of her skin.

"The starter's on the mantle," Nool says.

Pinkling finds the starter and kneels before the firecave. I watch her cup the firestarter in her hands and concentrate. The starter sparks, then catches. She lights the kindling, blowing on it gently to encourage the flame. There's a fragrance in the wood I can't name. It's sweet, like young leaves, but spicy, too. I breathe it in and feel clear-headed for the first time in days, though I'm still exhausted. I wish these doumanas would invite Pradat and me to sit.

The pinched-face doumana returns with bowls of mélange and cups of zwas on a rolling cart. Pradat seems ravenous, attacking the food. I have no appetite.

I take a sip of zwas. It burns my throat. The goblet feels heavy and nearly slips from my hand. My mind whirls. I set the goblet down on the floor.

The pinched-face doumana rubs a hand across her thin, sharp nose and asks, "Shall we throw the room open?"

Things are strange enough in the corenta that I wouldn't be surprised if the walls suddenly fell away.

Pinkling says, "Pradat's scheme has some good points. Perhaps we should start there."

Nool sets down her goblet. "The orindle is right that we need a diversion. Maybe a disturbance in the street outside the research center would draw out enough of the doumanas inside to let us get through."

"What kind of diversion?" Pinkling asks, turning her goblet slowly in her thick-fingered hands.

Pradat clears her throat. "Perhaps if two vehicles collided at the research center's door, maybe even pushing through the door."

"We don't have vehicles in the corenta," Nool says. "Who needs vehicles when your entire community, structures and all, travel as one? None of us knows how to pilot a vehicle."

Pinkling shifts her body, folding one leg beneath her. "Remember the Chimbalay helphand who claimed that the lens she purchased here was scratched and demanded it be replaced at no charge, even though she kept the other one.?We could storm the research center, demanding that the helphand pay what she rightfully owes. That would get us inside. While two of us stay to argue, making a lot of noise, the other could sneak through to find Azlii and the kler doumana with her."

Her name is Tanez, I want to shout.

The pinch-mouthed doumana draws her mouth into a line so tight that her lips all but disappear. "If we could find the captives. It's not as if the orindles and helphands are going to let us wander around freely. None of us have been inside Chimbalay. How will we find the research center? Even if we found Azlii and the other one, how would we get them out?"

My patience grows thin. Each moment wasted talking could be the last for Tanez and Azlii.

"I can lead you there," Pradat says.

"You can't go back," I say. "By now everyone in the research center knows that you helped me escape."

Pradat nods. "I can't go inside, but I can lead them through Chimbalay to the center's door."

"Unless they've alerted the guardians," I say. "If the guardians are looking for us, you won't be safe with one foot in the kler."

"We appreciate your offer," Nool says to Pradat, "but Khe is right. We can't chance being in the kler with you."

"There is a way that might work," I say. "Chances are that someone is looking for me—the guardians, or the orindles, or the lumani. If you took me to the research center, saying that I'd come to the corenta telling a confused tale, the orindles would let you in."

No one says anything. The home sends, *Yes. That might work.*

I flinch at the words. I've forgotten that the home is listening. I realize that what happens now is of as much concern to it as to any of the doumanas living in the corenta. The doumanas, beasts, plants, and structures are tied together in a way that's hard for me to understand, but I'd be foolish to forget it is so.

"That might get us in," Nool says. "But what if they take

you at the door, thank us, and send us on our way? It'll take more than you to rescue Azlii and the other."

"I'll be your diversion," I say. "I've already attacked a help-hand once. I'll put up a fight and make enough noise that it'll draw everyone's attention. That will let you sneak up to the seventh level, where the lumani have put Azlii and Tanez. With luck, you'll get them out."

Who will get you out? the home asks. No one else seems to hear the question, and I don't answer.

"Can you think-talk to Azlii once we get inside the research center?" I ask, beginning to see this escape in my mind. Beginning to see it might work. "Can you ask her where they are and follow her thoughts there?"

Nool nods. "If she's conscious."

"I think she will be. The lumani will want to question her and Tanez." I draw a breath. "You'll have to go fast. Get in and get out while the orindles and helphands are distracted by me. There's only one entrance to the building that I know of, but I think with all of us we can overwhelm the doumanas there and get out. Once we're on the street, things would get easier."

Nool strokes the knuckle of her thumb across her mouth. "It's a decent plan. We'll go into Chimbalay, with Khe as our excuse."

I glance from face to face. Pradat is clearly unhappy, the blue-red of anxiety glowing on her neck. The others show colors of emotions ranging from doubt to clear agreement. My neck isn't even warm.

CHAPTER TWENTY-SIX

"I am your instrument. Play upon me your tune."
—*Ninth Standard Prayer*

NOOL GETS TO HER FEET, walks over to a wall, and leans against it.

We're leaving now, she sends to the home. *Take good care of Pradat. Don't play any jokes on her. I'll be back before you have time to miss me.*

The home sighs and the door opens. I feel its worry. If the home had arms, I think it would grab Nool and keep her from going.

The sun has set but it is not yet dark as we set out across the corenta. A dusting of stars is scattered through a cloudless sky. Doumanas, singly and in small groups, stroll in the night air. All wear corenta-style clothing and no collars. The kler doumanas must have gone back to Chimbalay.

Fear slithers through me. Chimbalay.

"Nool," I say, "I'd like a favor."

"What?"

"I need to make a prayer and an offering for our safety. I know corentans don't believe, but I do. I need to do this."

Nool huffs under her breath. "All right. We'll come up to Community Hall quick enough. But be fast about it."

Community Hall in Kelroosh is a massive building, many times larger than the hall at Lunge. The high, plain wooden door is at the top of a set of twenty-five or thirty buff-colored stone steps. Walking through the corenta, I've heard the structures whispering among themselves. When we first came, the structures wondered who Pradat and I were. Now they all seem to know, and they whisper my name as we pass. But I'm not prepared for the surge of curiosity flowing from Community Hall, tumbling over me like water falling from a great height.

This doumana has come to make an offering to her protective deity, Nool sends to the hall. *Let her do it in peace,* she adds sternly. *No lecture from you for her, or for me.*

The hall gives no response for a moment, and then sends, *I hear that the stranger is versatile.*

She can hear and speak with you, Nool replies.

Oh! the hall sends, the thought-grains flowing faster. *To hear a new voice. I've been talking to the same doumanas, structures, beasts, and plants for far too long.*

Later, Nool sends. *We're in a hurry now.*

Community Hall opens its doors. Inside, the air is fragrant. I pick out several of the scents that I know from Lunge. I wonder why aromatics are burned here, since corentans make no offerings to the creator.

"You can use what's in that box," Nool says, and points with her chin to a small wooden chest.

I open it and find dried flowers and other aromatics inside. I choose denish, which helped keep me alive in the wilderness.

"Use the brazier," Nool says.

I put the denish in the brazier and pick up the firestarter lying next to it. As soon as I think of lighting it, the starter catches, throwing off a long blue cloud of flame that burns my hand. I drop the starter at my feet.

"Are you all right?" Nool kicks the starter away. "What happened?"

"I burned myself," I say, and hold out my singed fingers for them to see. They see what I see, perfectly whole flesh with no sign of damage.

"You were lucky," Nool says.

"You must have concentrated too hard," the pinched-face corentan says.

But I didn't. I hardly concentrated at all. The starter had gone off at my first thought.

My stomach clenches. Pradat said that Weast altered my electrical energy levels. Kicked them up to a faster level. What was I becoming?

I make a silent prayer, but I won't pick up the starter again. The creator will get words, but no offering from me. I hope it's enough.

"I'm ready," I tell the corentans.

The hall calls my name.

Go and be still, it sends as we leave.

The door closes behind us with a quiet thud. I crane my neck to look back over my shoulder, wondering what it meant by that.

We walk in two small knots—Nool and I side by side, Pinched-face and Pinkling together behind us. We don't talk. The only sound is the crunch of our foot casings in the snow. No one else is crossing the plain between Kelroosh and Chimbalay. If anyone is watching from the kler. We are in plain sight.

Even from a distance we can see that Chimbalay's great metal gate is closed.

"The gates are usually open until well after dark," Nool says. "What now?"

I pull my cloak tighter around me. "I'm not sure."

I think that maybe I am the reason they are closed, but that doesn't make sense—unless the lumani believe I'm still in Chimbalay.

"Maybe there's another entrance further around the wall," Pinkling says when we reach the high metal gate and see that it is indeed shut tight.

I shake my head. "Pradat would have said if there was another gate. I think this is the only way in or out."

"Look at this," Pinched-face says, pointing to what looks like a faint long, straight crack in the metal.

The crack extends up a bit higher than Nool's height, then turns and runs in a straight parallel to the ground. Another crack runs down the other side. Not a crack at all— a door. A door with no handle or knob on this side.

Nool leans her shoulder into the door, but nothing happens. She pounds the side of her fist hard against the metal, but there is no response.

"Open up in there," Nool yells, battering the gate with both of her fists.

The door opens enough to allow an unidentifiable face to peek out and then disappear. The door is left ajar. If we push it, we can get inside. The doumana behind the door says, "No need to scream."

I recognize Larta's voice. I don't know if I'm relieved or frightened that the First of Chimbalay's guardians is behind this door.

"It's Khe," I whisper.

"I can see that," Larta says. "Come inside. Hurry."

The door opens wide enough to let us pass. The corentans squeeze through the narrow gap. I hesitate. It seems too convenient that Larta happened to be passing just as we arrived.

"What are you doing here?" I ask Larta when we are all inside the kler. Across a stretch of snow-covered dirt are the backs of the squat black glass buildings that line the outer circle of Chimbalay. Not far from here is the refuse pile where Larta and I met.

"Watching out for an attack from the corenta," she says lightly.

The corentans laugh, low and under their breaths.

"Late this morning," Larta says, "a message came from the Powers, saying that an orindle at Research Center One had been spirited away by unknown doumanas. When I got there, everyone was in an uproar. The three guardians on assignment swore that a band of corentans had broken in and made off with Pradat. The rumor is that the corentans are coming back in force to take over Chimbalay."

The corentans snicker quietly.

"I know," Larta says. "Even if the whole of the sisterhood in the corenta decided to attack us, they couldn't get in and out without being seen. But the guardians at the research center believed what they said. Not one of them showed anything on her neck except fear and confusion—no sign of shame at telling an untruth. They've convinced themselves that corentans grabbed Pradat and made off with her."

"I was in Research Center One," I tell her. "Pradat helped me escape. Azlii and Tanez are still in there."

The muscles in Larta's face tighten. Her neck shows the brown-black spots of anger.

"I've been stupid," she says. "When the four of you didn't come back from Presentation House ... I've been trying to find out where you were taken. I never put what happened at the research center together with your capture at Presentation House. Pradat was there ... of course the rest of you were too." She rubs her neck and leans toward me. "Azlii and Tanez, you said."

I look her in the eye. "Inra has returned to the creator."

Larta turns away, but not before I see that all of her emotion spots are soft-gray with sorrow. My throat burns.

She turns back to face us. "You've come to free Azlii and Tanez."

I tell her our scheme.

"It's not going to work," Larta says with a finality that surprises me. "The whole of Chimbalay is a toe length away from panic. The only reason they haven't panicked yet is that I've ordered the gate locked and have let no one in or out since long before sundown. The guardian patrols have been increased threefold. Every doumana who isn't critically needed somewhere is locked up safe in her dwelling. Three corentans showing up at Research Center One, trah, I couldn't guarantee they'd leave again healthy."

"Azlii is our sister," Nool says. "We won't leave her here."

"Of course," Larta says. "Azlii isn't a sister to me like she is to you, but I have a fondness for her. But your presence at the center would make a bad situation worse, and make getting Azlii and Tanez out harder still, maybe impossible. Khe and I will go. No one will question me."

Nool takes in a breath and exhales it loudly. "Agreed. But you bring Azlii and Tanez to us straightaway. Straightaway, you understand?"

Larta opens the gate and the three corentans reluctantly leave. She shuts the gate behind them and slides five heavy metal bolts into place.

"We have some planning to do, Khe," Larta says. "Getting to the research center won't be hard. When we get there, I'll say that I received orders to bring you, a helphand from another kler, to help with the captives." She looks me up and down. "How fortunate that you're already dressed for it."

I'd forgotten I am wearing a helphand's hip wrap and cloak.

"We have to hope that no real orders have come from the Powers," Larta says. "And that the doumanas in the research center are still besides themselves with fear and worry and don't ask too many questions."

My mouth feels as dry as old bones. My neck warms. This plot also counts on us not being seen by either of the two helphands who could recognize me, and the lumani being too occupied to sense our arrival.

CHAPTER TWENTY-SEVEN

"*Patience. That which is central, that which is lumani, calls to her— like to like. She will return. She cannot do otherwise.*"

—*Weast, to its companions*

A PAIR of doumanas flanks the door to Research Center One. Light snow has begun to fall from purple-gray clouds. One of the doumanas stamps her feet and swings her arms to warm herself. The other tugs her hood into place against the drifting white flakes. Larta sets her hand in the small of my back and guides me toward the steps leading to the door. She seems calm and efficient. My breath feels stuck in my chest.

"Wretched night," Larta calls like a greeting. The doumanas' cloaks are fastened with the same guardian insignia Larta wears, but theirs are copper instead of silver. "Too cold to be stationed outside. Who assigned you to such a miserable post?"

"We pulled sticks to see who would stay inside and who'd

go out," the doumana who'd been trying to warm herself says. "We won."

Larta frowns. "They're still raving inside?"

The cold doumana nods and stares at me with open curiosity. I make a pretense of adjusting my cloak, letting it fall open to show the yellow hip wrap that marks me as a helphand. The doumana looks back at Larta and shrugs. Her companion curls her upper lip, as though she finds whatever is going on in the research center beneath contempt.

Memories of what was done to me within the walls and fear of what might happen now that I'm here again flood my mind. If it weren't for Tanez and Azlii, nothing would get me to cross that threshold.

"The orindles want this helphand," Larta says. Her voice turns to a grumble. "I don't know what's so special about her, but they insisted I fetch her."

The cold doumana waves her hand over a sensor mounted in the wall, and the door irises open. Larta and I step inside. The door closes behind us.

A small, thin helphand lets out a yelp and ducks behind a stone-topped table in the entry.

"She's the one who took Pradat," the helphand cries. "It's her."

I've never seen this helphand before. She couldn't have seen Pradat and I leave. Panic has made her accuse the first unknown face.

Four guardians race forward, stunners in their hands. My heart thuds in fear that the guardians will fire before they realize that Larta is behind me.

Larta grabs my upper arm, above the elbow, squeezing her hand tight, and screams at me, "Where is Pradat? What have you done with her?"

I stare at her, bewildered. She's thrown our scheme to the winds.

Another helphand says, "She's the one. I saw her too."

The four guardians keep their weapons pointed at my chest. One of them says to Larta as if apologizing, "The corentans overpowered us. She was with them."

I've never seen these guardians, but they must believe their own words—no shame colors glow on their necks.

"Have you nothing to say, corentan?" Larta yells in my face. She takes both my arms and shakes me.

I've sense enough to realize that Larta is telling me to keep silent.

"You'll tell me everything," she says, her voice hard. She turns to the guardians. "I want a room where I can question her."

One guardian nods and then leads us down the same hallway I took with Pradat. She opens a dark-blue-red door. "You can use this one."

Larta shoves me into the room. My feet tangle and I trip, landing sprawled facedown on the greenish-blue tiled floor. Greenish-blue, the color of hope. My hope is that Larta knows what she's doing.

I hear the door hiss close and then Larta whisper, "Are you all right?"

Rolling onto my side, I say, "I think so."

Larta extends her hand to help me up. I take her hand, but only pull myself into a cross-legged sit. My legs feel too weak to stand. In the empty room, there is nothing but the floor to sit on.

"Is it safe to talk here?" Larta whispers, and sits down next to me. "No Powers around?"

The room feels cool enough that I don't think Weast and its companions are with us. I don't see thought-grains moving in the room. Still, I'm worried that the lumani are watching us, listening in some secret way. I wish that Larta could think-talk, but she doesn't know how.

"You're the empath," Larta says, low. "Are we safe?"

I remember Azlii saying that Inra knew empathically when the lumani were watching, but not how Inra did it. Weast's emotions felt no different from a doumana's—happiness, confusion, and pride felt the same coming from it as from anyone. All I can think to try is to sense emotions around us that neither Larta nor I are feeling—curiosity, relief, satisfaction, anger. Resting my hands on my knees, I breathe slowly and feel.

Larta's more frightened than she lets on. Blue-red anxiety coats her body like a glaze. Greenish-blue hope trickles from the middle of her chest. I see distrust, a blackish-green smudge around her eyes, and it hurts to realize I'm the focus of it.

I look around the room slowly. There's no sign of the lumani. Probably I'm doing it wrong. Inra could tell when the lumani weren't paying attention. Inra knew what the lumani were doing when they were far away. Frustration howls through me. Larta and I have to assume the lumani are paying attention to us all the time.

Larta is sitting close enough that I can reach her without getting up. Taking her hand in mine, I trace on her palm an oval with two small lines rising from the top near the back—a stylized rendering of a dead doumana—the symbol for danger. I can only hope that Larta realizes what I mean, and the lumani don't.

Moving her hand from mine, Larta scratches her knee, then begins drawing waving lines on it. I watch her hand moving, but the lines mean nothing. She hasn't reasoned out what I meant.

Larta stops drawing. Propping her elbow against her knee, she seems to have found a sudden fascination with the inside of her lower arm. She traces the fingers of her right hand across the top row of dots on the inside of her left wrist. Larta has ten dots, a row of seven with a row of three beneath. I hadn't noticed before how young she is, how much life she has in front of her. I glance at the thirty-four dots on the inside of my wrist, and feel my muscles tense.

Self-pity vanishes in an instant. Larta does understand, and she's answering. She doesn't mean age, but the number seven. The seventh level, where Pradat said Azlii and Tanez are being kept. I try to think-talk to Azlii, to ask her where they are. I hope I can follow our thought-grains to the exact spot, but Azlii doesn't answer back. We'll have to do this the hard way—searching every room on the seventh level.

On the floor, near my foot casing, I draw a half circle with its opening facing right, the symbol for a question. How, I'm asking her, will we get past the orindles, guardians, and helphands, find the right room, get inside, and keep the lumani, if they are watching, from sending someone to stop us? Larta can't read all my wondering from that one small sign, but I imagine that the same questions are circling in her mind. I hope she has some answers.

Pulling herself to her feet, Larta crooks her finger as a signal for me to follow. I get up and stand next to her, thinking that I don't know how to get this room's door open. Pradat pressed a key on her textbox, or maybe a series of keys, like a code—I can't remember exactly. I can't remember at all how the helphands opened the doors to the two rooms I was in.

Larta stares at the door, her eyes roaming over the jambs and wall. Her mouth twitches. She rubs the corner of her eye —a sign, I think, that she's found the sensor—then waves her hand over a hardly noticeable depression in the wall. The door stays closed. The line of Larta's jaw tenses as she moves her hand in front of the depression again and again, coming at it from different angles and at various distances. Her spots light with frustration colors. The door stays locked.

The room begins to warm. I tap Larta's shoulder and then don't know what to say when she turns to me. Several lumani must be in the room, given how hot the air feels. Sweat breaks out on my forehead, but not from the heat. My neck burns. Larta's spots light up blue-red in alarm. She looks at me, wide eyed.

Nodding, I make myself breathe out slowly, forcing my muscles to relax, and search for the lumani's emotions. I feel disgust. Satisfaction. Relief. Hope. I try to put myself in the lumani's place, to think of Larta and myself as unruly preslets who have gotten loose and caused trouble, but now have been rounded up again. I think that must be how the lumani see us—as domesticated creatures of value only for the use they can make of us.

Emotions come at me from different places in the room. Four lumani are here, spread out—not clustered together. I work at staying calm, to hold on to the empathic connection. It's hard to keep my breathing level and to soothe my pounding heart. I walk across the seemingly empty room to the place from where I felt hope radiate.

Weast, I send. *I've returned.*

I am aware of that, Weast sends back. Its familiar voice sounds bland, but I feel desperation in Weast, a longing so strong it makes my eyes sting.

Where is the orindle who took you away? it asks.

The lumani's misunderstanding of what happened almost makes me smile. The research center doumanas claim that I stole Pradat, but Weast believes Pradat forced me to leave.

She's gone, I answer, and hope that's enough to quench Weast's curiosity.

I'd like to question her, Weast sends. *Spontaneous madness is little known in your species.*

Weast hasn't materialized. It's frustrating talking to

empty air. At least before, I could look at the semblance of a body, see how it moved and reacted to what was said.

All the lumani have stayed invisible. Larta stares at me. Confusion colors light on her neck. I must look absurd, standing near the room's center, saying nothing, staring at nothing. I send her a quick shrug, to let her know I haven't completely lost my senses.

What makes you think the orindle went insane? I ask Weast.

Her willful disobedience to our commands. Her theft of you. The damage she inflicted on us.

A collective shiver of remembered pain runs through the four lumani. I remember how I felt while Pradat twisted the dials, like I was burning inside. I wouldn't want to feel that again.

Larta is still looking at me, but my full concentration is on the lumani.

The orindle has returned to the creator, I send, in hope that this will stop the lumani from looking for her. *She fell and broke her neck outside the kler gate.*

But you did not return directly once the orindle dissipated, Weast sends.

There is no accusation in its voice, only a longing to comprehend why I didn't come running back to the research center the moment I could.

I was too weak to come back.

I feel Weast's emotions brighten, its hope rekindling.

You have become lumani enough that the orindle's treachery harmed you. That is good. Anger wells in the lumani. *The orindle's treachery also cost us our first chance at combining. It destroyed your offspring.*

I breathe deep, afraid that Weast will see how grateful I am for that destruction.

But that is of no consequence, Weast sends, its anger lessening. *We will begin again. You are strong. We have adjusted our machines. A new egg will form quickly.*

My stomach lurches. But the lumani's reliance on me to get what it wants is my protection. If I'm careful and sly, that desire might carry my companions and me safely out of this place.

The orindle said that the doumanas who were with me at Presentation House are here, I send.

Two are here, Weast replies. *The weakest one dissipated during testing. We are still testing the others.*

Emotions pour from the invisible lumani, a torrent of excitement, rivers of bright-blue and greenish-blue flowing from four distinct places in the room.

My chest feels squeezed. Larta takes a step toward me, but I warn her off with a look.

In what ways are you testing them?

I have taught you, Weast sends, *that the corenta-dwellers were left in their natural state. This is a first time—a corenta and a kler doumana side by side to evaluate their differences. We have questions about what physical differences in internal organ size and electrical or chemical makeup may have developed since the two groups separated.*

A wave of fear sweeps over me, wondering how the lumani might be finding the answers to their questions.

Larta opens her mouth to speak. I shake my head.

Weast flickers into sight for a moment and then disappears again.

Shall you see the doumanas before you and I begin our joining again? Weast sends. *I would find of interest your opinion of the information we have gained.*

Yes. I would like to see them, I send. *Will the other doumana come with us?*

Only you and us, Weast replies.

I don't let the disappointment I feel take hold. I want Larta with me. I need her help.

She can't hear us, I say. *I need to tell her with doumana speech that we are going and she will stay here.* I turn to Larta and say, "I'm going to see Azlii and Tanez. The Powers will take me. You are to wait here."

Larta's shoulders pull up and she shakes her head.

"I don't like it either," I say.

The door wheezes open.

Go into the hall and wait, Weast sends. *I will become visible to lead you to the doumanas.*

In the hall, Weast's vaporous form twists slowly in the windless space.

Through the third door, it sends.

The blue-purple door, the color of victory, is in the middle of the long hall. Pradat said that all the stairwells were at the hall-ends. If Tanez and Azlii are on the ground floor, getting them out will be easier than if they are still several levels up.

My heart is thumping while I wait for the door to open. Inside, the room is dim, but from the doorway I can make out two figures laying on cots, their faces turned away from the door. I also see several machines on three-legged stands. Three lumani are inside and visible. Weast was behind me, but it slips past me into the room. The millions of tiny bits that make up its form spread apart, flowing over me like a hot mist. My stomach knots in revulsion at Weast's touch.

I want to call to Tanez and Azlii, but can't—not if I want Weast to believe that I've become lumani enough to be only curious, not concerned, about them. One of the figures moans—Azlii, I think, by her body shape. The other doumana lies quietly. I want to run to her, but don't. Neither is secured to her cot.

Azlii turns her head toward me. Her face is puffy, her lips

cracked and dry. Ugly blue-black circles ring her glazed eyes. I think she recognizes me, but I can't be sure.

Are they drugged? I ask Weast.

Yes. But lightly. The small one is sleeping.

Can you wake the sleeper? I send. *I'd like to evaluate their states of awareness.*

Awareness? Weast sends.

To see if they are affected differently by the drugs.

The thin bands of all four lumani begin swaying. One of them coils in on itself.

A question of interest, Weast sends. *Yes, let us discover this. I will call an orindle to adjust the medications.*

Could I do it? I send quickly. I want control of the machines, and I don't want one of their obliging orindles in here with us.

You wish to learn, Weast sends. *Good. The sedatives dispense from the machine with green in the tubes. Slide the lever ground-ward. Do not lessen the dosage quickly, or shock will come on their minds.*

Next to each cot are two machines, each with a flexible tube no wider than four or five strands of beast fur. One tube from each machine is fixed into a small incision in each doumana's arm. One set of tubes is blackish-green, the other yellow-green. I stand over Tanez's cot and reach for the lever on the machine pumping the yellow-green fluid.

The other! The green! Weast sends. The agitation in its voice makes my heart knock against my ribs. But I'm relieved that Weast also doesn't want them hurt. At least not until the lumani finish finding out what they want to know.

I close my eyes a moment, then slide the lever down about one-quarter of the way. The bluish-red gauge on the machine's silver face records falling numbers as less liquid is pumped through the tubes. Weast watches me. I'm sure it knows the levels I can set safely, but wants to see what I'll do on my own. I lower the pressure as far as I'm brave enough to try. Tanez doesn't respond. When I go to Azlii's cot, she stares at me. A mix of fear and sorrow show in the colors on her neck. I press down her machine's lever further than I moved Tanez's.

How long before they are both fully conscious? I ask Weast.

If we knew that answer, it sends, *we would not need this experiment. I believe the corentan, in particular, will wake first. She has been stronger and more resilient through all the proce-dures.* The thin band of Weast contracts, then spreads into a small disk. *We suppose that living in one place, which is unnat-ural to your species, may have weakened the kler doumana. It will take further study to determine if only she is weakened, or if all kler dwellers are.*

I don't bother reminding Weast that the lumani are the reason kler and commune doumanas live in one place their whole lives.

The drugged dullness in Azlii's eyes seems to be fading. I push the lever down another quarter distance and do the same to the machine hooked to Tanez.

What are the other machines for? I ask Weast.

Its disk-like form swells and rounds, becoming a ball floating at my waist height, not more than an arm's length away.

Such curiosity, it sends.

I feel its happiness like a finger of pale-green stroking my neck. The color feels pleasant, but my stomach knots anyway.

Bending my knees to peer at a head-sized silver oval with several small, ridged black tubes sticking out, I send, *What does this one do?*

Worry emanates from all four lumani. The bits that form them move faster. The air grows warmer. Then Weast seems to decide that whatever threat the machine poses is not a serious one. Its whirling pieces slow back to their normal pace.

That machine analyzes energy output.

I can't grasp why that would make the lumani nervous, and think Weast is lying. Mounted on the cube's face is a black touchpad with twelve white squares arranged in a diamond. The squares are numbered in tens, from twenty to one hundred and thirty. Above the diamond's top point is a blank square. I touch this and the machine begins to hum.

There is no need to use that machine now, Weast sends.

I press the square marked forty. The humming tunes to a higher pitch. The muscles in my stomach cramp. I ball my hands into tight fists and then fling my fingers open, throwing off my tension.

I'd like to know if the doumanas' energy levels rise as they come back to consciousness, and if they do, at what rate, I send. *How do I make this machine show that?*

Pradat weakened Weast by disrupting the balance between the positive and negative bits that form it. She said that only the machine that created the artificial magnetic fields in the room where I was kept could have that effect. The lumani are worried about this analyzer. I think that even if I can't disrupt the lumani with it, I can at least make them uncomfortable. Maybe uncomfortable enough for me to escape with Tanez and Azlii. I press the button marked sixty. The pitch of the machine's hum moves higher.

My stomach clenches again and I gag on a sudden rush of bile in my throat. Sweat covers my skin. I push the levers on the drug dispensers lower. Azlii is fully awake now. Do the lumani know that? They seem busy, their bits moving fast. I walk the few steps to the machine by Tanez and push that lever completely down.

You must turn off the analyzer, Weast sends. *The calibrations will become wrong.*

There's fear in its tone. I look over my shoulder. Weast is compressed into a ball no bigger than my fist. The other three lumani have contracted in the same way. I step back to the analyzer and push the square marked one hundred—and double over in pain. My head swims. The muscles in my arms and legs cramp. A sizzling sound comes from the lumani, like water dripping onto red-hot logs. A sharp smell fills the air.

Tanez and Azlii are watching me, both awake and aware now. Neither seems to feel any effect from the analyzer.

Turn it off, Weast sends, and I feel its desperation. *Push the blank square.*

I want to do what Weast says. I want the pain to stop. Weast's elements are swirling crazily, the orderly orbit of two bits around one falling apart, single pieces flying away from the main body. Weast's companions are no better off. One of them spreads across the floor, its bits sparking. I push the button marked one hundred and thirty, and scream from the pain.

Azlii rolls off the cot and rushes to me. Her legs are wobbly and she nearly falls over me. She wraps one arm around my shoulders. Blood trickles down her arm, from where she's torn out the tubes.

"Khe," she whispers.

"Out," I tell her. My breath is shallow, my throat squeezed. "The door isn't locked. Larta is close."

I hope the door isn't locked.

Tanez is sitting upright on the cot, trying to pull out the tube that tethers her to the machine.

"Can you walk?" Azlii asks Tanez when the tube is out.

She nods and swings her feet over the side of the cot. When she tries to stand, she sinks to the floor.

"Get Larta," I tell Azlii, who seems the fittest among us. "Down the hall. In the room with the purple-blue door."

Azlii stumbles across the room and waves her hand in front of the wall near the door. The door whooshes open and Azlii goes through. The door stays open behind her. We might have a chance after all.

Weast has stopped sending to me. Its pain, the pain of each lumani, is worse than mine. I see their suffering like flaming yellow sparks careening through the room.

My legs give out. I grab at the stand supporting the analyzer, miss it, and crumple to the floor. Tanez crawls toward me. Our hands meet and clasp.

Then Azlii is at the doorway again, with Larta behind her. Azlii's face is pale, her movements stiff. Larta darts across the room, her arms supporting first Tanez to her feet and then me. That I can stand is a miracle. That my feet are moving, more amazing still. We walk down the hall toward the entryway—me leaning on Larta, Azlii and Tanez supporting each other. Helphands and orindles stare at us, mouths gaping, frozen in their places. The guardians point their stunners at us.

Larta calls to the four guardians, "We are leaving Chimbalay. You will come with us to the gate and ensure our safety."

Their weapons do not lower. Their emotion spots spark and glow with the orange-yellow of confusion.

"We are guardians," Larta says to them, "sworn to protect our sisters from all harm. Look at these doumanas. See what the Powers have done to them."

The guardians keep their weapons pointed at us. Larta's jaw tenses. The colors of determination show on her neck.

A guardian slowly lowers her weapon and steps up to Tanez. "Lean on me. It's a long way to the gate."

CHAPTER TWENTY-EIGHT

"*H*eat is a fine prod to action."
      —*Azlii*

THE SOFT PINK-YELLOW light of dawn awakens me. I open my eyes and see Pradat tapping away on her textbox.

"Tanez and Azlii?" I ask, as I've asked each of the two previous mornings.

Nool is sharing her sleep quarters with the four of us. The room is cramped with cots. Mine lies closest to the outer wall. Pradat is sitting at an angle that blocks the rest of the cots from my view.

"Azlii is in the meal room," Pradat says, looking up. "Tanez is sleeping."

"Still?"

Tanez has slept since we came to Kelroosh. She tosses and turns restlessly, muttering and sometimes crying out. I've spent much of the last two nights sitting on the edge of her cot, stroking her neck. It seems to comfort her.

"Do you want something to eat?" Pradat asks. When I shake my head, she frowns.

I have eaten some since we arrived here, but all food tastes bad to me, and none of it digests. It sits in my stomach like hardwood.

I sleep little now, maybe a fifth of the night, which leaves me plenty of time to think. My anger is so strong, I feel it will lift me from the cot. I am ashamed of what I have become, and wish that my spots still lit so others could know how I feel. But part of me merely notes each emotion with detached interest.

It is this part that thinks about Weast and the other lumani—how they and I reacted when the machines changed the magnetic fields in the room we shared. This part of me doesn't want to drive the lumani from our world. It is the part that schemes to destroy them.

"You were my great success, you know," Pradat says.

I sit up to encourage her to go on.

"Of the one hundred and twenty-six doumanas I'd treated for Resonance dysfunction, eleven showed new Talents. Ten went insane." Pradat looks at the floor a moment and then back at me. "But you didn't lose your mind. Simanca kept me informed. I knew every time you went to mating. I knew you were using your Talent to help your sisters at Lunge. I was thrilled when Simanca reported that you showed no ill effects from the restoration or from using your gift."

"She lied," I say quietly. The bitterness in my voice is like a shout.

"Yes," Pradat says. "I know how many years have passed since you hatched, and I can count the dots on your wrist. It doesn't take much to reason that something went wrong."

"Pushing the crops to grow better aged me."

Pradat winces as if I've struck her. "I'm sorry."

"It's not your fault," I say. "You did a good thing. I've always been grateful for the chance to mate and lay my egg."

"I tried twice more to come and see you," Pradat says. "Simanca put me off. I should have insisted."

I shrug.

"I didn't insist," Pradat says, "because I didn't want to call attention to you."

I listen, curious about her reasons.

"I'd kept you secret," Pradat says. "As First of Morvat Research Center, I reported to the Powers. It was they who devised the surgery that let you feel Resonance."

"I know," I say. "Azlii told me."

Pradat nods. "They tracked each patient with great interest. When the gifted doumanas began to go mad, the Powers ordered that all patients showing new Talents, sane or insane, be sent to Chimbalay immediately. Once they were there, no one ever heard from them again. But there were rumors—"

I see the gray mist of sorrow rise from her shoulders, a match to the colors on her neck.

"Whatever happened to those doumanas isn't your fault," I say.

Pradat sighs. "To save you from the Powers, I never reported you. I've lived in fear that Simanca would let the information slip. When the Powers called me to Chimbalay, I thought they'd discovered my disobedience, but they only wanted me to work with the babblers."

I think of Marnka and want to ask Pradat if she'd found a way to restore babblers' sanity, but this is not the time.

"One day the Powers informed me that they'd found a doumana who they believed would make a good candidate for breeding with them." Pradat rubs her throat as if to comfort herself. "This was too much, too great an insult to our species for me to help them. I'd already made up my mind to do what I could to spoil the experiment. When I saw that the doumana they'd chosen was you—I decided at that moment to get you out."

"Thank you," I say.

"I wish I'd gotten to you sooner. You are physically changed, Khe."

I nod, but don't say how changed I am. I don't tell her that when I look at the lumani now, I see not the hazy bands I saw at first, but all the individual swirling pieces that make up their form. I don't say that I've hardly eaten or slept in six days and that it doesn't seem to affect me.

I don't tell her the worst of it—that when I was in that room with Azlii and Tanez, I was truly curious and almost willing to let the lumani finish their tests, so I could know the answers.

"Pradat," I say, "I came to Chimbalay in hope of finding a way to get back my normal life-span. Is it possible?"

Her mouth draws into a line. "We'd need to know if your body is truly aging, or if the extra dots are the result of something else. Your Resonance sac was sealed. When it was opened, chemicals that had been kept from your body suddenly flooded in. Perhaps you are allergic to your own chemicals and the dots are a physical reaction to that, though there is no test or machine devised yet that could figure that out. Most likely, Khe, you are aging. I don't know of any way to stop that."

"Weast, one of the Powers, said that when they'd … changed me, I'd live longer than a doumana should. Almost double our life-span." I feel my heart begin to pound.

Pradat looks at me a long moment.

"Maybe," she says.

THERE ARE seven gathered in Nool's house for the night meal, including Tanez, who's finally woken and whose first words were "I'm hungry." Restlessness rumbles through me, Resonance-like—that feeling that I must move.

"Nool," I say. "I'd like to walk in the corenta. Is that allowed?"

"Go where you please," Nool says. "If you lose your way, ask any of the structures to point you back here."

Home sends, *Khe takes her own path*, and chuckles low, clearly pleased with its jest.

Nool rolls her eyes and gives a faint shrug. "Structures have bent personalities."

"What?" Tanez says, looking up from the meal she is devouring.

Nool waves her hand in dismissal.

I think that being able to hear structures talk when others can't is like being able to understand beast or bird talk—a second language, unintelligible to others. I think it is a great gift.

NO SNOW HAS FALLEN in a while. A hard crust of ice has formed on the ground, and I see the white puffs of my breath as I walk. Each step I take on open ground makes me happy. I feel refreshed and full. Few doumanas are out on this frosty night, but I nod and greet each one as if she were a sister. They respond back in the same manner. I know where I want to go, and head straight there.

I was hoping you'd come again, Community Hall sends as I climb the steps. When I reach the top, the tall wooden doors swing open.

I've come to offer a prayer to the creator, I send. *To ask its great mind for help.*

You are welcome to pray, though there is no mind greater than me here, Hall sends, and chuckles, a sound like distant wind. *Afterward, we will talk?*

I'd like that, I send.

Good. I'll be right here.

My lips crinkle. Structures do have their own kind of humor.

I choose several aromatics I find in a box and put a small handful of each in the brazier. Cupping the firestarter in my hand, I concentrate on keeping the flame under control, and am pleased that I succeed. I breathe in the spicy-sweet scent and make a small prayer of thanksgiving for my survival so far, and ask that the creator show me the way to rid our world of the lumani.

I take a deep breath and let it out.

Are you there, Hall? I send. *You haven't gone away, have you?*

I was thinking of leaving to visit some friends, but decided to stay. Now, what shall we talk about?

It's truly delightful to speak with a structure, and there is much I want to know.

My curiosity feels very lumani, and the peace within me is suddenly swept away. Weast has succeeded well with me.

But I was always one to ask questions and to think my own thoughts. Maybe I'm not so lumani after all.

Can you see as well as hear and speak? I ask.

Not so well as your species or the beasts, but better than the plants, judging by what I hear them say about it, Hall answers.

How do structures become aware? I ask.

Everything has consciousness, Hall sends. *From the smallest grains of sand and tiny drops of water on up. Consciousness is not all the same. A grain of sand knows it is part of a larger world, but doesn't know what that world is. The grain might know it was once part of a stone, but won't remember what that was like. For structures, as we are built, the pieces that form us begin linking their consciousnesses, growing stronger as the structure grows larger.*

I try to imagine being a grain of sand as Hall describes, and find it's not difficult. How different is that from my awareness when I lived at Lunge? I, too, knew I was part of a larger world, a world brought through the visionstage—with knowledge no larger than the instrument that delivered it.

At some point, Hall sends, *consciousness becomes intelligence. When that happens and how aware the structure is varies, depending on the materials used. Mud structures aren't great thinkers, but they have a fine sensitivity to the ebb and flow of the planet. Wall, being all baked mud and very large, is always the first structure to feel the change that marks Resonance for the doumanas.*

Structures made of stone are more aware than mud ones, and those that include wood are better thinkers still. Mortar made from animal blood brings a different, more aggressive intelligence to a structure. I am the oldest and largest structure in Kelroosh. I am made of stone, wood, and blood mortar. You may draw your own conclusions from that.

I laugh under my breath.

Do the structures hate the lumani the way corenta doumanas do? I ask.

Hall sighs. *Your question is like asking, does your arm feel the same way about the lumani as your leg feels? Structures, doumanas, plants, tame beasts—we are one thing.*

I shake my head. *Azlii—or any corenta doumana—isn't your arm or leg. She is herself. You are yourself. How can you all be one thing?*

Halls sighs again, more deeply. The sound is like wind through a cave. *Perhaps in time you will understand.*

Time is something I don't have much of.

Hall, I send, *were you here in the Before?*

Of course.

Over time, have you perceived any change in the feel of the lumani? Do they seem the same to you now as when they first came, or are they different?

Hall is silent. Then it sends, *When individual transportation vehicles were first developed in large numbers for those set-place doumanas to use at Resonance, the lumani seemed bothered. Resonance never bothered them before. It was the vehicles.* Hall makes a noise like a sniff. *This is the only thing the lumani and I seem to agree on—we don't like vehicles.*

Why don't you like them?

At Resonance, there are so many, zigzagging in every direction. Set-place doumanas are fools, running here and there to lay their eggs. Corenta doumanas all go together, with us, the way it should be.

But why do the vehicles upset you?

Resonance changes the energy of the planet. All those vehicles upset the balance even more. It hurts in every grain of my being when they come close to us. I suppose vehicles must hurt the lumani too.

Yes, I send, and pull myself to my feet. *Thank you. It's been wonderful to talk to you.*

If you want to talk again, Hall sends, *you know where to find me.*

CHAPTER TWENTY-NINE

"*R*aise a joyful song in praise of our sisters."
—The Expectation of Returning

THE MOON'S light reflecting off the ice-covered ground brightens the land around us. Azlii, Larta, Pradat, and I cast long shadows as we make our way toward Chimbalay's gate. Probably it would have been better to wait, to let Azlii rest another night and day, but we can't afford the time. In two days the corenta will pick itself up and leave for the faraway kler of Hawnya.

I wonder about my own strength. Kelroosh isn't far behind us, and already my legs and feet ache. I tell myself that it isn't physical strength that will matter once we are inside Chimbalay, but strength of will. And that has not weakened in me.

The snow that we slogged through the last time we passed between kler and corenta has melted and refrozen. We tread carefully across the slick ice. We'll need to tread even more carefully inside Chimbalay. Dressed in kler-style cloaks, the hoods pulled over our heads to hide our faces and necks as much as possible, we are as disguised as we can be. I worry that the lumani are watching for us. No disguise will fool them.

The high silver metal gate of Chimbalay and the smaller door within it are shut for the night. We expect the gate to be bolted and guarded, though Larta trusts that any guardian on watch will let her in and allow us to pass. I don't share her opinion. My thinking is that by now the lumani will have convinced everyone in Chimbalay that Larta is a babbler, at best.

She tries the small door. It opens easily. No guardians or kler doumanas seem to be nearby.

"Could someone have forgotten to lock it?" Pradat asks.

Larta shakes her head.

"It's an invitation from the lumani," Azlii says, and I agree.

Larta pushes the door further open and motions with her hand for us to follow. Azlii goes next, then me, then Pradat.

Light leaks through the small back windows of a few of the dwellings that form the outermost ring of Chimbalay. I catch the sound of voices coming from inside. We don't see anyone.

"Khe," Azlii says, her voice a near whisper, though there is no one but us to hear it. "You have to find the lumani now. Where are they?"

My throat tightens. I'm as fearful that I will find the lumani as I am that I won't. I search the only way I can think to find them, looking for emotions they alone would have. Leaning against the wall next to the gate, I seek out hatred.

Something like a fist knocks into me, slamming my head hard against the wall. Everything turns black—a hole into nothing. It hurts as if my life force is being wrung out. I fight through the pain, the blackness, to find the place where the hatred begins.

"Where are they, Khe?" Azlii says.

"Near." The word sticks in my throat. "Follow me."

I dive into the black current, struggling against the tide. I sense Azlii, Larta, and Pradat behind me—their worry and fear. I sense the lumani, many of them, together. I feel something else from them—hunger.

I'm running, both repelled and drawn by the lumani. The others follow. I cut across a pathway between streets, coming out on Crimson Circle. The emotions are stronger here, and I know I'm heading in the right direction. I take another pathway, crossing through Pale-Pink, on to Green. Doumanas fill the streets. Some look away quickly as we approach with a wildness and rush they never see. A few change direction when they spot us. I worry that they will alert the guardians, but they are not important. Only finding the lumani matters. I push through the black waters of the lumani's emotions. We cross circle after circle, emerging finally at the innermost heart of the kler.

I stop. I've found them. A feral hatred streams through me—my emotions, or the lumani's? My feet feel heavy. I can hardly lift them.

"They're in there," I say, and break the emotional connection I have with Weast and the other lumani. I stare at the ten-level-high building, trying to catch my breath. "What is this place?" I ask between gasps.

"Chimbalay's energy center," Larta says.

Pradat hunches into her shoulders. "Why would they come here?"

"They're feeding on the electrical field," I answer, suddenly knowing the answer as clearly as if I were lumani myself. My head aches where it hit the wall. If I'm still alive tomorrow morning, I'll have a good-sized bump to show. "They're weakened. I don't know why."

"Good," Larta says. "They'll be easier to defeat."

I tsk my tongue. "They've been feeding for a while and are growing stronger. We have to hurry."

"Now we know what the extra electricity the kler makes is being used for," Larta says.

Azlii laughs without humor. "I hope they choke on it."

"That would save us some effort," Larta says. "The large vehicles are stored on Bright-Blue Circle. It's a bit of a ways to go." She starts walking, taking the lead.

I've walked Chimbalay's streets twice now, and they've begun to feel familiar. I know that Bright-Blue is one of the kler's middle rings. In Chimbalay, as in Lunge, all vehicles belong to the community. The large hauling vehicles are stored mid-kler, so that no doumana need walk more than halfway through Chimbalay to get one.

We've decided on haulers to use against the lumani. They'll be more difficult to move into position than smaller vehicles, but we'll need fewer of them. Larta and Pradat have experience with vehicles and will be our pilots.

We take the pathways between streets, crossing the same circles that brought us to the lumani. Night has settled in. There are few kler doumanas out now. Larta turns right, heading up Bright-Blue Circle. Pradat, Azlii, and I follow. My legs throb. Twice I stumble and Azlii has to help me up. Pradat sends me a worried look, but I shrug and make myself walk with long, strong strides. The smell of coming snow is in the air. I send a small prayer to the creator, asking for success in our mission.

Do the lumani also pray? Are they as nervous and desperate as we are? Do they ask their creator to bring us to them? I shake the thought away.

Larta stops in front of a large building surrounded by a

low fence pierced by a black metal gate. The vehicles inside are neatly placed, the largest in front. All the biggest vehicles are painted white, the color of satisfaction. The smaller vehicles behind are bright-yellow, and behind them, the smallest vehicles are new-leaf green. I let out a breath, grateful that we won't have to move the haulers out from behind. It'll be easier this way.

She pulls on the unlocked gate, swinging it open. No one expects a doumana to steal a vehicle. My heart is pounding. The skin on my neck prickles. Larta licks her lips. She looks calm, but I know she's as nervous and frightened as I am. As we all are.

We pick two vehicles from the front row, big haulers that move by creating and collapsing magnetic fields of opposite polarity. The opposing fields repel each other, pushing the vehicle forward. Pradat and I head toward one vehicle, Azlii and Larta toward another. I spring open the foldaway metal ladder on the side of the towering vehicle and climb into the cabin. Pradat was faster up her ladder than I was and is already seated behind the controls.

My mouth is dry and my palms are wet. Pradat pulls a small black knob on the control box sitting on the floor between us. A low pinging ticks inside the instrument panel, but the vehicle doesn't start. My breath falls into the same awkward rhythm as the pinging, as if that could force the vehicle into action. The pinging stops. Pradat frowns, pushes the knob in, and pulls it out again. Nothing.

"Something's wrong with the energy storage unit," she says, and bends to look at a gauge tucked underneath the panel. She sucks in a breath between her teeth. She sits up and says, "It's totally drained."

I know enough about vehicles to realize that if the storage unit is empty, the hauler can't create the initial energy field it needs to start moving.

"Give it another pull," I say.

Pradat tugs on the knob. We hear two quick pings and then silence. And the clang of someone climbing the ladder on Pradat's side of the vehicle.

Larta's face appears in the window next to her. "We've tried three haulers. None of them will start."

My teeth clench in anger. We can't fail before we've even begun. I think of the firestarter, and how the lumani have changed me. I lean over and pull on the black knob.

Electricity jolts through me, making my fingers twitch and sting. The sting spreads up my arms and through my body. My heart shudders, beating too hard, then stops, only to pound again. I concentrate, pushing the incoming electrical flow outward. I feel the energy reverse, magnify, then spurt from my core out to my hand. My arm shakes. The stinging grows, becomes pain. My eyes water and my ear holes ring. Blue sparks fly from the knob. The air smells like something burning. A jab of electricity knocks my fingers off the knob. The machine hums to life.

Larta stares at me, wide eyed.

"Try one of the other haulers, Khe," Pradat says. "See if you can start it."

I slump against the seat, staring at her, trying to get my breath back. But I know she is right. We need two haulers, and time is passing.

My knees are wobbly as I make my way to another hauler. I open the door slowly and reach for the starter. I don't want to feel that draining again, my own energy being sucked out through nerves and skin and into the vehicle's starter. I take the knob and pull, holding on to it even when my whole body is shaking and my teeth rattle in my head. The hauler starts. Azlii and Larta clamber inside.

We glide through the open gate and onto the street. The haulers move with a silent grace. I slump in the seat between

Azlii and Larta, my head lolled to one side. My bones feel splintered, my muscles crushed. Larta glances at me. Concern is in her eyes, in the purple-gray haze I see coating her skin, and in the lit spots on her neck. She strokes my throat and pulls her focus back to piloting the hauler.

My strength slowly returns, enough to realize what miserable, uncomfortable machines the haulers are. The seats are hard, the cabin cramped. The vehicle floats forward with nerve-wracking slowness.

No one is on the streets now, which is a blessing, and nearly all the dwellings are dark. We reach the energy center and move the vehicles into the positions we've already decided on, one on each side of the tall structure where the lumani are. The magnetic fields the vehicles make will push the negative bits of the lumani in only one direction. To push the bits first in one direction and then the other, forcing the pieces to collide, the field's sources have to be alternated.

Azlii and I have to stay within sight of each other, to coordinate the powering up and shutting down of the vehicles. We're going to have to be fast, to weaken the lumani quickly before they can flee or attack us in return. My heart pounds and my throat prickles. I push open the door, lower the ladder, and climb down.

The moment my feet touch the ground, energy rushes through me. A profound sense of well-being seeps through my foot casings to my feet, rising through my legs to my belly. It's like the energized peace we feel in Resonance, but many times stronger. The feeling races upward through my chest, warming the skin on my neck, putting a flush on my scalp. The spot where I'd bumped my head stops hurting.

The feeling is so unexpected that I shake for a moment. In that moment I realize what is happening—that the planet itself is giving me this gift. The idea makes no sense, but I know it is true. I spread out my toes, stretching the fabric of my foot casings, to increase my connection with the ground. A long, slow breath whispers over my lips.

Azlii is already in place on the other side of the center, waiting for my signal. Pradat, too, has her eyes on me. Pradat will start her vehicle first. Then Azlii will signal Larta to fire up her machine.

"The Song of Returning" leaps into my head. A happy song with a lively beat, *tat a tat tum, tat a tat tum*; it was always one of my favorites. I tap my foot to its rhythm and raise my hand to tell Pradat to power up and then turn my palm to signal that it's Larta's turn. I don't know if the song's cadence is the right one to disrupt the lumani, but I use it to keep a steady beat.

Pradat said that if the lumani pieces bang together hard enough, they will explode. Like lightning, she said, which occurs when cloud tops and bottoms get too much buildup of positive and negative charges. My heart begins to pound. I struggle to keep the beat even for the hauler pilots. If one explosion starts another, we could destroy the entire kler.

My foot taps. My palm swings toward Azlii and Larta, then toward Pradat, then back again, signaling them when to turn the engines on and off. If all of Chimbalay is blown to fragments, it will be worth it to stop the lumani.

The hum of the haulers is so quiet that I can't use sound to know if Pradat and Larta are in rhythm or not. I watch Azlii signal to Larta. The gloom of night deepens.

A soft crackling sound tingles my ear holes. The smell of something acrid burns my nose. I concentrate on the song, on keeping the beat, on helping Azlii and Larta and Pradat keep the magnetic field inversions quick and even. *Tat a tat tum, tat a tat tum.*

It is no use, Khe, Weast sends, its voice drilling into my mind. *We are all here together. We are strong together. We will make you stop.*

The air feels as hot as the end of Bounty Season. The lumani are invisible, their heat all around me. I swing my hand back and forth, *tat a tat tum, tat a tat tum*, ignoring Weast's threat.

We knew you would come, Weast sends. *We left the gate open. We have been waiting for you.*

CHAPTER THIRTY

"*A*nother swears she hears the future in the wind."
—*Pradat*

MY STOMACH KNOTS. Tapping my feet and moving my palm, I keep my eyes on Pradat. Her mouth is drawn taut in concentration. Her shoulders lift and fall as she turns the hauler's engine on and off at my signal.

Cease now and we will allow your companions to go, Weast sends.

I smile weakly at Weast's bribe. I'm tiring. My chest feels tight, my arms as heavy as if I were carrying the entire kler. I stop tapping my feet. I've lost the beat.

Take her now, Weast sends to its companions.

The ground beneath me falls away. My body feels light and stretched to an impossible length. Wind whistles in my ear holes as I'm lifted into the air by the lumani. Their touch is hot and brutal. I am burning in their grasp. Azlii said this— how the lumani snatched up beasts and fieldgoods, and doumanas. That none ever returned.

We race through the hot air. I try to find my eyes, to open them, to see where I am, but I have no eyes. I try to scream. I have no mouth. But I feel that we are slowing, then speeding again, only to slow once more. I feel the lumani's hold on me tighten, loosen, tighten, loosen. I feel myself falling—a rock through water. I bang into the snow-crusted street, shoulders and hips first. I lie still, panting. A sharp pain radiates in my side.

I am on the street again, but not where I stood before. I'm closer to Azlii. The lumani dropped me. Or couldn't hold me. They've weakened since the days Azlii spoke about.

We give no second opportunities, Weast sends. *Stop your companions now or we will destroy them.*

But not me. Me they still want for their combining.

I pull myself to my feet and run to the structure side where Azlii and Larta are. My leg muscles shriek. The air is hotter in some places than in others. Where the air is hottest a turbulence rages, like the spot where two strong winds from opposite directions meet. Am I passing through the lumani? Is the turbulence caused by the orbits of their elements breaking down, or by their anger?

Azlii is still signaling, finding a rhythm of her own to use. Larta continues starting and stopping her vehicle. I need to see the lumani, to know if the pieces are swinging back and forth, hitting one another. My mind whirls, trying to think of a way to make the lumani materialize. I come up with nothing.

Your opportunity is lost, Weast sends. *Your companions will be destroyed. Come with us now and you can still save them.*

Kindness is not in the lumani makeup. If they had the strength to stop us, they would have done it.

I'm such a fool, I realize. I don't need to see the lumani to know if their elements are disrupting. I stand still and feel for their emotions. Fury blasts over and through me, knocking me back a step. Behind the rage there is panic. Beneath the panic lies anguish.

The burning smell grows stronger, almost overwhelming. The air feels prickly, the way it does before a storm. Larta's hauler begins sliding. Not forward or back, but scraped sideways over the paved courtyard, crashing against a wall. I see Larta's panicked face, her hunched form as she desperately yanks on the pilot stick. This is my fault. Why didn't I listen to Weast? The hauler grinds across the pavement, the metal creaking and groaning. Larta throws open the door and leaps out.

Metal shrieks, crushed under pressure. Sparks, like tiny lightning bolts, fly from where the hauler scrapes against the energy center wall. I'm amazed to realize the hauler is still running. Part of me watches in horror, and part in fascination. How can the lumani move the hauler when they need their servant-doumanas to run the simplest machinery, when they can't even carry me off?

Larta and Azlii run toward me, Azlii holding Larta upright, pulling her along. I watch them with my seeing eyes. My empathic eyes still search for the lumani. I find them clustered near the vehicle, twenty-seven emotional centers. Twenty-seven. The number of lumani Weast said were in our world. It must take their combined efforts to move the hauler, and they had to come close. Their emotions burn through me, and I double over in pain. I break off the connection.

Azlii turns Larta loose, who wobbles a bit on her feet, but finds her balance. Azlii grabs my arm, spinning me toward her. When she touches me, my muscles contract, stung.

"Think, Khe," she shouts. "We can still destroy them. There's a way. I know it. What is it?"

The answer is in her touch, in the static electrical charge

that leaped between us. I motion to Pradat to join us, yelling out, "Leave the hauler's engine running."

Pradat shoulders open the door, hustles down the ladder, and runs to where we are.

"The lumani are by Larta's hauler," I say quickly when Pradat reaches us. "The hauler is still producing a field, but it's not enough. We have to amplify it."

"How?" Azlii asks.

"We have to get as close as we can to the lumani and then, in unison, focus our own electrical impulses on them."

Pradat draws a harsh breath across her teeth.

"No different from sending the impulses from our bodies down a strip of metal to spark a firestarter," I say. "The lumani's electrical bits are in confusion, but it isn't enough to destroy them. We have to add our energy to the haulers' fields. The extra will overload the flow of electricity through the lumani enough to push apart their disordered bits. Enough to kill them."

If it works, I think, but don't say. If.

Azlii grabs Pradat's hand and starts toward the hauler. Larta and I follow. Our cloaks lift and pull in the turbulent air. Puffs of snow scatter across the ground like dead leaves. I lean forward, fighting against the lumani wind. Sweat washes my skin.

In the distance I hear the sound of running feet, the slap of foot casings against paving stones. The lumani have called their servants to stop us. Commands are called out, but the words slide over me, meaningless. I see twenty guardians, maybe more. I see raised arms, hands with stunners clutched in them.

"Stay back," Larta screams at them. The guardians stop and look at each other, confused.

We reach Larta's hauler. I feel the lumani around me, a

hot, wet cloud. I pull Azlii to my left side, Pradat to my right, so that we are touching.

"Larta," I say, "come next to Pradat. Closer."

The energy flows between us, as if we four were one doumana. We are linked, stronger combined than separate. The air crackles.

"Now," I call, and focus my electrical energy, zinging it through my body and arms, out through my hands. My arms rise as if they have thoughts of their own. My hands turn palms down, my fingers spread out, the tendons stretching. I see that the same thing is happening to my sisters.

The air grows hotter and hotter, the lumani wind more violent.

I feel the lumani knocked back, but rebounding. I feel their hold tighten on me.

"It's not enough," I say. "We're not enough. We need help."

Larta gapes at me, not understanding. "The guardians?"

I have the answer now. "The structures. This structure. The energy center. We need it to help us."

I think-talk to it. *Please. We can drive away the lumani. Whatever it is that distresses you, we will try to fix it. But you have to help us now.*

Azlii's gaze slides toward me. I see her thought-grains floating out toward the gate and beyond. *Hall. Help us. Talk to this structure.*

Pradat runs out of strength, and her arms fall to her sides. The lumani's grip on me is almost too much to resist. I focus all my energy on them. I hear Community Hall's voice, but the words sound like another language. Pradat forces her arms up and adds her energy to ours again.

It's not enough. My own arms are shaking from the effort, the muscles ready to give out.

Please, I send to the energy center. *Help us.*

I hear Community Hall speaking on and on.

A new smell rises in the air, acrid and electric. Sparks bounce on the outside walls of the energy center, winking like stars against the dark glass. The black lines that run through the glass begin to glow faintly gray-red.

I grit my teeth and send out as much energy from my body as I can. My arms tremble.

More sparks bounce on the glass and fall toward the ground. We duck our heads. I look up. The black lines glow bright red.

See what you have done, Weast shrieks.

The lumani become visible. The steady two-around-one orbit of Weast's elements is gone, the fundamental fragments blown apart. The positive bits rise; the negative pieces drop. Sparks of uncontrolled energy shoot in all directions. The reek of burning fills the air.

The oval of Weast convulses, its form winking from visible to invisible and back again, expanding each time it becomes visible, the glowing elements burning brighter. The acrid smell in the air is overwhelming. Next to me, Pradat is coughing.

The guardians still stand where they stopped. They stare open-mouthed at the glittering form that is Weast, visible to everyone now. The smell grows stronger. Sparks fall through the air like rain. The glass around the energy lines buckles and groans.

"Run," I yell. We are already in motion, heading away by the time the word leaves my mouth. The acrid air makes my eyes water. I recognize the smell now. I know what will happen.

"Run to the gate," I scream at the guardians. "Run."

I am no longer strong. Pradat, Larta, and Azlii outdistance me. I chase my companions, straining on weak legs that won't let me keep up. I hear the pounding feet of the guardians behind me. Pradat glances back and starts to slow. I shake my head, and she quickens her step.

The sky explodes with a violent white light. In the sudden radiance, the street's buildings gleam, hard-angled stone in still water. A shattering boom tears the air. The force of the sound boils against me, shoving me like a storm wind. I'm pushed forward, almost losing my balance.

The light fails as quickly as it came, plunging the buildings into shadow, the night into darkness all the blacker for the light that had been. I barely run another two steps before the sky explodes again. The follow-on boom rattles the air. Glass and lumps of twisted metal rain over the street, the metal hissing when it touches snow-dusted pavement. The sky lights again.

Ahead of me Larta, Azlii, and Pradat are running with their heads down, their arms thrown up to protect their necks. I run in the same awkward position. The air reeks of melting glass and metal. The light and the sound come so quickly now that one blends into the other and I can hardly tell which is which.

Panicked doumanas stream out their dwellings. I yell, "Run. Run." They are like stunned beasts. They stand and stare. Then one runs, and another, until the streets are filled with doumanas, some screaming, all of them bumping, and pushing into each other, the quickest shoving their slower sisters from their paths.

My feet pound on the snowy pavement. My heart feels ready to burst, but I keep going. Azlii, Larta, and Pradat stand at the gate, its huge metal arms swung open. I look over my shoulder. Thick black smoke chokes the air above Bright-Blue Circle. Azlii grabs my hand and pulls me through the open gate.

"I've sent a message to Kelroosh that we're coming," she says, panting hard. "They're preparing to leave."

My mind is too jumbled for the words to make much sense. I only know that we are running again across the icy plain, slipping and sliding, but moving forward.

Kelroosh has its gate open. Larta grabs my arm, hauling me through the gate that slams shut the instant we're inside. But something's wrong. The ground beneath my feet is shaking.

"Lie down," Azlii yells, and throws herself onto the ground. "Spread out your arms and legs."

Pradat, Larta, and I do as she says. Kelroosh rumbles and shakes and begins to move. I dig my fingers into a sturdy bush and try to hold on.

And realize, suddenly, that in Chimbalay, I didn't feel what the lumani felt. I wasn't affected by the changing magnetic fields.

CHAPTER THIRTY-ONE

ELROOSH

"RIDING OVER LEAF and brush
  In a new land,
  The windblown seed blossoms."
  —*The Song of Growing*

DAYLIGHT SLANTS through the small window of my sleep quarters. I sit in a chair and watch the doumanas outside rushing here and there, some already dressed in green gowns, as they finish the preparations for Commemoration Day.

Not only are there doumanas on the street, but also a few males from a corenta that has set down so close to Kelroosh that a hand could barely fit in the space between the walls. Males! Walking among doumanas, stopping to talk, their delicate hands moving in concert with their speech, as if it were the most natural thing on the planet that doumana and male should be together outside of Resonance. Maybe it is. The way Hall sees it, it wasn't until fifteen days ago, when Kelroosh's guide contacted the males' corenta and invited them to set down with us outside of Hawnya kler—and they did—that the true healing of our planet began.

Not only are the males visiting Kelroosh, but many of the doumanas of Hawnya kler have ventured into the males' corenta for trading. Some of our doumanas—curious to see the inside of a kler—have gone to Hawnya. Tanez went this morning. She says the kler is smaller than Chimbalay and poorer in the wonders that a kler can offer. Still, I would like to walk its streets and stare up at its tall structures, to see a kler with eyes that are wide open and fear free. Azlii and I plan to go there together soon.

The lumani are gone. All of them. I didn't count the explosions at Chimbalay, but know in my heart that all twenty-seven are dead. Everything feels different now—as though during all of my life a storm had raged across the planet, but now it has passed. I wish Inra were here. I would like for her to know how sweet this peace feels.

Word about Chimbalay has come over the visionstage. The explosion didn't destroy it, as I'd feared. The energy center completely collapsed and the buildings on either side of it were badly burned, but the rest of the kler escaped relatively unharmed. Tanez, Azlii, and I watched the presentation together, in what is now our home. When the smoldering shell of the energy center was shown, Tanez hid her head against my shoulder. When the rest of the undamaged kler was presented, she breathed a loud sigh at the same moment Azlii and I did.

The snows of Barren Season have melted. With First Warmth upon us, the slumbering trees have awakened and pushed their roots deep into the rich soil outside Hawnya.

Seeds from plants that live only one year have sprouted, their shoots stretching up and up, reaching for the light. I sit outside often. Sometimes the plants and I talk, but mostly I simply watch the pictures of their thoughts as they chatter among themselves.

All the doumanas in the corenta speak with the plants, but it seems they can't help them grow. While Pradat watched in amusement, I tried an experiment with Nool and two of her homemates. After I explained how I thought the plants into growth, we each planted ten seeds in identical soil and asked them to sprout. None of the corentans' seeds showed above ground in less than seven days, but the seeds I tended came up the day I set them in the soil. We tried the experiment other times with other doumanas. The results were always the same, except with Tanez, who seems to have a bit of the grower's touch.

Kiiku grows in the garden here, along with denish bulbs, golden-flowered fedephloc, aromatics, and other staples. I'm using my Talent to push the plants a little, to ensure that Azlii and Tanez have an abundant crop this Bounty Season. Probably both would disapprove if they knew what I'm doing, but I reason I've earned the right to do as I please with the gift I've been given.

Pradat would likely disapprove as well. After recalibrating her machines to account for what the lumani did to me and running a series of tests, she is convinced that if I save my strength, I won't return to the creator until I reach my true thirty-fifth year.

Sometimes I'm afraid that she's right. I fear that Weast has kept its promise to extend my life and that I will live a long, long time the way I am—with legs that can no longer support me well and arms that can barely lift. Pradat says I should eat, but admits that I am no thinner despite having taken almost no food since we returned to Kelroosh forty-five days ago. She says that although my muscles are weakening, otherwise I am as healthy as any doumana. She has no explanation for what is happening to me.

But I know. The lumani's tinkering did this. I am changing from the inside out, my muscles and bones melting —the elemental bits of me pushed into faster energy orbits. The longer I live, the more I will become like the lumani.

And yet I am not lumani any more than I am soumyo. I am something else. The lumani existed by consuming electricity. The soumyo eat plants and animals. I am nourished by the planet. Each time my feet are on soil, I sense the pulse and flow of the planet surging through me, feeding me, keeping me alive. The same pulse and flow I felt during Resonance.

I think that maybe the reason we do not need food or drink during Resonance is that the planet sustains us then, but we are too blind with the desire to mate to notice. All that extra eating we do in advance isn't necessary. Corentans don't gorge before Resonance and come back none the worse for not eating, though they don't know why.

Home, where I live now, makes the soft *kroot kroot* sound that means it wants my attention and sends, *Tanez is coming.*

Thank you, I reply, and shift my chair around to be facing the door when she enters.

Tanez and I share these sleep quarters. Azlii and Home wanted to build one more room, to give us each our own. I said that seemed unnecessary since I would be with the creator soon, and have no need. Azlii's face had darkened and her spots lit dark-gray-purple in frustration.

"Pradat says that you might be with us another twenty years. That's a very long time to share such small quarters with someone," she said.

Spoken like a true corentan. But I am commune bred and Tanez is from a kler. I have slept alone under the stars, but neither Tanez nor I have ever had, or wanted, sleep quarters to ourselves. We like having our sisters near.

"I came to help you dress for Commemoration Day," Tanez says, striding across the room. My heart leaps up when I see her, as it always does. "Pradat and Larta will join us later for the walk to Community Hall."

The signs of her ordeal with the lumani are completely gone. To see her cheerful face now, you'd never know that she'd felt a moment of sorrow or pain. And yet her face is changed, grown wiser somehow. The face she wears now is exactly the one I would have wished for her.

As she comes across the room, a gold cord as thick as her wrist stretches out from her chest and reaches toward me. I saw this gold cord for the first time the day Pradat, Azlii, Larta, and I returned from the destruction of the lumani. It was only a thread then, but it leaped from her with great force, sped through the air, and wrapped itself around my waist. A similar gold thread reached out from me back to Tanez.

Gold is a color with no emotion we name attached to it, but gold is the color of my feelings for Tanez. There is no word in our language for the love I have for her—this kind doumana with a face that seems to merge mine with the male of my second Resonance.

"Green or scarlet?" Tanez asks, standing by the gown chest.

I know what she's asking. Scarlet gowns are worn by Returning doumanas only. "What do you believe?" is her unspoken question. Do I expect to feel the tug of the creator on my soul this year, or not for another twenty?

I want to reach for the green. I want to believe that my life will go on. I want to know what happens next.

I'm curious to see if Kelroosh's guide and the guide from the males' corenta will decide, as some have suggested, to join their communities together. If Pradat will accept the offer to stay in Kelroosh and begin training orindles and helphands here. If Larta and Tanez will choose to stay in Kelroosh or return to Chimbalay.

Of them all, it's Tanez's future I think about most. Tanez, patiently standing before me with a gown in either hand—a green and a scarlet. I look at her, and the gold strand of my nameless emotion leaps from my chest, reaching for her like a hand.

"The scarlet," I say, because in truth I already feel the touch of the creator, feather light, the blessing of acceptance and peace. If I am wrong, next year I'll gladly wear the green.

Tanez frowns. She starts to say something, but seems to change her mind. Gathering up the gown to make it easy to put on, she slips it over my head. It's an effort for me to stand, but I do, and tug the gown down until it hangs in a flowing red sweep to my ankles. I sit again and gaze up at Tanez. She gazes back and shrugs.

Tomorrow Pradat and I will head out to search for Marnka. I owe the babbler a debt and hope to pay it with restored sanity for her. Pradat had some success using aruna with the babblers in Chimbalay. She has a new idea, using a naturally fermented aruna, which she thinks will work even better than the compound she used at Chimbalay. The wilderness is a long way, but Pradat and I will find a way to get there. Maybe Kelroosh's guide can secure a vehicle for us.

"Are you a mistake?" Marnka once asked—before she found her name again, when she was simply a babbler living in a cave and I was an angry doumana fleeing those I believed had wronged me, running toward a hope of salvation.

Perhaps I was a mistake. Certainly, those who made me what I am never meant me to be the source of their destruction.

"Who are you?" Marnka, and later Azlii, asked. I say now what I said each time then: I am Khe. There is no answer beyond that.

– – –

WANT to know when more books are coming? Sign up for my New Release Alerts **here**. I value your privacy as I do my own and will never sell or give away your email address.

ALSO BY ALEXES RAZEVICH

Science Fantasy

The Ahsenthe Cycle

Khe

Ashes and Rain

Gama and Hest

By the Shining Sea

Urban Fantasy

Ice-Cold Death Oona Goodlight book one

Barbed Wire Heart Oona Goodlight book two

Vulture Moon Oona Goodlight book three

Chalice and Blade Oona Goodlight book four

The Mermaid's Lament Shay Greene book one

Historical Urban Fantasy

The Girl with Stars in her Hair

Contemporary Fantasy

Shadowline Drift

If you'd like to be among the first to know when new books arrive, I'd love for you to sign up for my VIP Readers Group by clicking *here*. I respect your privacy and would never sell or share your information. As a thank you, I'll gift you a copy of my urban fantasy novella, *Bird Song*.

ear Reader,

WHEN I WAS in the Fourth Grade, I had a wonderful teacher named Mrs. Hoffman who assigned the class to write a poem. I wrote a blatant rip-off of Carl Sandburg's "The Fog," but Mrs. Hoffman praised the imagery. Later that year, she had us write plays. I jumped at the opportunity to tell a whole story. My play was one of three chosen by the class to be performed. There was no going back after that. From that first poem to my first published novel, fifty years passed, but I wrote through all of them—poems, short stories, unpublished novels, promotional literature, press releases, sales brochures, you name it. As long as I'm putting words on a page, I'm happy.

But the truth is, words without readers are just scribbles on a page. It's you, the reader, who makes the story live. Thank you for breathing life into these characters.

Khe explores several themes I'm interested in: life and death, of course, but also the push/pull of wanting to belong and longing to be yourself. I wanted to explore and detail a society that was completely different from the one in which I, in which most of us, live. I'll read most anything, but the novels I most enjoy take me somewhere I've never been before. I hope I've provided that experience for you. Plus, I'm a sucker for a good adventure story.

Khe's story continues in *Ashes and Rain* and concludes in *By the Shining Sea*, available on Amazon in both paperback and as an ebook.

A companion book, *Gama and Hest*, a story of love, loss, and carrying on anyway, set long before Khe's lifetime, is also available on Amazon

If you would like to receive an early email notification and a special Premier Day-only discounted price for future e-book releases, please sign up for my **VIP Readers Club**. I promise not to inundate you with Spam.

Thank you.

Alexes Razevich

ACKNOWLEDGMENTS

Many thanks to Dan McNeil, Meg X, Paul Dillon, Randy Jackson, Richard Casey, Sue Marschner, Alfred Martino, Cathy Bruhn, Mary Lou Reed, Janet Reiner, and Nadine Trenton, wonderful writers all, for their help in shaping Khe and her world.

Much love to Chris, Larkin, and Colin Razevich, who make every day a joy.

Cover art by Tony Honkawa, Tony Honkawa Design

ABOUT THE AUTHOR

Alexes Razevich lives in Southern California with her husband. When she isn't writing, she can usually be found on a hockey rink or traveling somewhere she hasn't been before.

Alexes is always happy to hear from readers and welcomes new friends on Facebook and Twitter.
Email: **LxsRaz@yahoo.com**
New Releases Mailing List:
http://eepurl.com/08229
Website: http://www.alexesrazevich.com/

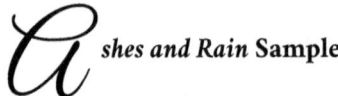 *shes and Rain* **Sample**

A THICK, gray silence smothered the world. Silence, and the smell of dirt — wet, sweet, and deep.

"Khe," Pradat said.

Soil — rich and loamy — crumbling between my fingers.

"Are you all right, Khe?"

"Fine," I said.

The chair beneath me was generously padded and probably comfortable, maybe even comforting, in a different situation. I sat with my back straight, knees together, feet dangling above the wood-planked floor. My nerves hummed and my skin itched from nervous sweat. I coughed into my fist.

"Do you need water?" Pradat adjusted her machines, small black orbs covered with spindly silver tubes that pinpointed colored lights on my body, and clearstone bowls of purple-red or clear liquids that pumped into my arms.

She'd brought her tools with her from Chimbalay to Kelroosh, where I lived now with my new sisters, Azlii and Nez.

"No," I said. Better to stifle the cough and finish the treatment sooner — and hear Pradat's judgment on whether it was working or not.

It would have been easier for me to go to Pradat, but the doumanas — the females of our kind — of Chimbalay had no love for me. I didn't blame them; I'd reduced much of their city to ashes when my sisters and I destroyed the lumani, who had been the secret rulers of our world.

I hadn't set out to destroy them; I'd wanted only to escape Simanca and her relentless pressure to push the crops to greater yield, even when she knew it was killing me. I'd wanted to find the orindles who might heal me. I'd found Pradat, but the lumani had found me, and had changed me into an abomination.

Pradat adjusted another light. I flinched at the sudden sting.

I had other reasons to stay away from Chimbalay. There were those there who might think what Pradat and I were trying to do was wrong. Those who would say that I'd had my rightful time — 'see, count the age dots on her wrist' — and it was unnatural to try to stop the returning to the creator that all doumanas embraced during their thirty-fifth year. But it wasn't yet my time. It was only thirteen years since I'd broken free of the egg and stood on the world, first as a downy hatchling, and then as an emerged, smooth-skinned doumana. I wanted those years back. It was the most natural want there could be.

The day was growing old and the room felt chill. Pradat peered at her palm, consulting the instrument she wore strapped around her hand.

I watched her neck, but with Pradat you rarely knew

what she felt unless she told you. It wasn't that she was unfeeling, not like Simanca or her cold-necked unitmates back at Lunge commune. Pradat had told me once that orindles spent years learning to keep emotions from showing on their necks. A patient could be frightened or get a wrong idea about her health because of an orindle's fleeting worry or concern. Orindles stifled their emotion spots out of courtesy to their patients — a sacrifice they made for their sisters. No orindle could be certified until she'd proven her control. I'd asked once what the trials were, but she'd pulled her lips into a thin line and refused to speak. I'd not asked her about it again.

A light-blue circle of light that focused on a spot between my eyes darkened to nearly purple. Heat on the back of my neck and base of my spine told me Pradat had lights focused there, too. I coughed again, harder and longer this time. She came around and stood in front of me.

"I'm fine," I said. The shame of that lie didn't show on my emotion spots. The lumani had changed me so no one would ever see my emotions again.

Pradat ran her hand over her smooth scalp, turned, and dialed off the machinery.

I sighed, glad it was over.

"There's a chance this worked," she said as she gently pried the tubes from my arms. "The calculations predict a probability, but I can't make promises."

I rubbed the spots where the tubes had been inserted. My throat prickled again, started to burn. I brought my hand up to my mouth, but couldn't stop coughing. It went on and on, a deep choking cough, my upper body pounding against the chair-back with each convulsion.

"Khe?" Pradat said.

Her voice sounded far away. My earholes felt on fire. A

ringing in my head grew louder and louder. I couldn't breathe.

No! Not yet.

Thirty-five dots showed on my wrist. I'd known this was coming — had chosen to wear the scarlet gown of a Returning doumana last Commemoration Day. I'd thought — I'd believed — I would shoulder right up to that day before I fell.

Pradat moved quickly, laying things on the back of my neck, trying to put something in my arm. I was coughing so hard and shook so violently she couldn't set in the tube.

The room spun and grew dim, the walls and floors fading from my sight.

The smooth, gray silence settled over me again. The smell of loam, of Lunge commune; I welcomed it, and sank into the silence, breathing the word, "Nez."